The Wipeout Round

'A fun, action-packed crime romp set against the backdrop of the good ol' British pub-quiz scene. This story plays out so naturally you almost forget it's a novel. Hugely satisfying.'

Charlie Gallagher
Author of the Maddie Ives Books

Also in this series

The Write Way to Die

Bang to Rights

Other books by Jo Bavington-Jones

Lucy Shaw's Not Sure

Lucy Shaw Wants More

A Giraffe Thing

The Bonfire Buddleia

The Wipeout Round

Jo Bavington-Jones

The Wipeout Round

Published by Hut 22 Books in the United Kingdom 2025

Tel: +44(0)7921 887519

www.hut22books.com

jo@hut22books.com

Print book ISBN 978-1-0683088-1-9

eBook ISBN 9781839787485

Copyright © Jo Bavington-Jones, 2025

The moral right of Jo Bavington-Jones to be identified as author of this work has been asserted in accordance with the Copyright, Designs and Patents Act 1988.

All rights reserved.

Typesetting and Cover Design by: Charlotte Mouncey, www.bookstyle.co.uk

Printed and bound in Great Britain by Clays Ltd, Elcograf S.p.A.

Nobody likes a smart-arse.
Anon.

For Sam, always, and for the Mutineers: Dirk,
Gwynne, Janice, Paul, Chris and Russ –
the best quiz team that ever wiped out.
And for Kev: die-hard West Ham fan
and quizmaster extraordinaire.

CHAPTER 1

The fellowship of the quiz

A whole-life order. That's what the killer got. He'd never be released from prison. *Rightly so*, Amy nodded to herself as she switched off the radio. Jeff Teller, who'd terrorised Amy's hometown of Folkestone the previous summer, on a killing spree to match that of Robert Seymour only a year earlier, would never see the outside of a prison again. Amy took comfort from the fact that she'd played a big part in putting Teller away. Justice had been done.

Of course, Amy was serving her own, self-imposed, whole-life sentence. She may not have been put behind bars like Teller, but she was imprisoned in her own mind. She'd killed Seymour, 'The Exhibitionist' serial killer, and got away with it. *Had justice been done?* she still wondered from time to time. Had he deserved to die? And had she had the right to carry out his sentence? She'd found an uneasy kind of acceptance – most of the time – but there were still days, and nights, when the spectre of Robert haunted her dreams. Times when she relived the awful moment when she snatched the gun and felt the recoil as she put a bullet in his head.

On those days, she usually called on Jenny, her best friend and literal partner in crime.

'Hey you. Did you hear the news?' Amy asked, when Jenny answered the phone.

'Yup. Still too good for him though. Bring back the death penalty, I say,' Jenny said. She was thinking of her friend, Bella, the beautiful young reporter, who'd been one of Teller's victims.

Amy pictured her pink-haired friend at the other end of the phone, face mutinous as she expressed her thoughts on Teller's prison sentence. 'I know what you mean. A life for a life and all that. I'm trying to take some comfort from the fact that there won't be any more victims with him behind bars, and that's largely down to us.'

Jenny harrumphed. 'I'd still like to see him strung up.'

'Hm ... public hangings ... Not sure I want to see them brought back,' Amy mused.

'Oh, I dunno. I can see a crowd happily gathered around Memorial Arch to watch someone like Teller swing.'

'Handy for McDonalds afterwards,' Amy chuckled, getting into the spirit of things. 'They could change Happy Meal to Hanging Meal.'

Jenny laughed. 'I'd like to see the toy you'd get with it!'

'Ronald McDonald in a hangman's hood?' Amy suggested.

'Ha! Yeah, stringing up the Hamburglar.'

'Isn't there an Officer Big Mac too?' Amy asked.

'Bloody hell, we're doing the work for them. We should be on commission.'

'I think we'd be a pretty good marketing team, actually,' Amy said. 'Can you imagine writing the advert for the job of hangman?'

'Hang-*person*, if you please. Let's be politically correct about these things.'

'Oh, frightfully sorry, hang-*person*,' Amy exaggerated. 'Next you'll be telling me you put your personal pronouns on your emails.'

'Doesn't everyone?' Jenny said seriously, even though she didn't. 'You need to woke up, old girl.'

Amy groaned. 'I think I'm just a little bit too old to cope with all this wokeness. I've always just accepted people the way they are anyway. It's quite difficult for my fifty-three-year-old brain, with its grammar school education, to accept that they/them aren't simply plural pronouns.'

'You old fart,' Jenny said.

'Charming.'

'Why should anyone who doesn't identify as male or female be lumbered with traditional he/she pronouns?' Jenny asked.

'I'm sure you're right, Jenny. It's just slightly harder for most of our generation to get their heads around. Speaking of things to get my head around, I saw my first furry the other day.'

'I reckon I probably identify as a cat half the time,' Jenny told Amy.

'When did you last see a cat with pink fur?'

'Fair point. Maybe I'll dye it tortoiseshell next.'

'Oh God. Please don't. I won't be seen out with you until it grows out. Unless you wear a hat.'

'How am I going to fit a hat over my cat ears, dopey?'

Amy glossed over that. 'Is it true that a school in America put litter trays in the loos for the furries?' Amy asked.

'What? No! I think that's probably an urban myth.'

'Hm. Can you imagine if someone had miaowed at a teacher when we were at school?'

'Bloody hell, no. They'd have got the board rubber chucked at them and detention for a month.'

'Yeah, simpler times, eh? You knew where you stood back when we were kids. You were either naughty or nice, he or she, grammar school or not.'

'It was only simple for you because you were "nice" and "grammar school" as you put it,' Jenny said. 'Imagine being one of the "naughty" ones, who were written off when all they needed was a bit of understanding as to why they were naughty, or struggled with reading, or something.'

'I hadn't really thought of that,' Amy admitted. 'Looking back with what we know today, about spectrum disorders and things, I do see what you mean.'

'Maybe there's hope for you after all, you old fossil,' Jenny relented. 'And we prefer neuro-spicy, thank you very much.'

That was a step too far for Amy, baby steps and all that, and she turned the conversation back to the requirements for a hang-person.

'Applicants should have good people skills …' Jenny said.

'Sense of humour an advantage …' Amy chipped in.

'Oh yes. Can't beat a bit of gallows humour.'

'Experience in knot-tying preferable but not essential, as full training will be given.'

'Might suit a former Boy Scout with their knot-tying badge,' Jenny suggested.

'Person Scout, thank you very much,' Amy corrected, earnestly, using Jenny's political correctness against her.

'Frightfully sorry!' Jenny imitated her friend. 'Actually, I think they're probably just called Scouts now,' she added.

'You're forgiven,' Amy told her.

'The question is, who's going to train the trainer, eh? Can't be many qualified hang-people around these days?' Jenny continued.

'True. You volunteering?'

'Depends on the salary. And the perks.' Jenny paused. 'Although they rather speak for themselves, don't they?'

'Sicko,' Amy joked. 'There's probably a standard operating procedure in a government file somewhere.'

'How hard can it be though? Really?' Jenny asked.

'S'pose. Not exactly the sort of thing you can practise though, is it?'

Jenny chuckled. 'Not if you want good reviews on Trustpilot.'

'Two out of ten, would not use again. My neck's still hurting three weeks later.'

Both friends were laughing now. Their own gallows humour had become something of a coping mechanism since the awful events of the past two years.

'Right, I need to do some work; this book's not going to write itself,' Amy said, thinking of the work in progress languishing on her laptop.

'Okey dokey,' Jenny said. 'Are we still going to check out that pub quiz on Wednesday?'

'Yeah, definitely. Willem and Finn are up for it too, so I'll see you Wednesday at the latest,' Amy confirmed.

'Cool. Look forward to it.'

'See if you can come up with any genius team names before then,' Amy added. 'Put that brilliant marketing brain to work.'

'Okey dokey, pig in a pokey. Toodles.'

The friends hung up and Amy went off to make a coffee, which she took to her office.

Amy's desk looked out over the railway viaduct which spanned the valley in front of her house. Consisting of nineteen arches, the tallest of which towered one hundred feet in the air, or four-and-a-bit giraffes as the sign below pointed out, the viaduct was Grade Two listed and had been carrying trains across since 1843. Amy never tired of the view and was fascinated by the history of the structure. According to local legend, dead horses were buried in the legs. She wondered why they'd never scanned the arches like they had at the Loch nan Uamh one in Scotland, revealing the remains of a horse and cart. The thing Amy loved most about the viaduct, though, was the fact that at the other end of it, directly across the valley, lived Willem, the photographer she had started seeing, and who had become embroiled in Amy and Jenny's amateur sleuthing shenanigans.

Amy spent far too much time gazing out of the window daydreaming when she should be working, and kept a pair of binoculars on the windowsill, with which she could read the messages Willem sometimes stuck in his window. As she sipped her coffee, Amy smiled at the prospect of seeing Willem again for the quiz.

At that particular moment, Willem de Groot, a fifty-seven-year-old Dutch South African, was doing much the same thing. Instead of coffee, he had a mug of strong black tea, but he too was staring across the valley, and thinking about Amy. It was only Monday, and he wasn't due to see Amy until Wednesday when they were trying out a local pub quiz. He'd been trying to think up good names for their team, but these days, no matter what he was trying to think about, he always ended up with a picture of Amy in his head.

His one-eyed cat, Cat, often had to remind him several times to feed him both in the morning and the evening, as his human's attention wandered. Cat regularly found Willem staring out the window, his blue eyes fixed on the house opposite, running his heavily tanned, and now slightly gnarled fingers, through his steely grey curls. Willem glossed over the noticeable thinning when he reached his crown. Cat had perched on the windowsill once or twice, to try and see what the attraction was but, apart from the occasional seagull on the lean-to roof, he saw nothing of note and quickly lost interest.

For Willem, meeting Amy had definitely been both blessing and curse, though. As smitten as he was with the lovely writer, she was not without baggage. Amy was almost always to be found with her friend, Jenny. They were pretty much a double act and, since the apprehending of Jeff Teller, Willem saw them very much as partners in crime. Not so much Cagney and Lacey, more a slightly younger Jessica Fletcher from *Murder, She Wrote* and a grown-up Velma from *Scooby Doo*, he chuckled. While Willem liked Jenny very much, he found himself expecting her to pop up from behind a tree every time he met Amy. He realised, though, that if he wanted to keep seeing Amy, and he very much did, then he had to accept that Jenny was part of the package.

As he continued to gaze out of the upstairs window, Willem wondered what Amy was doing. Was she sitting at her desk? Was she thinking about him? Or was she off with Jenny somewhere, fighting crime? Or, more likely, eating gluten-free cake and drinking an oat-milk cappuccino with her. The thought of coffee and cake triggered a mental alarm as Willem remembered he was meeting his friend, Finn, in town for breakfast. He looked at his watch.

'O vrek!' he cursed, switching to Afrikaans, as he often did when exclaiming anything. Almost tripping over Cat, who was lurking in the doorway, Willem rushed downstairs, threw a toothbrush round his mouth, grabbed his keys and was out before Cat had a chance to remind him about breakfast. He remembered halfway down the road, and hurried home to empty a pouch of food into Cat's dish. Cat hissed at him before tucking into his very late breakfast. 'Don't you start, animal! Don't forget who took you in off the street,' he said, wagging his finger at the animal, who proceeded to ignore him.

Setting off once more, Willem half jogged the ten-minute walk into town, acknowledging gratefully that he was still in pretty good shape for his age, despite his hair's attempts to suggest otherwise. It was a mild autumn day, the blue sky criss-crossed with contrails; a day when it felt good to be alive, and Willem smiled and waved when he spotted Finn already seated at an outside table at their favourite place for breakfast, Djangos.

The younger man lifted a hand in greeting. 'OK sitting outside?' he asked.

Willem nodded. He preferred sitting outside until the temperatures dictated otherwise. 'Good morning, Finn. My apologies for being late. You can blame Cat. Or my failing memory. Ach, or both,' Willem said, shaking his head.

'No apology needed,' Finn smiled. 'I ordered you an Americano.'

'Thank you, thank you, my friend,' Willem said, as he pulled out a chair and sat down with an 'oof'.

Finn was much younger than Willem, at only thirty-four, but the pair had hit it off at once when Willem had joined the members of Coastal Creatives, a group of artists who shared a shop together. They had beards in common, while Finn's was black where Willem's was grey, a dry sense of humour, and an inability to suffer fools gladly. One such fool no longer had to be suffered, gladly or otherwise, as Gloria de Dieu, self-appointed shop manager, and all-round bossy-boots, had been another of Teller's victims. Rather than speak ill of the dead, the two men rarely mentioned her these days. They had, by common agreement, taken over the day-to-day running of the Coastal Creatives shop, and very much enjoyed working together. They were currently working on a project that involved the Folkestone lighthouse and both Willem's photography and Finn's pyrography. Amy's novels were also sold in the little shop, which was how she and Willem had met.

'How was your weekend?' Finn asked.

'Pretty good, thanks. Now that we're in autumn, sunrise is not quite so hideously early. It's getting harder and harder to get out of bed for those early morning shoots now,' Willem said. 'I got a cracking sky yesterday morning, down on the Sands,' he said, referring to the town's only sandy beach. 'I'll have prints ready for the shop tomorrow. How about you?'

'Had a quiet one. Visited my folks for Sunday lunch, which was nice. Made the mistake of mentioning the pub quiz to Dad, and he was all up for joining us! Bloody hell, can you imagine?' Finn raised his eyebrows.

Willem chuckled. Finn's father, Brian, was nothing like his son, who tended towards introversion. Willem could just imagine how embarrassed Finn would be by his dad's raucous behaviour.

'Well, it would certainly not be dull with your dad on the team,' Willem said.

'Jesus, that's an understatement. He'd have us calling

ourselves ... I dunno ... Big Fact Hunts, or Hoof Hearted,' Finn groaned.

Willem chuckled. 'I take it you talked him out of it?'

'Bloody right I did. Told him we already have a full team.'

'But we only have four at the moment ... you're allowed up to six I think,' Willem said.

'Well, unless you want my crazy parent there, I suggest we find two more people asap.'

'I think it would be very funny to have Brian there,' Willem said.

The look on Finn's face disagreed, vehemently. Willem quickly changed the subject, and the friends spent a happy hour drinking coffee, eating Djangos 'Colossal' breakfasts, and discussing mirrorless Nikons and cordless pyrography pens.

CHAPTER 2

Let's get quizzical

Wednesday evening rolled around soon enough, and saw Amy, Jenny, Willem, and Finn at the venue for their first ever pub quiz together. Finn and Jenny had only met, briefly, a couple of times. The four hadn't found anyone else to join them yet and were sworn to secrecy should any of them bump into Finn's dad. They would hopefully find another couple of team members at some point. For now, though, they were game to give it a go against undoubtedly bigger and better teams.

They'd arrived early so they could settle in, size up the opposition as they arrived, and also come up with a team name. Once drinks were bought, they bagsied a table in the window of Griffin's Alehouse, so called after a character created by H. G. Wells, the author having lived in the area for several years.

'Cheers!' Amy said, lifting her Bathtub and tonic.

'Cheers!' the other three responded, raising two pints and a rum and Coke. The rum was Willem's. Jenny was on the pints.

'Right, so, team name? Suggestions, please,' Amy said, taking charge.

'Big Fact Hunts,' Jenny immediately threw in. 'You know, when you say it, it sounds a bit like big fat c—'

'Yes, thanks, Jenny. We get the idea!' Amy interrupted.

Willem nearly spat out a mouthful of drink and couldn't meet Finn's eyes, but he could feel them glaring at Jenny. He quickly made a safer suggestion. 'What about the Invisible Men?'

He was met with silence as the others tried to make sense of his idea. It was Amy who realised. 'Ah! Griffin was the name of H. G. Wells' *The Invisible Man*, wasn't it? Very clever,' she said.

'Very sexist,' Jenny muttered into her pint.

Trying to move them to safer ground, Amy chipped in an idea she'd had. 'I was thinking we could play on the word Folkestone. Something like Stoned Folke, or maybe Toned Folkes? What do you think?'

'Have you ever been stoned in your life, Amy?' Jenny asked, eyebrows raised.

'Well, no, but does that matter? I'm not particularly toned now either,' Amy pulled a face and breathed in, thinking of the extra weight she now carried, and hated, around her middle.

Jenny shrugged.

Easy for you, skinny Minnie, Amy thought, sighing internally.

'I quite like Stoned Folke,' Willem said.

'Willem, your choice of friends has no bearing on tonight's proceedings,' Jenny said, straight-faced.

Amy giggled. Jenny was as sharp as she was skinny.

Finn still hadn't said anything at this point.

'Or we could play on the word four, as there are four of us,' Jenny suggested.

'We might not be four forever though,' Amy pointed out.

'Yeah, s'pose,' Jenny admitted. 'What about Who Farted? But we write it as Hoof Hearted. That would get a laugh when the quizmaster said it.'

'Quiz-person,' Amy corrected automatically.

Jeez, was Jenny channelling her inner Brian? Willem wondered.

Finn continued to glower into his beer, and Willem and Amy began to wonder if the mix of Jenny and Finn was less agreeable than gin and tonic, or indeed rum and Coke. Their eyes met and they both grimaced.

The pub was filling up by now, and most of the teams seemed to have the maximum six members.

'We definitely need to pressgang a couple of brainiacs before next week,' Amy said, looking round in apprehension. 'I don't want to come last. I hate losing.'

'We won't lose, Amy,' Willem reassured her. 'We might just surprise you.'

'So, what's your specialist subject then, Willem?' Jenny asked.

'Maybe geography. Or history. Although I think I know a little about a lot of things,' Willem replied.

'What about you, Finn?' Amy asked, trying to pull him into the conversation.

'Um ... music and film, I suppose. And I keep up with the news, so ...'

'Great! That's current affairs sorted,' Amy said. 'And Jenny's got celebrity gossip covered, haven't you?'

'Amongst other things,' Jenny nodded.

Cats and sewing, Amy thought, knowing them to be Jenny's two greatest passions these days.

'And I'll attempt to not disgrace myself with literature questions,' Amy said, pulling a face that indicated she may well disgrace herself.

'Your specialist subject is crisps,' Jenny said. 'And chocolate.'

'And gin,' Amy agreed, raising her glass. 'We still need to decide on a name before we win or lose.'

'Shall we just go with Stoned Folke for now? We can always

change it down the line,' Willem suggested.

With that agreed, the four of them settled back in their chairs and waited for the quiz to begin.

It was only a couple of minutes before the quizmaster introduced himself. 'Good evening, quizzers, and welcome to the Griffin. My name's Barry and I'll be asking the questions tonight.'

'Oh my God, Barry's escaped from Butlin's!' Jenny hissed.

'Butlin's Filey, by the sound of that accent,' Amy added, having detected a hint of Yorkshire in Barry's voice.

Bald-headed, sixty-something Barry was indeed wearing a red jacket reminiscent of the Butlin's Redcoats, and which matched his jolly round face. Jolly and jolly round, that is.

'He does look like he could have been a Redcoat in a former life,' Amy giggled, remembering childhood stays at the holiday camps.

'Hi-de-hi, campers!' Jenny said, in her best Ruth Madoc Welsh accent.

Willem shushed them both then, earning a hard stare from Jenny, and they returned their attention to what Barry was saying.

'I can see a couple of new teams here tonight,' Barry said, nodding in the direction of Amy's table and to one other which was occupied by six rather older quizzers, who turned out later to be called Saga Crews.

'With a bit of luck, half of them will pop their clogs before the halfway point,' Jenny whispered, a little too loudly. 'Increase our chances of winning.'

'Well, I can see one of our new teams is going to be a bit of a handful,' Barry said, laughing rather unconvincingly. 'And what might you four be calling yourselves tonight then?'

Jenny opened her mouth to speak, but Amy put a hasty hand on her friend's arm and spoke up. 'Er … Stoned Folke,' she said sheepishly. 'You know, a play on the name of the town …' she began to explain.

'Just as I thought!' Barry exclaimed, putting his hand dramatically to his now slightly sweaty forehead. 'This lot's gonna be trouble, ladies and germs. Hold onto your hats!'

Amy and co were starting to wonder what they'd let themselves in for as Barry went on to explain the format of the quiz. While he was talking, a rather frumpy middle-aged woman with a beige cardigan and a bad perm, who turned out to be Barry's wife and his 'glamorous assistant', came round and collected the two-pounds-per-person entry fee, which she took off to count.

'First is the picture round. You'll get ten minutes to look at that before a round of twenty general knowledge questions. Then we have a specialist round – if you've seen the hint on Facebook, you'll hopefully have mugged up on Elvis Presley for that …'

Everyone at Amy's table groaned.

'For fuck's sake,' Jenny said. 'Do any of you know anything about Elvis-fucking-Presley?'

'I know his middle name wasn't "fucking". It was Aaron,' Amy informed her in hushed tones, not wanting to let everyone know in case that was actually a question.

Barry went on. 'The music round this week is, naturally, an Elvis round …'

Amy and the others groaned again.

'Shall we just leave now?' Amy said.

'Come on, Amy, get in the spirit,' Willem said, reaching over and squeezing her hand.

'Yeah, Amy, drink your gin. And channel your inner Elvis,' Jenny added.

'Sorry, you're right. We can do this, although I'm not sure I have an inner Elvis,' Amy smiled apologetically. 'Positive mental attitude. I'm positive Jenny's mental and got an attitude,' she added, sticking her tongue out at Jenny.

'She's not wrong,' Jenny shrugged, and took a big swig of beer.

They'd missed whatever Barry had said after the joyful news of an Elvis music round, and the next thing they knew, he was handing out the picture round, giving Amy's team two copies. Amy wisely let Willem share with Finn.

'What is it then?' Jenny asked, as she looked down at the sheet. 'Fuck my life. Famous-fucking-bridges? I'm gonna need more beer.' With that, Jenny got up and went to the bar.

'Oh lordy. I only recognise, maybe, two of them,' Amy groaned. 'Willem? Finn?' To her surprise and pleasure, the two men had put their heads together and were already rapidly filling in the names of the bridges in the spaces provided on the answer sheet they'd been given.

'We've got this, Amy,' Willem smiled at her.

'Our knight in shining armour. Be still my beating heart,' Jenny said, arriving back at the table holding two pints, sarcasm dripping from her words like condensation down a glass.

'Jenny! Play nicely,' Amy reprimanded, while thinking it was nice that Jenny had got Finn a drink.

Jenny rolled her eyes and plonked both pints down in front of her. Amy sighed.

'Just one we don't know,' Willem said, after a few minutes.

'Brilliant!' Amy said. 'Well done, you two. Sorry we weren't much help. Can we have a guess at the missing one? Better than leaving it blank.'

Willem wrote down the name of a bridge they hadn't used.

Before proceeding, Barry then announced that they were playing for £108, and a big 'ooh-ooh-ooh' went up around the pub. Stoned Folke hadn't got the memo and just looked at one another, open mouthed.

Round two, the general knowledge round, came next, with Barry calling out the question number each time.

'Question seven …' he began.

'SEVEN!' the pub responded loudly, in the style of Len Goodman from *Strictly Come Dancing*.

Stoned Folke looked at each other and laughed. It really was a bit like being at Butlin's.

'I bet he runs bingo somewhere too,' Jenny observed.

'Oh, we should definitely go to that!' Amy grinned.

Willem and Finn didn't look quite as enthusiastic.

Round two went surprisingly well, and it turned out that between them they actually knew quite a lot of random stuff. Finn came into his own on many of the questions and finally seemed to relax a bit.

'Bring on Elvis,' he said, smiling shyly.

Round three was somewhat less successful as any Elvis knowledge they had, had apparently left the building. One of only three answers they were sure about was indeed his middle name.

'No, Jenny, we can't write "fucking".'

There was a short break then, and Willem and Finn went

to the bar to get another round in while Barry cued up the music round. They'd half expected him to swap his red coat for a bejewelled white number and perform the songs himself, and were relieved when the first song came over the speakers.

'Okey dokey, point for the song title and point for the year,' Barry told them.

'I'd prefer a point for the artist,' Jenny said.

The King of Rock and Roll drowned out any further comments from Jenny, and they tried their best to identify the eight songs, having an educated guess at the years.

'Well, that was ten minutes of my life I'll never get back,' Jenny said, when the round was over.

'What's next?' Amy asked.

The other three shrugged, no one having heard what Barry had said.

'Whatever it is, it's got to be better than Elvis,' Willem said, as they waited to find out.

It wasn't.

'Righty-oh, my quizzy rascals, round five is upon us and it's mythology.'

Amy looked round the table and grimaced. The others didn't look as horrified as her though and she began to feel a bit better. Once again, Willem and Finn came to the rescue, and they had a good stab at more than half of the questions.

'Is it nearly over?' Jenny asked, yawning.

Amy shrugged.

But Barry hadn't finished with them yet. 'Okay, time to swap your papers. Don't forget to mark your opponent's paper as you'd like yours to be marked.'

'With a pen,' from Jenny.

'And then we'll have our final round: the wipeout!' Barry finished.

The four of them groaned as one at the news of a wipeout round.

Willem took the job of marking the other team's answer sheet. It belonged to the other new team, Saga Crews, who had all survived the evening thus far, much to Jenny's disappointment.

They were neck and scraggy neck by the time they reached the Elvis rounds, but were overtaken by the oldies after marking them.

'It's not exactly fair, is it?' Jenny moaned. 'I mean, those old buggers were around when Elvis was grinding his hips for real. They probably bought his records and played them on their gramophones.'

'Well, hopefully another week it'll be eighties music and we'll thrash them,' Amy said.

Jenny grunted something but didn't look convinced.

They pulled a couple of points back on the mythology round but were seven points behind going into the final round.

'Everybody swapped their papers back?' Barry asked. 'Okay, into the final round: the wipeout! There are ten questions, and if you get all ten answers correct, there's a five-point bonus.'

Another 'ooh-oooh' went up from the pub. Clearly this was something they always did, much like the earlier 'ooh' and the 'SEVEN!'.

'And remember, no answer is not an incorrect answer, so if you're not sure, leave that line empty. Unless you're the gambling types and prepared to risk it all!' Barry threw up his hands dramatically. 'But one wrong answer and you get nothing for the round! Nul points! Nada, nichts, rien!'

'Ooh! Barry's gone all continental,' Amy chuckled.

'Any other continent would be preferable. I reckon Saga Crews only sail to incontinent-al these days,' Jenny smirked. She was on her fourth pint, and it had definitely sharpened her razor tongue.

'Right, drumroll, please, ladies and gentlemen. Let the wipe-out begin!' Barry announced theatrically.

A tabletop drumroll commenced, and Amy giggled again.

CHAPTER 3

Les Quizerables

After the quiz had finished and Barry had left the building, Amy and the others decided to stick around for one more drink and a post-quiz-mortem. Jenny went to the bar and came back with a round of shots.

'Just congratulated that lot on winning,' Jenny said, nodding across the pub at a team called Scrambled Eggheads, as she carefully deposited four shot glasses on the table. 'Smug bastards didn't even say thank you, just smirked at me like I was shit on their sensible shoes.'

'Oh dear. Well done for being the bigger person, anyway,' Amy smiled at her friend.

'Oh, I wasn't,' Jenny grinned. 'I told them to go fuck themselves.'

Amy and the other two groaned.

'Well, what did we think of it?' Amy asked, moving swiftly on from Jenny's insult to the winning team, and screwing up her face as she knocked back the now much-needed shot, the fiery liquid burning her insides. 'The quiz, not the shot.'

'I rather enjoyed it,' Willem said, smiling.

'Yeah, I didn't mind it,' Finn shrugged. 'Better than sitting in front of the telly.'

'We thought it was hilarious,' Jenny said. 'For all the wrong reasons.'

'We did much better than I'd expected. Don't feel I

contributed much though,' Amy said.

'Not at all. I think it was a good team effort, and we all chipped in answers,' Willem said, graciously.

'Yep, if it wasn't for that pesky wipeout round, we didn't do too badly at all,' Finn said.

'Yeah, fancy getting the first nine answers right and then wiping out on number ten! Who does that?'

'Us apparently.'

'Hm. Lesson learned for next time.'

'There's going to be a next time?' Jenny said.

'Come on, admit it, Jenny. You loved every minute of it,' Willem teased.

'Oh yeah, like I enjoyed every minute of that root canal I had done last year. By the world's most sadistic dentist.'

'Well, I'd like to come back,' Amy said, 'but I'm more than happy to try some other quizzes too.'

'I don't know about other quizzes, but I'm ready for a week at Butlin's after that. All warmed up. Unlike holiday-camp breakfasts,' Jenny said.

Amy turned to Finn. 'She's not always like this, honestly.'

'Yes, I am,' Jenny said.

Amy pulled a face. 'Yes, she is.'

'Beer just makes me more me,' Jenny added, burping. 'And more burpy.'

'Charmed, I'm sure,' Willem laughed. 'Finn, you'll get used to her.'

Finn looked doubtful, but attempted a smile.

'Right, are we off then?' Amy asked.

The others nodded and they got up to leave, Finn waving as he set off in the opposite direction to the others.

Amy and Willem offered to walk Jenny home. They didn't want to run the risk of a mugging or something. By Jenny, that is, not to her.

As they walked, conversation soon switched from the quiz to the recent trial and sentencing of the serial killer, Jeff Teller. When the three friends had last seen Teller, he was trussed up in the back of his own van, with a taped confession, and a bullet in his knee, nicely gift-wrapped for the police. Shooting him hadn't been part of the plan, but when Jenny saw images Teller had taken of her friend Bella's murder, she'd lost it. Amy was secretly pleased that Jenny had shot Teller. It somehow tied their fates together even more inextricably than they had been following the fatal shooting of Robert Seymour by Amy a year earlier.

'I still can't believe what's happened these past two years,' Amy said. 'What are the chances of our little town by the sea having two serial killers in two years?'

'A hundred per cent, apparently,' Jenny said dryly.

'If you think about it, they were connected though, weren't they? The original ideas came from both men together, so in a way they were just one killer,' Willem put forward.

'I see what you're saying,' Amy mused. 'Well, whatever the case, it's over and neither of them can ever hurt anyone else.'

'Unless Teller kills people in prison,' Jenny added, just as they reached her house.

'Well, on that cheery note, we'll say goodnight, Jenny!' Willem said.

Amy hugged Jenny and said she'd see her soon, and they waited until she was safely inside before setting off once more. Willem took Amy's hand, and they walked in silence for a time.

When Willem finally spoke, it was to ask Amy to dinner the next night. 'I'll cook,' he said.

'That would be lovely,' Amy smiled, squeezing his hand, 'thank you.'

When they reached Amy's door, she hesitated on the doorstep. She knew Willem was hoping to be asked in, and she didn't want to hurt his feelings by not doing so, but Amy was holding back. It was a matter of self-preservation.

A timely yawn gave her the get-out she needed.

'Sleepyhead,' Willem smiled at her. 'You need your bed. I'll see you tomorrow. Around seven?'

'Sorry, yes, look forward to it. Let me know if I can bring anything,' Amy smiled up at him, and he pulled her into a hug, kissing the top of her head.

'Goodnight, Amy,' Willem said.

Amy opened her front door and stepped into the house, turning to blow a kiss after Willem as he made to leave. Closing the door, Amy leaned back against it and shut her eyes tight, trying to hold back the tears that were threatening.

'Fuck fuck fuck!' she cried, pressing her fingers into her eyes. 'Fuck!'

Taking a deep breath, she shrugged off her jacket and hung it on the hooks at the bottom of the stairs. Wandering into the kitchen, Amy wondered if she needed another gin. Or if chamomile tea would be more sensible. Deciding to compromise on a lavender-scented bath and a glass of wine, she trudged upstairs and turned on the taps. Five minutes later and she was submerged in the bubbles, leaning back with a sigh that spoke of both pleasure and sadness. What was she going to do about Willem?

Amy had been making excuses for weeks now, putting Willem off when he clearly wanted to take things to the next level, and either stay the night at her's or have her stay at his.

This was the first relationship Amy had been in since that fateful night when she shot and killed Robert Seymour. While she may have found some sort of peace and acceptance with what she'd done, she couldn't be sure that Willem would understand. He might be so outraged that he'd go to the police. No, Jenny was the only person she could trust with this. Anything else was simply too risky. No way could Amy go to prison.

She was sure Willem suspected she was hiding something. But what choice did she have? Really? He was such an honourable man. He might feel he *had* to do the right, the lawful, thing and have her arrested. Amy took a big glug of white wine, and tried to work out what she should do, but everything just kept going round and round in her head.

Should she end things with Willem before they got any more serious? Save them both some of the heartbreak. Did her secret mean that she could never be in a proper relationship again? Ever. For the rest of her life. A big fat secret like this was no way to start, or indeed carry on, a relationship, was it?

Maybe it's time to get a cat? Or a dog, Amy mused unhappily. *How can I share a bed with anyone when I might talk in my sleep and give myself away?* Having been a somniloquist since childhood, Amy knew this was a very real risk.

Being no closer to an answer, Amy tried to think of something else, but her brain wouldn't let her, and she continued to think herself round in circles until the water grew lukewarm and she dragged herself off to bed. She could only hope that the alcohol would allow her to slip into a dreamless sleep, but she feared the faces of Robert Seymour, Jeff Teller, and all their victims would be waiting for her when she crossed over into the land of nod.

Across the viaduct, Willem was sitting in the garden nursing a glass of rum and smoking a cigar. He was wide awake and wondering, looking for answers in the cloudless night sky. He didn't notice the chill in the air. He'd watched Amy's bedroom light go off a short while ago, and lifted his glass to her, with a sad smile. 'Goodnight, Amy,' he said quietly.

Amy was, of course, the reason for his restlessness. He had sensed early on that she was holding something back. It was like she'd put a wall up between them and he couldn't find a way around it, over it, under it, through it, any which way he looked at it. He could admit that he was falling for her, and he was pretty sure she felt the same, but something was stopping her from moving forward with him. He was afraid to broach the subject for fear of scaring her off, but it was as clear as the North Star in the night sky that something had to happen if the relationship was to grow.

At her house, Jenny had passed out on the sofa, all thoughts of anyone forgotten, including her cats, which had made themselves comfortable around her.

CHAPTER 4

Taking care of quizness

The next morning, Thursday, saw Amy manning the Coastal Creatives shop on the Old High Street, the town's cobbled little hill, alive with galleries and arty shops. She was feeling rather tired and flat after another night of tossing and turning, and was torn between wanting a quiet shift where she wouldn't have to engage with anyone, and being swamped by customers to keep her busy and occupied. Rather than preoccupied, which was how she felt most of the time these days. Stopping in at the aptly named Steep Street Coffee House on the way down the hill, Amy picked up a large coconut-milk cappuccino to go, grabbing several sugars too.

She'd only been settled behind the counter for a few minutes when Finn came in.

'Hi, Amy,' he said, smiling at her. Finn always seemed more relaxed in a one-on-one situation. Or any situation where Jenny wasn't, Amy thought, after the quiz.

'Hello!' Amy smiled back. 'Have you recovered from last night?'

'Just about.'

'You caught Jenny in sparkling form,' Amy chuckled.

'She's quite a livewire,' Finn said, eyebrows raised.

'That's a polite way of putting it,' Amy grinned at him. 'She has a razor-sharp wit at the best of times. And when she's on pints, it can be a little overwhelming to the uninitiated. She's a pussycat really, though, and an incredibly loyal friend. Once she's accepted you into her ... what's the collective noun for cats ...?'

'Clowder,' Finn answered at once.

Amy's eyebrows went up in surprise.

Finn shrugged. 'Quiet days in here I mug up on stuff sometimes. A couple of weeks ago I took a pass at collective nouns.'

'Oh my God, you should join a quiz team,' Amy laughed.

'Funny you should say that ...' Finn grinned, his dark brown eyes catching the smile that lit his face. Amy couldn't help thinking he should smile more often.

'Well, quiz-astrous first quiz results aside, what can I do you for this morning?'

'I'm meeting the lady who might be taking over from Harry here at quarter past, see if we think she's a fit for the shop.'

Harry was the resident ceramicist, although of course Amy always said 'potter' to customers. Harry was moving up to London for an IT job and they were all sorry to see him go.

'Ooh,' Amy said. 'What does she make?'

'Knitted stuff as far as I can make out. Although it could be crochet. Not my area of expertise,' Finn said.

'Would be a good fit space-wise,' Amy said. 'As long as it's not all knitted loo-roll covers and tea cosies,' she grimaced.

'I asked her to bring some samples of her work, so I guess we'll find out soon enough.'

Soon enough came even sooner than expected as the door swung open at five past ten. Amy looked up with a smile and a hello that soon turned into a frown as she tried to place the face of the woman who'd just come in. She definitely recognised her from somewhere. The penny obviously dropped for Finn at exactly the same moment and his eyes met Amy's as they realised it was 'Mrs Barry', the 'glamorous assistant' from last night's quiz.

Finn made the introductions. The woman's name was actually Pauline, and when she took off her coat, she was wearing another beige cardi. Close up and in daylight, Pauline looked to be in her early sixties, her face devoid of makeup and her perm and outfit straight off a nineteen-seventies knitting pattern.

'Hello, Pauline,' Amy said. 'Nice to meet you.' She wondered if Pauline recognised her and Finn too. She didn't have to wait long to find out.

'Oh, hello, nice to meet you too, Amy. Although I think I'm right in saying we sort of met last night. At the quiz,' Pauline said. Amy's keen ear detected the same subtle hint of a Yorkshire accent as that of her husband, Barry.

'Yes! You're absolutely right, I thought I recognised you,' Amy said, mentally retracting all the bitchy comments they'd made about Barry's missus. 'You'll know then that we wiped out rather spectacularly,' Amy said, pulling a face.

'Beginner's bad luck,' Pauline smiled sympathetically. 'I'm sure you'll do better next time. The main thing is did you enjoy yourselves?'

'Oh yes! It was great fun,' Amy said, ignoring the images of bridges and the Elvis soundbite filling her head.

'That's good,' Pauline nodded. 'Hopefully we'll see you back for more next week?'

Amy looked at Finn who shrugged.

'Yes, hopefully we'll be able to make it,' Amy said, thinking it was time to change the subject. 'So, Finn says you're interested in a space in the shop?'

'Yes, dear. I've brought along some samples of my work,' Pauline said, rummaging in the capacious-looking bag she was holding. 'You might have seen some of my bits around the town actually,' Pauline continued, all the while pulling out brightly coloured knitted items.

Putting thoughts of Pauline's 'bits' firmly out of her mind, Amy asked, 'Oh really, whereabouts?'

'Oh, all over the place really. On top of bollards, letter boxes, railings ... anywhere I can brighten things up.'

'I think I have seen some of them!' Amy exclaimed. 'Did you do that amazing post-box topper on Sandgate Road? With the octopus?'

Pauline smiled proudly. 'Yes, that's one of mine.'

'Oh, Finn, sign her up at once,' Amy enthused. 'I almost wanted to take up knitting when I saw the post box.'

While they spoke, Pauline continued to pull items out of her bag, making Amy think of Mary Poppins' magic carpet bag.

Finn was smiling at the exchange taking place. 'Well, the only thing we really need to talk about is whether you can cover weekends, Pauline. Harry, the guy who's leaving, does alternating Saturdays and Sundays.'

'That wouldn't be a problem, dear. Barry does like to watch his snooker and darts at the weekend, so it would be a blessed relief if I'm honest. I usually just take myself off into my knitting room and listen to a bit of Burt, Bacharach that is, or catch up on my soaps.'

'Great!' Finn said.

'Can we have a look at your work anyway, seeing as you've gone to the trouble of bringing it in?' Amy asked.

They spent the next ten minutes admiring Pauline's

handiwork. As well as her own amazing knits, which ranged from bags and dolls to bunting and jumpers, she also sold knitting kits for all levels of ability.

'Have you got one for a doll's scarf?' Amy asked. 'I reckon that would be about the limit of my skill. Unfortunately, the knitting gene seems to have died out with my granny.'

'Never too late to learn,' Pauline said.

Unconvinced, Amy said she'd leave it to the experts.

With shifts agreed, they wrapped up the meeting and Pauline packed everything back into her Mary Poppins bag. She refused Finn's offer of keeping it all in the shop.

'That's very kind of you, dear, but I'd like to make sure everything's nicely presented and all priced up before I bring it down,' Pauline smiled.

Finn and Amy waved her off.

'Do you think she's going home to knit Shreddies now?' Amy asked.

Finn laughed. 'She is a proper knitting nana, isn't she?'

'I think she'll be a good addition to the shop. Something, and someone, completely different.'

'I agree. As long as she doesn't think she's going to have Burt Bacharach blasting out when she's here. Who even is Burt Bacharach?' Finn frowned.

'Probably the featured artist for the next music round at the quiz,' Amy laughed.

'I'd better give him a listen then,' Finn said.

'That's going above and beyond, young Finn. It's one thing swotting up on group nouns …' Amy said, pulling a face.

'Did you find it curious that for all the colourful knitting she does, her cardigans have both been beige?' Finn observed.

Amy cocked her head and thought about it. 'Hm ... that is interesting. Maybe beige is for business, but when she lets her hair down in the knitting room, she's all Joseph-and-his-amazing-technicolour-dream-coat?'

Finn laughed. 'Yeah, maybe. Or maybe she doesn't want to steal the limelight from Barry, the walrus of quizzing.'

'She should knit him a toupee,' Amy giggled.

'I'll let you suggest that, Amy. Anyway, we'll see how it goes; it's the usual three-month trial period. Right, I need to get on. Got a commission for a huge piece on a tiny deadline.'

'Eek! Good luck,' Amy said.

'Thanks! I'll hopefully see you next Wednesday at the latest.'

Amy nodded.

'Have a good day. Sell everything!' Finn said, as he waved from the door.

With the shop to herself again, Amy's thoughts drifted back to their default setting of preoccupied. To try and shake herself out of it, she googled Burt Bacharach and started listening to 'I'll never fall in love again'.

'Urgh. Not helping,' she grumbled, thirty seconds into the song.

Opening Google again, she typed in *capital cities* and set about memorising them. She'd only got to the Bs when the shop door opened again.

CHAPTER 5

Beer today, gone tomorrow

Jenny walked in, wearing oversized dark glasses.

'Morning, Jackie,' Amy said, smiling at her friend.

'Eh?'

'The sunglasses. Very Jackie O,' Amy explained.

'Oh,' said Jenny.

'Exactly,' said Amy.

'It's too early and way too bright for humour, thank you very much,' Jenny groaned, coming over to the counter and plonking herself down on the stool recently vacated by Finn. 'Why did you let me drink beer?' she asked, as she removed the aforementioned glasses.

'Hey, don't blame me when you decide to put your beer goggles on.'

'You know beer makes me obnoxious.'

'Does it? I hadn't noticed.'

'Twat.'

'Takes one to know one,' Amy smiled sweetly at her hungover friend.

'Child.'

Amy stuck her thumbs in her ears and waggled her fingers while simultaneously sticking her tongue out.

Jenny sighed theatrically. 'I do feel rough this morning.'

'So you should. See it as your penance for wishing half of Saga Crews dead and dissing the King.'

'King Kong? The King of Pop?' Jenny did a Michael Jackson-style 'ow'. '"The King of Wishful Thinking"?' Jenny launched into the Go West song. She soon stopped and put her hands to her head. 'Ow.'

'The King of Rock and Roll, Mister Elvis-Fucking-Presley, stoopid.'

'Oh yeah. Actually, I do remember that. Unfortunately.'

'To be perfectly honest, I'd be happy to forget most of last night. I think we should try a different quiz. There is one in Canterbury I used to go to before Covid which was good fun, if we can tempt Willem and Finn out of Folkestone.'

'I'm game,' Jenny nodded. 'Anything's got to be better than Butlin's Bazzer.'

'Okay, cool, I'll suggest it when I see Willem later. He can ask Finn. You've just missed Finn actually.'

'Probably just as well,' Jenny muttered.

'Ooh! That reminds me, I just met the new lady who's joining the shop when Harry leaves. You'll never guess who it is in a million years.'

'You'd better tell me then. I haven't had breakfast yet.'

'Does beige cardi ring any bells?'

'Um ... my Auntie Doris?' Jenny asked.

'You haven't got an Auntie Doris. Have you?'

Jenny shook her head.

'Give up?'

Jenny nodded her head. Then grimaced.

'It's Butlin's Barry's wife! You know, the lady who collected the money last night!'

'Huh. Small world. What does she make?'

'Knitted stuff.'

'Beige cardis?' Jenny queried, mentally picturing an army of beige-cardigan-wearing zombie grannies taking over the town.

'Thankfully not. It's actually really nice, colourful stuff.'

Jenny nodded her head gently and then appeared to drift off.

Amy cast her eyes back to the list of capital cities she'd been trying to learn. *Baku, Bamako, Bandar Seri Begawan.* 'Sod this for a game of soldiers,' she muttered.

Jenny suddenly came back to life again. 'If you were a colour, what colour would you be? Like, Mrs Barry's beige.'

'Mrs Barry's name is Pauline. Um ... Dunno ... maybe green? Or blue?' Amy shrugged.

'I'd be black,' Jenny announced. 'Or shocking pink. Depending on the day.'

'And the hangover?'

Jenny didn't disagree.

'What are you up to today, anyway?' Amy asked.

'Got to pop into a couple of shops that are interested in stocking my stuff. Need to eat something fried and have some caffeine before that though. Probably pop into Miss Gingers to look at fabrics too.'

'That's great,' Amy said. 'I'm so happy you're starting to make money from your sewing. Maybe one day you'll be able to come in here?'

'Yeah, maybe,' Jenny said noncommittally. 'Not sure I fancy the shifts though.'

'It's only a day a week.'

'We'll see. For now, though, you've got Mrs Beige coming in.'

'She sounds like a Cluedo character,' Amy grinned.

'In the library with a knitting needle,' Jenny said.

Amy had just opened her mouth to speak, when the shop door opened, and the first customer of the day came in. Jenny slipped her sunglasses on and waggled her fingers at Amy as she got off the stool and made her escape.

'Catch up later,' Amy called after her, before greeting the lady customer. 'Good morning,' she smiled. 'Just shout if you need any help.'

'Thank you. I'm looking for a birthday present for my husband.'

Five-or-so minutes later, and Amy was bubble-wrapping one of Willem's framed lighthouse prints. She always took extra pleasure in making a sale for him. 'Thank you,' she said to the customer as she was leaving. 'I hope your husband likes it.'

With the shop to herself again, Amy suddenly felt a little low. Capital cities weren't going to cheer her up. Opening a new search window on her phone, she typed in *pub quizzes Canterbury Folkestone* and began researching.

A short while later and Amy was creating a WhatsApp group chat for Jenny, Willem, and Finn called 'Sherlock Homies'.

So, there's a quiz on Friday nights at the Merry Monk in Canterbury if you're all up for it? It used to be really good fun a few years back when I tried it.

She didn't have to wait long for three affirmatives to come back.

I'm game from Finn.

Only if we can be called 'In dog beers, we've only had one' from Jenny.

And *I'll drive* from Willem.

Yay! Amy typed back. *And Jenny, if it's still the same quiz, you have to make up your team name on the night based on criteria the quiz-person gives you.*

With the quiz to look forward to, Amy felt a bit better. She also had dinner with Willem to look forward to. And she *was* looking forward to it. But she was still anxious about what might happen after dinner and the strong possibility that Willem would ask her to stay the night.

The rest of the day in the shop was uneventful. Amy was happy to sell a couple of her books and also something else for both Willem and Finn. She just had time to get home for a quick shower and change before heading to Willem's, with a brief stop en route to grab a bottle to take with her.

She took a deep breath before she rang Willem's doorbell, telling herself to relax.

'Amy, hi, come in,' Willem said, smiling broadly as he opened the door.

'Hello, you. Thank you,' Amy said, holding out the wine.

'Thank you, but you don't have to bring something every time you come round,' Willem told her.

'Sorry. I promise to bring you absolutely nothing next time. Oh, except good news – you had three sales in the shop today.'

'That is good news, thank you.'

'Something smells good,' Amy said, as she followed Willem to the kitchen.

'I hope it tastes good too. I'm attempting my first ever tagine. Lamb and apricot, with couscous.'

'Sounds yummy. I sort of forgot to eat today.'

'That's no good. You'll waste away.'

'Fat chance,' Amy said, breathing in.

Willem laughed. 'I think you're perfect just the way you are.'

Amy blushed and tried to accept the compliment gracefully, but the little voice in her head was telling her to run for the hills.

As it transpired, Amy didn't have to worry about what came after dinner. She got a frantic call from Jenny saying she'd found ticks on one of her cats and needed Amy's help. NOW!

'I'm so sorry, Willem,' she said, hating herself for being secretly relieved. 'I promise I'll make it up to you. Jenny won't rest until we've dealt with this. Her cats are her babies.'

'It's okay, really, you go. I'll see you tomorrow for the quiz. Pick you up around six forty-five?' Willem said.

'Perfect, look forward to it,' Amy smiled.

They kissed goodbye on the doorstep and Amy made her escape.

When she arrived at Jenny's a few minutes later, she was greeted by her friend holding out a bottle of vodka and a pair of tweezers. 'We're ready for you, doctor,' Jenny said.

'So I see. Is the vodka for me or the ticks?'

'Neither,' Jenny said, taking a swig.

Amy laughed.

'I would have had a go at removing them myself, but I was too worried about leaving a bit behind,' Jenny said.

'It's no problem, you did me a favour actually,' Amy said, explaining her dilemma to her friend.

In response, Jenny passed the vodka bottle. Amy shook her head. 'Thanks, but I'd better keep a clear head for surgery.'

Jenny had shut the cat in the kitchen with the promise of Dreamies if she behaved, and Amy made short work of removing the ticks, by dowsing them in vodka, grasping them close to the cat's skin and then giving them a firm tug. She then made a big fuss of the cat while Jenny dispensed tuna-flavoured treats. *If only all problems could be so easily resolved*, Amy thought with a sigh.

CHAPTER 6

Risky quizness

At just after seven the next evening, Willem was parking the car in Canterbury. Amy had very wisely elected to sit in the back with Jenny, leaving the front passenger seat free for Finn. Although Jenny had promised to stay off the beer, Amy wasn't taking any unnecessary risks.

'So, I rang up and booked a table, just in case,' Amy said, as they walked to the pub. 'I hope it's the same woman doing it. She's got even more of a potty mouth than our Jenny.'

Finn looked at Amy doubtfully, his expression asking if that was even possible.

The Merry Monk was warm and welcoming, with a real fire burning in the hearth and a vast array of gins, which made Amy very happy. With drinks purchased, they found their table and settled in. They found four raffle tickets on the table, but Amy couldn't remember what they were all about.

'I s'pose we'll find out at some point,' she shrugged.

The quiz kicked off at seven thirty.

'Oh good, it is the same woman as before,' Amy whispered to the others. 'If Barry is Butlin's, she's an eighteen–thirty holiday in Magaluf.'

The first thing Mrs Magaluf, real name Gemma, did was explain the basis for the week's team names. 'So, imagine Boris Johnson's government was named after a musical,' she said, giving the simple example of *Cats* to *Rats*. 'The ruder the better,' she added. 'A round of shitty shots for my favourite.'

Amy and the others immediately started brainstorming.

'Just throw out all the names of musicals you can think of,' Amy said.

The suggestions started off quite tamely.

Chess. Mess.

Joseph and the Amazing Technicolour Dreamcoat. Boris and the Amazing Technicolour Yawns.

School of Rock. School of Cock.

Then Finn threw out *Chitty Chitty Bang Bang*, and they had their team name.

'Pretty Shitty Gang Bang,' Amy announced when their turn came. A gratifying laugh went round the pub, and the next thing they knew, they were being presented with a round of shots, which apparently came from a bottle of spirits plucked at random by the bar staff from a selection that had been languishing on the shelves, gathering dust, for some time. Hence the 'shitty' bit.

'Well, we're off to a good start,' Willem said. 'Although, as I'm driving, I probably shouldn't have this …' He held up the shot glass.

Wasting no time, Jenny reached over and took it from him, downing it at once. 'You're welcome,' she said, smiling sweetly at Willem.

Willem had the good grace to laugh.

'Jenny! For fuck's sake!' Amy exclaimed.

'What? He didn't want it,' Jenny said.

Amy just shook her head.

'Right, you lovely lot, let's make a start,' Gemma said. The noise in the pub didn't abate. 'Oi! Shut the fuck up you 'orrible lot so we can get started!' Gemma shouted, glaring at one particularly noisy table at the back of the pub.

'You wouldn't get that at the Griffin,' Willem chuckled.

'Perish the thought. Pauline would wash Barry's mouth out with soap,' Amy giggled, earning a hard stare from Gemma. 'Sorry,' she mouthed, before drawing an imaginary zip across her lips.

'That's more like it, people,' Gemma said. 'Right, round one is geography.'

Willem came into his own for this one, ably assisted by Finn. Amy was beyond delighted when the final question of the round was *What is the capital of Brunei?*

'B,' was Jenny's contribution.

'Ooh, ooh, I know this!' Amy said excitedly. 'It's ... oh bugger ... um ... three words ... B ... B ... Band ... Bandar Seri Begawan!'

'How the hell did you know that?' Finn whispered, suitably impressed.

'I followed your example and did a bit of swotting while the shop was quiet. I only got as far as the Bs, but that was enough!'

'Nice,' Fin nodded.

'Okay, moving swiftly on to round two, which is collective nouns,' Gemma announced, sending a groan around the pub. 'If you don't fucking like it, you can fuck off,' Gemma informed them.

Amy looked at Finn and smiled broadly. 'Oh my God, it's our lucky night!'

They smashed round two, with Jenny and Willem astounded by Finn knowing every answer, even earning them a bonus point for being able to name three of the five possible answers for group nouns of cats: clowder, clutter, and pounce.

Round three turned out to be a picture round and they were encouraged to use their ten allotted minutes to get drinks. Amy tried to encourage Jenny to get a soft one.

'Don't be a fucking killjoy,' Jenny said, obviously channelling her inner Gemma.

Amy and Willem ordered Cokes, Finn a cider, and Jenny a double VAT in keeping with the government theme.

Amy couldn't help thinking she was glad they hadn't driven over in her car, the way Jenny was drinking. She thought it would probably be best if they drove back with the windows open and a carrier bag to hand.

The picture round was like a gift from the gods. Make that a gift from the dogs. It was *Name twenty breeds of dogs and cats*. Between Amy's vet knowledge and all-round love of animals, and Jenny's cat-aholic-ism, they answered nineteen of them with no trouble at all. The twentieth one was a hairless dog that looked like it was inside out.

'Just put "ugly",' Jenny suggested.

'Um ... shall we just have a guess at Chinese Hairless?' Amy suggested, and Willem wrote it on the answer sheet.

'S'pose eating hairless dogs saves a lot of hassle,' Jenny mused.

After a very successful picture round, Gemma told everyone to grab a raffle ticket each. Amy actually had her lucky number, eighty-nine. 'It never fails me,' she said. Gemma explained to the newbies that she would pick a number at random, and the winning team would be asked one question which, if they answered it correctly, would win them a prize.

'Tonight's winning number is ...' Gemma said, rummaging in a hat full of raffle tickets, '... number eighty-nine!'

'I knew it,' Amy said excitedly. 'Every time!' She held the ticket aloft and waited for Gemma, who sauntered over and held out three white envelopes.

'Seems to be your lucky night,' Gemma said. 'So, one envelope is a round of shitty shots, another is a scratch card, and the third is fifty quid to spend behind the bar,' she informed Pretty Shitty Gang Bang. 'Get the answer to the next question right, and you can choose one envelope.'

Amy looked around the table grinning and held up crossed fingers. Willem and Finn smiled and crossed their fingers too. Jenny was busy thinking about the possibility of winning another free round of shots.

'Tonight's raffle question concerns the King of Rock and Roll, the one and only Elvis Presley,' Gemma continued.

'Elvis-fucking-Presley,' Jenny mumbled.

Amy's grin widened. *What were the chances?*

'Listen up, team. What was the name of Elvis Presley's pet chimpanzee?'

If they hadn't been to the quiz at the Griffin just two days earlier, they would never have known. They'd guessed 'Peanut' when Barry had asked them the very same question. Now, Finn and Willem nodded at Amy, and she gave the answer.

'Scatter,' Amy said confidently.

'Scatter it is!' Gemma confirmed, to the team and the pub in general. 'Elvis's chimp, Scatter, was by all accounts a bit of a bugger. He'd tear apart dressing rooms on film sets, swill whisky if left unattended, and masturbate in public. Until he was allegedly poisoned by a maid he bit.'

'Sounds like my spirit animal,' Jenny looked impressed. 'Apart from the masturbating in public bit. I draw the line at that.'

'Good to know,' Finn muttered into his drink.

Gemma was now wafting the three envelopes in front of them.

'You pick, Amy,' Willem said.

Amy reached out and selected the middle one, which she tore open and held up. 'A round of shitty shots,' she said.

'Yesss!' from Jenny, as she punched the air. Groans from Willem and Finn.

When the shots arrived, Willem simply handed his to Jenny.

'Down the hatch!' she said, knocking back both hers and Willem's.

Amy downed hers too. 'Was that Malibu?'

Jenny answered with a rum-and-coconut-scented burp.

Round five kicked off then and was general knowledge. Amy's team knew about fifty per cent of the answers and made educated guesses at the rest. The final round, thankfully not a wipeout one, was a connections round. The first four answers were connected in some way, and that connection was the answer to question five.

Pretty Shitty Gang Bang answered questions two and three confidently and had the names 'Carrie' and 'Miranda'. They were trying to come up with a connection so they could sort of reverse-engineer questions one and four.

Jenny had pretty much given up by now and was slumped in her seat, but the others were deep in thought. Amy and Willem were gobsmacked when Finn quietly suggested a connection.

'Could it be *Sex and the City*?'

Amy thought for a couple of moments. 'Oh my God, yes, I think you're right. The answer to question one could be Charlotte. That makes three characters from *Sex and the City*.

I don't know about the rock band though.'

'Tell me some other names from the show,' Willem said. 'Something might ring a bell.'

'Um ... Samantha's the only other one I can think of,' Amy said. 'Finn?'

'There was Mr. Big,' Finn said, again surprising them with his knowledge of the TV programme.

'That's it!' Willem said. 'That's the name of an American rock band; I'm sure of it.'

'Brilliant! Well done,' Amy said, watching as Willem filled in the missing answers.

They swapped papers then, and the marking began. Gemma collected up the answer sheets then and went off to double-check the final scores.

'I wonder if we've done enough?' Willem said.

'We smashed most of the rounds,' Finn pointed out.

'I suppose it all hangs on the general knowledge round,' Amy said. 'We were so lucky with the other topics.'

'I know, I can't believe it,' Finn agreed.

'Lady luck was certainly on our side tonight,' Willem nodded.

Jenny hiccupped.

'Right, you lot, we have a winner, and I have to say this team absolutely smashed it tonight on their first time here.'

Amy held her breath. *It must be ...*

'The winners are Pretty Shitty Gang Bang!'

'Oh my God, we did it!' Amy exclaimed.

Finn and Willem grinned at her.

Jenny had her eyes closed and her head was nodding.

Gemma handed over their winnings of £122, and Willem

divided it between them.

'Thirty pounds and fifty pee each!' Amy was delighted.

'Not forgetting two free rounds of shots,' Finn said, nodding at the nodding Jenny.

'More than makes up for the disaster at the Griffin on Wednesday,' Willem smiled.

'It really does! I'm definitely going to mug up on some more topics too,' Amy said.

'Maybe we could each take on a different subject every week,' Finn suggested.

'That's a great idea,' Willem agreed.

'Right, shall we make a move then?' Amy asked.

The two men nodded and Amy poked Jenny. 'Time to go. Jenny, wakey wakey.'

With Amy and Willem each taking an arm, they got Jenny back to the car and into the back seat, with the window open next to her. She promptly closed her eyes again. The drive back to Folkestone was, thankfully, uneventful as Jenny fell asleep, and Willem helped Amy to get her indoors and upstairs after they'd dropped Finn home. Dropping Amy off last, Willem kissed her goodbye and drove home, where Cat greeted him with a stretch and a yawn at the door.

CHAPTER 7

Too much liquor makes me quizzy

Amy woke late the next morning, Saturday, and took her coffee back to bed. She was thinking about Jenny. Her friend's behaviour of late was worrying her. She thought it was time to find out what the hell was going on with her. Deciding it was probably wise to wait a while before messaging Jenny, who probably had a very thick head that morning, Amy got up, had a shower and breakfast, and did a few jobs before messaging.

Morning, pisshead, she typed at about eleven thirty.

Bleurgh came the response.

That good huh?

Oh yeah. Did we win? Or was I turning tricks last night? I found a load of money on my bedside table.

Amy laughed. *We did indeed win. Absolutely smashed it in fact. Me too.*

Amy could picture Jenny, looking decidedly worse for wear and wondering what day it was.

I vaguely remember something about Elvis's chimp. Feels like it pissed in my mouth to be honest, Jenny typed.

Charming, Amy replied. *Do you feel up to meeting for lunch today?*

Yeah, I s'pose.

Cool. Django's at half twelve? If we can't get a table there, we can just go next door.

OK. See you then.

Amy returned to her jobs to kill a bit more time and left the house at about twelve fifteen to make the short walk into town. She bagsied a table in the window of the bistro and waited for Jenny to arrive.

'Jackie,' Amy greeted her, when Jenny arrived wearing the enormous sunglasses again.

'Fuck off,' came the response.

Amy laughed, watching her friend as she sat gingerly down.

Once they'd placed their lunch order, Amy didn't waste any time and got straight to the point. She'd learned that there was no point pussyfooting around Jenny. She'd respect you a lot more if you just got straight down to brass tacks.

'Right, missus, what's going on with you?' Amy asked, looking directly at Jenny, who was still sporting the shades.

Jenny put on her best I-don't-know-what-you-mean face, shaking her head.

Amy reached over with both hands and removed Jenny's glasses, forcing her to make eye contact.

'Fuck me, I didn't know I was having lunch with the fun police,' Jenny said, pulling a face.

Amy just raised her eyebrows and continued to stare at her friend, making it clear that she wasn't going to let Jenny off the hook.

'For fuck's sake!' Jenny exclaimed. 'Alright, alright, if you must know, I'm not sleeping all that well.'

'There, that wasn't so hard now, was it? Do you know why?' Amy smiled gently at her friend, her good cop taking over.

Jenny leaned her elbows on the table and pressed her fingers into her eyes. 'Because every time I close my eyes, I see that bastard. I see Teller. And I see the pictures of Bella, of what he did to her. Jesus, even their names rhyme. Teller, Bella, Teller, Bella, going round my head in a fucking nightmare loop,' Jenny shook her head as if trying to dislodge the awful images.

Amy reached over and put her hands on Jenny's, pulling them away from her face and holding them on the table. Just then, two iced teas arrived, and Jenny yanked her hands away, looking down at her lap.

'Thank you,' Amy smiled at the waitress, and waited for her to move away. 'I get it, Jenny, really I do.'

'I wish I'd killed him, Amy!' Jenny blurted out. 'I wish I'd killed the fucker!' she spat, looking up at Amy with angry tears in her eyes.

The other diners looked round with shocked expressions. Amy smiled round at them, trying to reassure them that there was nothing to worry about.

Jenny's head was lowered once more as she tried to compose herself.

'No, you don't, Jenny. Trust me on that,' Amy said quietly.

'I do,' Jenny said tearfully. 'I bloody do, Amy.'

Digging a tissue out of her handbag, Amy passed it across the table. Jenny dabbed at her eyes and blew her nose.

'Killing Teller wouldn't stop the nightmares, Jenny. I know from bitter experience,' Amy leaned in and whispered to her distraught friend. 'Taking another life, even scum like Seymour and Teller, isn't something you can truly come back from.'

Jenny risked a glance up at Amy. 'It couldn't be any worse than this,' she said quietly, shaking her head.

'Oh, it could.'

'I don't see how.'

'Well, for starters, I'm probably going to have to finish things with Willem because of the secret I carry. I honestly don't know if I'll ever be able to share my bed with anyone ever again.'

'Just get cats,' Jenny tried to smile.

'Oh, I've thought about that, trust me.'

'I do get what you're saying, really I do,' Jenny began, 'but it's just eating me up that he's still breathing, while beautiful Bella is dead.'

'I know, but wouldn't death have been too good for him? Surely being locked up for the rest of life is more of a punishment. He can't suffer if he's dead.'

'Maybe he'll get shanked in the shower,' Jenny said grimly.

Amy flinched. 'Yeah, maybe.'

'Or some giant of a man called, I dunno, DeShawn, will take a fancy to him.' This prospect seemed to cheer Jenny slightly.

'What? Are we in an episode of *Prison Break* now?' Amy smiled.

'I just want him to suffer, Amy, for what he did to Bella. And the others.'

'I get that, I do. But all killing him would have done would have been to change you forever and, potentially, get you locked up instead,' Amy tried to reason.

Jenny gave a huge sigh and seemed to deflate.

Just then, two jacket potatoes arrived, one with prawns and one with tuna, and the pair fell silent again as they focused on their food.

After a while, Amy spoke again. 'How can I help you? What do you think might help you?'

'I honestly don't know,' Jenny shrugged.

'Well, you know you can talk to me any time. It might help.

Get it out of your head. You know you can call me any time, day or night.'

'I know, and I appreciate it. I suppose it's going to take time.'

Amy nodded. 'And maybe lay off the booze a bit?' she suggested, putting her fun-police hat back on.

Jenny maturely stuck out her tongue, but she knew deep down that Amy was right. She'd been a bit of a twat lately. 'I probably owe Willem and Finn an apology,' she grimaced.

'Or two,' Amy chuckled. 'I'm sure they'll forgive you. Well, Willem will. Finn may still think you're a potty-mouthed lush.'

They were both laughing now and, for the first time in a while, Jenny felt a small spark of happiness. Maybe it would be all right. Not yet, sure, but maybe one day.

CHAPTER 8

The fab four

The four quizzers didn't meet up again until the following Wednesday, having decided to brave Barry's quiz at the Griffin Alehouse again. Willem had been away for a few days photographing in Northumberland. He'd invited Amy, but she'd made her excuses, feeling guilty again that she was deceiving him.

Amy and Jenny walked to the pub together and Amy handed her friend a gift bag. 'It's just a few things to help you sleep,' she told her. 'Open it when you get home.' Amy had bought Jenny some items that had helped her over the past months: a lavender pillow spray, relaxing bath oil, chamomile teabags and some essential oils. She'd wrapped them all up with a funny cat eye mask.

Jenny stopped and hugged her friend. It had already helped a great deal to have talked things over with Amy, and the bond the two shared was stronger than ever. No one else could ever understand what they had been through together.

Finn and Willem had arrived before them and were settled at the same table they'd had the previous week. They both had pints of bitter in front of them. Willem made to get up at once, offering to go to the bar to get drinks for Amy and Jenny, but Jenny stopped him.

'Thanks, Willem, but I'll get these,' she said. 'Can I get you two anything?'

Willem and Finn exchanged glances, wondering who this woman was and what she'd done with Jenny. They both said 'no, thanks' and the two women went to the bar. When Jenny ordered a Coke, Amy did the same, thinking if Jenny was laying off the booze, she would too. Solidarity and all that.

'So,' Amy began, when they were all seated round the table, 'have you all been genning up on tonight's specialist subject?'

Amy had found the Facebook page that BB – that's Butlin's Barry – had mentioned last week and found out that the specialist round was on fauna and flora of the British Isles. She and Jenny had volunteered to take flora, although they would both have preferred fauna.

Three heads nodded around the table.

'It looks like all the same teams as last week,' Willem said, looking around the pub.

'Yeah, I see the Saga Louts are back,' Finn joked, nodding in the direction of the Saga Crews team.

The others laughed. Amy was happy to see Finn coming out of his shell a bit.

'And the smug bastards that won last week,' Jenny added, smiling saccharinely at the Scrambled Eggheads and waggling her fingers at them. 'Hello, smug bastards,' she mouthed, through her big fake smile.

'I wonder what the music round will be this week?' Willem said.

'Guns N' *Roses*?'

'Kate *Bush*?'

'How about A Flock of *Seagulls* or the Boomtown *Rats*?'

'What are we going to call ourselves this week?' Finn asked.

'Smarty Pints?' was Jenny's rather tame suggestion.

'Shining Wits? I do love a good spoonerism,' from Amy. She got blank looks until the others worked out what she meant and laughed.

Willem couldn't help thinking it was a shame she didn't love a good spoon.

They finally settled on Menace to Sobriety in Jenny's honour.

Barry appeared then, this time wearing a yellow golfing sweater.

Jenny did her Ruth Madoc impersonation again.

Barry made the usual announcements while the lovely Pauline, this time sporting a beige knitted waistcoat over a white blouse, came round to collect the entry fees. She stopped at Amy's table for a minute, and they introduced her to Willem as the lady who was joining the shop.

'Lovely to meet you, Pauline,' Willem smiled.

'And you, Wilhelm,' she said.

Amy giggled.

'Well, good luck tonight,' Pauline went on. 'Be nice if a different team won for a change. Those blooming Scrambled Eggheads haven't lost for weeks.' As she spoke, Pauline was frowning at the team in question. She went on to explain that the group of middle-aged, well-to-do-looking men and women were all teachers and university lecturers. 'It's time they ruddy well gave the other teams a fighting chance,' she grumbled.

Pauline moved away then, patting 'Wilhelm' on the shoulder and wishing them all luck once more, as she went off to continue collecting the money. The team turned to Barry who was telling everyone that the music round was on the Beatles.

The four agreed that they each had a smattering of Beatles knowledge but were not overly confident that they'd do any better than with Elvis.

'Let's hope it's a better picture round this week,' Amy said. Although Willem and Finn had known the bridges, Amy was hoping for something she could join in with.

Amy's hopes didn't last long, however, as Pauline deposited two copies of the picture round on their table.

'Shipping-forecast areas?' she groaned. 'You must be kidding me?'

The others were laughing, but not with joy as they all felt the same way.

'I literally don't know any of these,' Jenny admitted, as she studied the map with its numbered sections.

'Me neither,' Amy said, screwing up her face.

Willem and Finn didn't look much happier but were having a stab at it. They both knew some names they could chuck in – Dogger, Humber, Wight, and Fastnet to name a few – but neither of them could place them on the map with any degree of confidence.

'Yuck,' Amy said, when they'd done the best they could.

'Yuck indeed,' Willem agreed. 'We could conceivably get a big fat zero on this round.'

'The Scrambled Eggheads are looking smug already,' Jenny informed them, having just glanced over at their table.

'Well, if they knew all those shipping-forecast thingies, I feel sorry for them. They need to get out more,' Amy said.

'Hear hear,' Jenny agreed, lifting her Coke. 'Boring twats.' She wasn't gone completely, Amy smiled to herself.

Putting the disastrous picture round to one side, mentally and literally, the team had two reasonable general knowledge rounds, and did pretty well on the specialist round, with the homework paying off. The Beatles music round wasn't as bad as feared although, as with the Elvis songs, they had to guess all the years. By the time they'd marked the first five rounds, however, they were in joint second-to-last place. The boring twats, aka the Scrambled Eggheads, were way out in front, with the Saga Crews an unseaworthy second.

With just the wipeout round remaining, Menace to Sobriety were debating the pros and cons of going for it or playing safe.

'We've got nothing to lose by gambling, have we?' Jenny was saying. 'We can't possibly win unless we do.'

'Or …' said a naturally more cautious Amy, 'if we play it safe and get some guaranteed points, other teams might wipe out?'

'I think we have to go for it,' Finn was saying. 'Jenny's right. What have we got to lose?'

Had Finn just said Jenny was right? Whatever next? Amy wondered.

'I don't mind, to be honest,' Willem said. 'Why don't we see what questions come up and decide as we go along?'

They finally agreed that this was an acceptable compromise.

'I hate the wipeout round,' Amy declared. 'It's not good for my blood pressure.'

By the time Barry asked the final, tenth question, they had five definite answers. Amy was still arguing for sticking.

'It won't be enough though,' Jenny insisted.

'But it might stop us from being last,' Amy pushed.

'Go big or go home, I say,' said Finn.

Who are you and what have you done with Finn? Amy looked at him in surprise.

'I'll go along with the majority,' Willem said, knowing that meant siding against Amy.

'Fine!' Amy said, holding up her hands. 'I know when I'm beaten. Unlike the fecking Scrambled Eggheads,' she grumbled.

They'd been making educated guesses on a spare piece of paper as they went along, and Willem now filled them in on the official answer sheet.

Amy sat back with a sigh as the teams swapped papers and marking commenced. It was no surprise when they wiped out on the fourth question, scoring a big fat zero for the round, and last place overall.

To nobody's surprise the Scrambled Eggheads stormed home with a full fifteen points for the final round. You couldn't help noticing that the applause for them was decidedly lacklustre though, and there was a definite air of disenchantment in the pub. Amy caught a glimpse of Pauline's face, and she did not look at all happy that the same team had won, yet again.

A smiling Barry handed over the winnings of £106 and gave everyone a bit of a pep talk. Apparently, it was about the taking part.

'Is it fuck as like,' Jenny disagreed. 'I could really use the money at the moment.'

'Yeah, and it's not as if that lot need it, smug gits,' Finn agreed with her.

Willem and Amy just looked at each other and wondered if there was something in the air. Or their drinks.

'I think we should try and find two more people to join the team,' Amy suggested. 'See if you can come up with any ideas for suitable candidates.'

The others nodded and they finished their drinks and got up to leave.

'Walk you home?' Willem asked Amy.

'Um ... I'm going back to Jenny's tonight actually,' Amy smiled at him, feeling a lump in her chest at telling another lie. She felt Jenny's eyes flicker in her direction, but her friend said nothing, simply linked her arm through Amy's and pulled her away from Willem.

'Yeah, you can't have her; she's my friend, so there, nur,' Jenny said, pulling a face at Willem.

'Well, while you two fight over Amy, I'm off,' Finn announced, setting off down the road.

'Bye, Finn!' the other three called after him.

Amy disentangled herself from Jenny and went over to hug Willem goodbye. 'Speak to you tomorrow?' she said.

Willem muttered something unintelligible and pulled out of the hug. 'Bye, Jenny,' he called, as he walked off into the night.

'What was all that about?' Jenny asked Amy when Willem was out of sight and of earshot.

'Sorry! I didn't mean to put you on the spot. I just couldn't face making excuses to Willem again about why we can't spend the night together,' Amy said, sighing deeply. 'What am I going to do, Jenny?'

'I don't know, but if you're not careful the decision will be taken out of your hands. Willem wasn't a happy bunny just then.'

'I know. I feel terrible. I can't keep lying to him. But what's the alternative?' Amy could feel tears pricking her eyes.

'You have two options as far as I can see. You either tell him the truth and take your chances, or you end it,' Jenny said, reaching over and tucking Amy's hair behind her ear.

'What if I hate both options?' she said sadly.

Jenny simply shrugged. 'You can't go on as you are, can you?'

Amy shook her head as a single tear rolled down her cheek. 'Fuck.'

'Indeed.'

'I think I need to sleep on it.' Amy sounded as tired as she felt.

'I take it you're not really staying at mine?'

Amy shook her head. 'No, I need my own bed. And you have to try out some of your goodies,' Amy reminded her.

'I do, don't I? Thank you,' Jenny smiled, holding up the gift bag Amy had given her earlier.

'I hope they help. I have a feeling I'm in for another restless night.'

'You need to make a decision. Until then you're just going to be going round in circles. And I know all about those buggers.'

'I know you're right. It's not easy though.'

'I know. Anyway, whatever you decide, you've always got me,' Jenny said, throwing her arms in the air, and almost losing the contents of her gift bag.

Amy gave a half-laugh and smiled at her crazy friend.

Soon afterwards, the friends hugged and went their separate ways, and Amy trudged up the hill to her house. She didn't switch on any lights as she made her way through the house, banging her shin on the corner of the coffee table in the lounge when she went in to close the curtains.

'Ow! Bugger!' she cursed. 'This is ridiculous, Amy,' she muttered. She'd just reopened the curtains in case Willem had been watching her house and would know the curtains had been left open when she went out. She grumbled her way around the house in the dark, getting ready for bed and cleaning her teeth with no light. Creeping into her bedroom, she had to duck under the window, thinking as she did so that she would have to sleep with the curtains open. 'For fuck's sake,' she swore as she fumbled by the bed for the phone charging cable. Deciding to risk the bedside lamp for the briefest of moments, Amy flicked the switch and illuminated the room for all of five seconds to plug her mobile in. Finally, she crawled into bed and lay there, wide awake. She would normally read herself to sleep. 'Arseholes,' she said, closing her eyes and waiting for sleep to come.

Across the viaduct, Willem was sitting in his back garden with his telescope and a cigar. He could swear he saw a light flick on momentarily at Amy's house across the valley. He smiled sadly.

At her house, Jenny was climbing into a bed that smelled of lavender ('Ew, old ladies') and pulling her new cat mask over her eyes. Both cats took one look and made themselves scarce.

It was about 2 a.m. when Amy finally gave up trying to sleep. Padding downstairs, she went through to the kitchen, closed the door so no light would shine through to the front of the house, and switched on the light, yawning as she filled the kettle. A few minutes later and she was seated at her kitchen table with a mug of Pukka night-time tea. She was so tired, she could cry, but she didn't even have the energy for that. Her soul was weary. 'Arse-souls,' she said tiredly. She knew, deep down, that she wouldn't get a good night's sleep until she dealt with the Willem situation. She thought, not for the first time, that she might as well be in prison for her crime, because she couldn't live a normal life on the outside anymore.

'Stop feeling sorry for yourself, you sad cow,' she said. 'You made your bed ... Oh, very funny,' she sighed from her place on the kitchen chair. She had made her bed and it looked as though she'd be the only one who *would* ever lie in it. She knew what she had to do. Amy's head sank and big fat tears began to plop onto the kitchen table.

Willem was lying in bed staring at the ceiling. Glancing over at the clock, he saw it was 4 a.m. He might as well get up and go out with the camera. Dawn was still a way off, but that just meant he could drive further away to photograph. Maybe he'd just keep on driving ...

Jenny was snoring her head off, lulled by lavender, and enjoying the first good night's sleep she'd had in ages.

CHAPTER 9

Gin'll fix it

The following morning, after a few hours of fitful dozing, Amy lay in bed looking out at a grey and mizzly day. Autumn was definitely making its presence known.

'Suits my mood,' Amy sighed. She was no nearer to a decision about Willem than she'd been eight hours earlier and was wondering about the practicalities of a) joining a convent, or b) running away to join the circus, or c) moving to a remote croft in the Outer Hebrides. There were plenty of pros for becoming a nun: easy decision on what to wear each day, no need to do your hair, no dating dilemmas ... not believing in God might be a bit of a stumbling block though. As for b, did people even still do that? She didn't have any real circus skills anyway, unless you counted hula hooping. The croft had the most appeal – she could get a dog and write to her heart's content – but she'd miss Jenny. And besides, she really did love Folkestone, serial killers and all.

Sliding out of bed and crouching down as she passed the window – 'For fuck's sake, you're ridiculous' – Amy padded downstairs to make coffee. She was surprised to find a letter on the doormat. *Way too early for the postman*, she thought, frowning. Unless she'd missed it in the dark last night. Turning the envelope over as she went into the kitchen, Amy recognised Willem's handwriting.

Amy's heart did a flip, right up into her throat.

She focused on making coffee before opening the letter. Her heart was still firmly in her mouth, and she couldn't swallow the coffee, as she tore open the envelope and took out a single sheet of paper.

Dear Amy,

By the time you read this I will have gone. Not forever, but for a while. For a few weeks at least. I think it's for the best, don't you?

I care a great deal for you, and I think, thought, you felt something for me too, but I am so full of doubt now. There has been something between us, a barrier, ever since we met. I kept waiting, hoping, that whatever it was would disappear as you came to know and trust me. But it hasn't happened, and I can feel you holding back all the time.

Maybe you've been hurt before, I don't know, but you have put up a wall I can't get past. I think I've been patient, but I can only take so much rejection, Amy. This old heart of mine has too many battle scars already, and I'm too old to play guessing games.

I wish things could be different, but the fact of the matter is you've been lying to me, and I can't get past that. I can forgive many things, but not dishonesty. Whatever it is you can't tell me, I can't begin to imagine. What could be so awful? Perhaps I'll never know as you keep it locked inside so deeply.

Take good care of yourself, Amy. I wish you only happiness and I hope you find peace from your demons. Perhaps we can pick up our friendship one day. Until perhaps ...

Willem

Amy was sobbing, and Willem's words were smudged where her tears had fallen unchecked onto the letter. Grabbing the kitchen roll, she wiped her face and blew her nose, hiccupping as she tried to get the sobs under control. Then, as a thought struck her, she ran upstairs and grabbed the binoculars, focusing them on Willem's house across the valley, convinced that he'd have had second thoughts and there'd be a big smiley face in the window. *Only joking! Ignore the letter! Silly me!*

Nothing. The window was empty.

But what about Cat? He couldn't just leave like that, could he?

Could he?

Amy got dressed quickly and was out of the house and in the car heading for Willem's house before you could say *you're dumped*. She rang his doorbell a few short minutes later and waited. No answer. She tried again. Nothing. She was trying to phone his mobile when the neighbour's door opened.

'He's gone away,' the woman said.

'What? No …' Amy shook her head. 'He can't …'

The woman shrugged. 'That's all I can tell you.' She smiled at Amy and closed the door.

'But what about Cat?' Amy asked as the door closed. 'What about me?' she whispered.

Getting back in her car, Amy tried calling Willem, but it went straight to voicemail. The tears were flowing again as Amy started the engine and drove off. She didn't go home and was soon ringing Jenny's doorbell.

If Jenny was surprised, she didn't show it as she opened her front door and gestured for Amy to come in before wrapping her arms around her.

'He's dumped me!' Amy said, through the tears. 'Willem's dumped me.'

'I know. Let's go into the kitchen,' Jenny soothed, leading the way.

Once they were settled at the kitchen table with cups of tea, and Amy was a bit calmer, she seemed to realise what Jenny had said.

'What do you mean, you know?' Amy asked, dumbfounded.

'Willem called me. Said you might be needing a friend. I put two and two together and … here you are. It wasn't rocket science. Please don't ask me to learn that for a quiz by the way.'

'You got a call? I got a sodding Dear John letter.'

'I don't think it's called a Dear John letter when it's addressed to a woman. I think you'll find that's a Dear Jane letter,' Jenny said helpfully.

'For fuck's sake, you knew what I meant,' Amy said crossly, thinking now was not an appropriate time to be correcting her. 'Either way, I'm dumped, and he didn't even have the decency to tell me to my face!'

Jenny raised her eyebrows. 'Because that would have been so much better for you both?'

'Yes. No. I don't know!' Amy wailed.

'The way I see it, Willem's done you a favour and made the decision for you. At least you can stop agonising over it now.'

'But I wasn't done agonising over it!' Amy whined. 'And I might have decided to tell him!'

Jenny screwed up her face. 'Really? Would you? Be honest, Amy.'

'Fuck it! Honesty is overrated.'

'Well, not as far as Willem's concerned, eh?'

Amy seemed to deflate then. 'I don't blame him for finishing it. I wasn't being fair on him. And I hated lying to him. He deserved better. But it's not fair.'

'I know. Life rarely is.'

They sat quietly for a few minutes and drank their tea. One of Jenny's cats came and demanded some attention, reminding Amy of Cat.

'Apparently Finn is looking after Cat until Willem gets back,' Jenny reassured her.

The mention of Finn made Amy think of the shop. 'Bloody hell, it's my day in the shop!' she said, jumping up. 'Oh God! How am I going to get through a day in the shop? And I'm going to be late! I have to go home, shower, change, have breakfast. I'll never be ready in time.'

Jenny shushed her. 'Finn's opening up for you. Willem spoke to him too. You can go in later if you feel up to it. No pressure.'

'Oh my God, he thought of everything. He's such a lovely man, Jenny. What have I done? Have I buggered up the best thing that ever happened to me?' Amy was crying again.

Jenny passed her a tissue. 'Well, no, obviously I'm the best thing that ever happened to you but, yes, this probably comes a close second.'

Amy snorted, not knowing whether to laugh or cry anymore.

'I am sorry, Amy. Neither of you deserved this.'

Amy nodded, snuffling into the tissue.

'And being single's not so bad, is it?' Jenny smiled.

Amy shook her head. 'No, I s'pose not.'

'You s'pose snot. You certainly do. Here, have another tissue.'

Amy blew her nose and sat back with a sigh.

'So, what are you going to do with this unexpected day off?'

Jenny asked her. 'You're welcome to hang out here with me.'

'Um ... thank you. I think I could actually do with some time on my own. Might go down to the Warren for a walk and a mope. Then go and buy all my favourite foods and pig out in front of the telly.'

Jenny nodded. 'Good plan. No one to stay slim for now, eh?'

'Fuck off!' Amy said, but she was laughing now.

Amy left soon afterwards and made her way home. She thought briefly about just going back to bed but, after texting Finn to thank him for covering her shift, she drove down to her favourite wild beach and let the sea take her worries with the tide. She would survive this. She'd survived much worse. When she got back to the car just over an hour later, she composed a message to Willem:

I'm so very sorry. I wish I could explain. Know that I care a great deal for you, and I hope we can find our way back to friendship one day. Take good care of yourself. Amy xx

CHAPTER 10

Two's company

With Willem gone, the quiz team was in danger of fizzling out. Amy wasn't sure if Finn would still want to go without Willem. Even off the booze, Jenny was an acquired taste, and Amy wasn't sure if she was a sufficient buffer on her own. She did think it would be a shame to stop though, and she for one needed all the distraction going.

Willem had been gone for five days and Amy hadn't heard from him at all. She had just about stopped expecting the phone to ring or her doorbell to go, and for Willem to be there, saying it was all a big mistake and could they try again? She had started to type many a message before deleting it with a sigh. She knew she had to respect his decision to cut off all contact and disappear from her life. She wondered where he was though, and hoped he was okay. In the meantime, she just had to get on with her life as best she could. She had tried losing herself in her writing, but nothing was flowing. Except gin.

Jenny, as usual, had been her rock and seemed to be back on an even keel most of the time. They'd visited Bella's grave and laid flowers, sitting on a bench close by and talking about Jenny's friendship with the younger woman. It had proved cathartic and Jenny was definitely beginning to find some sort of peace and acceptance, with less and less frequent blips and trips to the offie.

Amy had been wracking her brains for suitable candidates to

join the quiz team, and thought back to her old writing group which had been killed off by Covid. Pippa would be a lovely addition, but she thought Finn would feel the odd one out if they were joined by yet another middle-aged woman. They needed another man or two. *Story of my life*, Amy mused. It was a shame Harry the potter was moving away – he would have been perfect. There was always Finn's dad, Brian. He'd liven up proceedings. Finn would never forgive her though.

Amy was still pondering when the doorbell rang. Her heart leapt as her thoughts went immediately to Willem. Closing her eyes for a moment, Amy shook her head and went to answer the door.

'Morning, you sad single person.'

Jenny.

'Morning, dickhead.'

'What you up to?'

'Er ... not a lot. Supposed to be writing, but ...'

'Yeah, yeah, I know. You're too sad and single ...' Jenny said in mock sympathy.

'Fuck off,' Amy told her.

Jenny just grinned. 'Thought we could go for a walk while the sun's shining. Do you good to get out.'

'Because I'm so sad and single?'

'Yep. Can't have you moping around the house feeling sorry for yourself forever. Get your lazy arse into gear.'

'Lazy *fat* arse, if you please,' Amy groaned. 'I've barely moved lately.'

'I know, you fat cow, that's why I'm here.'

'How very rude.'

'Accurate though, eh?'

Amy sighed and nodded and Jenny followed her back into the house long enough for Amy to grab a jumper and jacket and pull her boots on.

'Where are we headed?' Amy asked, as they set off down the hill towards the town.

'Harbour?' Jenny suggested.

'Yeah, okay. Maybe head along the boardwalk, blow the cobwebs away?'

Jenny nodded and they walked on in silence for a while.

'Thanks for this. It is good to get out,' Amy smiled at her friend, and took a deep breath as the sea came into view. It never failed to lift her spirits and she wondered why she hadn't been down before now. But she knew, deep down, that she'd needed to hide away and lick her wounds for a while.

After grabbing takeout hot chocolates from Harbour Coffee, the two friends made their way across the old railway platform and picked up the boardwalk which ran along the pebbly beach towards Sandgate and Hythe.

As they passed the Pilot Bar, Jenny had a flashback to the day she'd met a friend from London there, and he'd slipped her the gun she'd asked for. She shuddered. Amy noticed.

'You okay?'

'Yeah, yeah. Just thinking about Spud.'

'Your dodgy friend from London?'

'One of many,' Jenny confirmed.

'And supplier of small arms?'

Jenny nodded. 'Aye.'

'Spud gun,' Amy said. 'Do you remember them? Had one as a kid. You pushed the tip into a raw potato and then fired a potato pellet.'

'I think Teller would have laughed if I'd fired a spud gun at him, don't you?'

'He'd have had a job with his mouth taped up,' Amy said. 'Imagine him telling the police … "Crazy bitch shot me! Look!" as he pulls a bit of mashed potato out of his leg.'

'Still wish I'd killed him,' Jenny muttered.

Amy switched her drink to her other hand and linked arms with her friend. 'I know you do, but shit happens. Or not. Anyway, we have more important things to think about, namely the quiz team.'

Jenny pulled a face. 'Hardly more important, Ames.'

'Yes, it is. Teller's in the past. We're done with serial killers. Two is quite enough for one lifetime. The quiz is just the sort of distraction we need: me from Willem, and you from brooding.'

'Does Finn even want to carry on quizzing?' Jenny asked.

'Ooh, carry on quizzing! What a great team name! Remember the *Carry On* films? God, I used to love them as a child.' Amy saw that they were about to pass the spot where Jenny had discovered a particularly gruesome murder scene, where Teller had left his female victim's mutilated body parts staged in one of the art installations. She shuddered inwardly as she remembered the sordid details, and was relieved when they were past the spot without Jenny making any reference to it.

'Yeah, *Carry On Screaming* was my favourite.'

'Mine too. Brilliant! I think that was made in the sixties. I wonder if Finn's even old enough to be aware of the films? Bloody hell, we're getting old.'

'Maybe we should check with Finn before we carry on anything?'

'S'pose. Although there's no reason why we can't still go without him,' Amy said.

'The Gruesome Twosome?'

'Well, I was thinking we could find some more people to join us. What about Pippa? Do you think she'd be up for it?'

'Actually, that's a very good idea. Pippa's fun and brainy. I reckon she'd say yes.'

'What about her husband? I don't really know him.'

'Dave. He's a nice guy. Pippa might enjoy getting out without him though, I think. Only one way to find out.'

'Okay, let's ask Pippa and check with Finn too.'

They were nearing the end of the boardwalk now and headed up into the Coastal Park. The bright colours of the summer planting had faded to green, but it was as beautiful as ever.

'Thanks for getting me out, Jenny. You were right, it was exactly what I needed.'

'You're welcome, any time,' Jenny smiled. 'Now, hurry up, I want to have a go on the zipwire. You can help scare off any pesky kids.'

CHAPTER 11

Serious quizness

By the time Wednesday evening arrived, the quiz team had swelled to six members, with Amy, Jenny and Finn being joined by Pippa, her husband Dave, and one of Finn's friends, James, who was home from a year travelling in the Far East. Amy was obviously far too upset about Willem to notice James's chiselled good looks, floppy brown hair, and physique that screamed gym.

It was strange without Willem, and Amy experienced a bit of a wobble which presented itself as a lump in her throat. She swallowed it down and forced a smile onto her face, determined to relax and have some much-needed fun.

After introductions were made all around, and a round bought, the team settled themselves at the table in the window they now considered theirs, and talked team names. They figured a new team warranted a new name. Besides, it was a good icebreaker.

It was actually James who came up with the winner.

'What about Gryffindor? But replace the y with an i?'

'Yes! Brilliant! That gets my vote,' Amy said, high-fiving James, who looked a little taken aback at being high-fived by a middle-aged woman he'd only just met.

The others agreed it was the perfect name, with the venue being the Griffin Alehouse, and the specialist round being Harry Potter. Amy had thought again what a shame it was that Harry the ceramicist had left the town when she'd found out the theme from BB's Facebook page. It had been years since she'd read the book series or watched the films, but Amy was reasonably confident that she had a good smattering of HP knowledge. Jenny had just pulled a face when she'd found out. She wasn't a fan, declaring, 'Harry Potter can fuck off.'

The music round was the nineties, which suited Finn and James, and there was an optimistic vibe around the table. Pauline had been all smiles too when she came around and collected the money.

'Hello, hello!' she said brightly. 'Lovely to see you all again – and with some new faces,' she continued, looking round the table. 'Welcome, welcome … but where's Wilhelm?'

Amy blushed and looked down at the table.

Jenny saved her. '*Wilhelm*'s away at the moment. Photographing lighthouses or something.'

Amy looked gratefully at her friend.

'Oh, well, that's very nice I'm sure. And you're a full complement tonight too. You might have heard that one of the Scrambled Eggheads died suddenly, so they're down to five. Terribly sad, such a nice man, Stanley. And by far the strongest quizzer in the team,' Pauline finished, shaking her head before she moved on to the next table, with a 'Good luck!' over her shoulder.

The optimistic vibe took a bit of a knock when the picture round arrived.

'Fucking-kings-and-queens-when-they-were-young-what-the-actual-fuck,' was Jenny's reaction.

Amy felt the same, but was controlling her language in front of the newest team members.

What Amy and Jenny hadn't known about Pippa was that she was a bit of a royalist and they gladly handed the answer sheet to her and let her get on with it, while they talked in hushed tones about the member of the Scrambled Eggheads who'd died.

'It was that beardy bloke. Slim, glasses, very studious-looking,' Jenny was informing Amy. 'Wardrobe-full-of-jackets-with-patches-on-the-elbows-and-avid-watcher-of-University-Challenge type.'

Amy screwed up her face as she tried to recall the man. 'I think I know who you mean. He didn't look all that old, did he? Maybe mid-sixties? I wonder what happened.'

Jenny shrugged. 'Dunno. Salmonella? Should've listened to Edwina. Was pretty sudden, wasn't it?'

'Looks that way. I'm a bit surprised the rest of them are here tonight, aren't you? Seems a bit disrespectful.'

'Yeah, you'd think they'd have at least taken a week off to mourn old Stan the man.'

Any further discussion about the death was halted by Pippa. 'I've done my best. I'm pretty sure about seven of them—'

'SEV-EN!' Jenny interrupted.

Pippa looked at her with bemusement before carrying on, '... but I'm not sure about the rest. I can have a guess if you want.'

Amy looked at Finn and James who looked about as interested as she and Jenny did, and who both shrugged. 'Go for it, thanks, Pippa.'

'Well, at least with Stan popping off, we've got a slightly better chance of winning,' Jenny said, getting straight back to the subject of the dead quizzer. 'Although, I reckon we'd need a couple more to shuffle off to really be in with a chance.'

'Jenny!' Amy remonstrated.

'What? I'm only saying what you're thinking. Besides, I think we'd need the Saga Crews ship to sink too if we want to be in with a real chance of taking home the spondoolicks.'

Amy raised her eyebrows, but any further comment was impossible as Barry was introducing the next round. The mix of ages and sexes in the team proved pretty successful, with Finn and James smashing the music round – they must surely pull some points back from the oldies there – and Amy getting all but the most obscure Harry Potter questions right.

'I mean, who knew Hogwarts had 142 staircases? Or all seven of the ingredients that go into Polyjuice potion? For God's sake,' Amy had muttered.

'Yeah, but fancy not knowing that Dumbledore has a scar above his right knee that's a perfect map of the London Underground,' Jenny had mock reprimanded.

The rest of the evening was uneventful: nobody died, Jenny didn't insult anyone, and team Griffindor finished third, a dramatic improvement on their last performance.

Who needs Willem anyway, Amy thought to herself. She ignored the little voice that answered back: *I do*.

CHAPTER 12
The Old Town Bar

Life settled into some sort of routine for Amy and she began to write steadily most days, pushing any intrusive thoughts about Willem to the back of her mind as they crept in. She knew they were festering there, but out of sight and all that. She had to admit there was an element of relief at no longer having to fend off any romantic advances which she simply couldn't indulge. Amy didn't allow herself to think too much about the fact that she might never be able to have a serious relationship again either. It had crossed her mind in a moment of madness that there might be a dating site for ex-cons, and that perhaps she could settle down with a fellow murderer. Just as long as they'd only killed someone who deserved it, of course.

The rest of her life revolved around the shop, Jenny, and the pub quizzes, which she looked forward to each week. As well as Butlin's Wednesdays, she, Jenny, Finn and James had also been back to the Merry Monk in Canterbury. They'd decided Pippa and Dave were far too genteel to cope with Mrs Magaluf, Gemma, and her filthy mouth.

Their second visit to the Merry Monk had been a more sober affair. Amy volunteered to drive and Jenny was limiting herself to two alcoholic drinks per quiz (barring any shitty shots they might win, of course). Finn and James were on pints of lager, but could clearly handle them a darn sight better than Jenny.

Gemma opened the quiz by telling them what they should

base their team name on. 'Something rude you might hear at the supermarket,' she told them. 'Remember, the ruder the better; that's how I like it.'

The four sat quietly, each trying to come up with something rude enough for Gemma's gutter-mind.

'Um ... what about something to do with organic?' Amy offered. 'We could change it to orgasmic maybe?'

'Orgasmic fruit and veg? Don't think so, Amy,' Jenny said.

The other two pulled faces. They were clearly not feeling it either.

'Or something to do with a clean-up in the aisle?' James suggested.

'Clean-up in the orgasmic cucumber section? Nope,' from Jenny.

Finn piped up next. 'How about Unexpected item in the tea-bagging aisle?'

James spat out some of his drink. 'Nice one, mate.'

Amy and Jenny looked at them blankly.

'Don't get it,' Jenny said.

Amy was busy typing on her phone.

'Well, you learn something new every day,' she giggled, passing her mobile to Jenny.

'Ew. Yeah, let's go with that,' Jenny said, nodding approvingly.

Amy nodded her agreement too and they waited for Gemma to ask them what they'd gone for. She laughed like a very approving drain, clearly not needing the help of a dictionary, and soon they were knocking back a shitty shot each, Amy declaring that she could have one drink.

'What the hell was that?' she asked a moment later, shuddering and pulling a face as she coughed into her hand.

'Battery acid?' Jenny suggested, eyes watering.

Finn and James took the shots in their stride, making the two women feel like complete lightweights.

It was a fun evening again, although they didn't have the same lucky streak as the first time round: no winning raffle ticket and a mid-table finish. James said he'd enjoyed it and would happily come again, but he also knew of another quiz back in Folkestone on the same night which he'd heard good things about and might be worth trying.

'It would certainly be more convenient – save the drive and someone having to be designated sensible person,' Amy said.

'But you do it so well,' Jenny said sarcastically.

Amy very maturely ignored her.

'Okay, I'll get the details and message Finn,' James said.

'Cool,' Finn said. 'I can let Amy know then.'

Amy thought of the WhatsApp group they'd started with Willem for quizzing updates, and wondered if she should suggest another one. 'Might be easier to have a WhatsApp group, d'you think? Save multiple messages.'

'Good idea, let's do that,' Finn and James agreed.

'Yeah, no need for multiple things, organic or otherwise,' Jenny nodded, straight-faced.

And so it was that the following Friday, the unlikely foursome rocked up at the Old Town Bar to tackle a new quiz. As it was in Folkestone they'd all made their way on foot, Amy and Jenny arriving before Finn and James, and bagsying a table in the front section of the pub. Amy had come prepared, as ever, with pens and spare paper 'just in case', earning her the usual sarcastic comment from Jenny, 'thanks, Mum'.

Finn and James arrived a few minutes later, got their drinks and settled themselves at the table with Amy and Jenny.

'This must be like being out with your mums,' Amy said, as they sat down. 'Or mad aunts.'

'Ahem. Older sisters will do, thank you very much,' Jenny corrected.

'Nah, you're alright,' Finn smiled.

'Yeah, for old birds,' James added.

'Oy!' Amy and Jenny said in unison.

'Cheeky sod,' Jenny added.

'Yeah, watch it or we'll send you to your room,' Amy tutted.

'To do your homework,' Jenny finished.

The quiz was due to start at seven thirty, but it was almost eight when the quizmaster finally came round to collect money and hand out pens and paper.

Jenny waved the offer of a pen away. 'It's alright, the head girl brought some,' she said, nodding in Amy's direction.

Amy blushed, but held up the four pens she'd produced from her handbag to prove Jenny's point.

The quizmaster laughed and introduced himself. His name was Kev. He was wearing West Ham shorts and T-shirt even though summer was long since over, had a completely bald head and a cheeky grin. Amy put him at about fifty years old.

'Kev seems nice,' she said. 'His legs must be cold though.'

'Yeah. I reckon he's a postman – probably wears shorts all year round,' James said.

Amy nodded and returned her attention to the job at hand, namely coming up with a team name once more. 'Suggestions?'

'Um ... not sure. Play it safe until we know what sort of quiz it is?' Finn said.

'The prefects?' Jenny threw out. 'In Amy's honour.'

Amy glared at her. 'Sod off.'

'James and the giant peaches?' James suggested. He'd clearly found his cheeky side around Amy and Jenny.

'You can fuck off too,' Amy said.

'Yeah, go to your room and squeeze your spots or something,' Jenny added.

James just laughed. 'Sorry, aunties, my bad.'

'Shall we just go with Stoned Folke for tonight?' Finn proposed, the relative voice of reason.

With that settled, they waited for Kev to get started. The pub was busy and noisy, so one of the young women working behind the bar tapped hard on the microphone a few times to get everyone's attention. And irritate the pants off them at the same time. She then handed the mike to Kev and they were off.

''Ello and welcome to the Old Town Bar quiz. A few new faces 'ere tonigh', so welcome. Before we begin, I just wanna raise a glass to one of our regulars 'oo sadly died at the weekend. To Norm. 'E 'ad a good innings. Rest in peace me ole mucker.'

Everyone raised their glasses and joined in the toast: 'To Norm.'

'I'm starting to think quizzing's bad for your health,' Jenny said. 'That's the second person who's popped their clogs in as many quizzes.'

'He might have been ancient,' Amy said. 'Kev did say he'd had a good innings.'

'No he didn't. He said 'e 'ad a good innings,' Jenny corrected.

Any further thoughts of Norm were quashed as Kev continued. 'We're startin' off with a round of twen'y general knowledge questions. Question one: 'ow long is 'adrian's wall?'

Amy's team looked at one another and giggled. Kev 'ad clearly never said an 'aitch' in his life.

'Is that *Hadrian's* Wall, Kev, or *Adrian's* Wall?' a young man from another team piped up.

All eyes turned to Kev. 'Fuck off, Jon, the aitch is silent.' It was clear heckling was something Kev was used to.

Everyone laughed and the Stoned Folke began to relax even more as they gauged the level of the quiz: somewhere between Barry's Bognor Butlin's and Gemma's smutty gutter.

'Question two,' Kev began after he'd allowed some thinking time for the first question. Or guessing time in Amy's team's case. 'Svetlana Sav … its … kaya …' he began, struggling to pronounce the unfamiliar name, 'was the first woman to do what?'

'Could you repeat the name please, Kev?' another member of Jon's team said, straight-faced.

'Svet …' Kev began. 'Some Russian bird,' he finished.

'Could you spell it?'

'Yeah, I. T.' Kev said.

The remaining eighteen questions were relatively incident free, although there were dropped aitches all over the floor, along with a good smattering of tees by the end of the round.

Stoned Folke had known about fifty per cent of the answers and were having a good time.

After round one, the teams all swapped papers for marking and Amy went off to exchange answer sheets with a team seated just around the corner of the bar.

'You'll never guess who's on that team,' she said, indicating with her head as she sat back down.

'I think we've done enough guessing for one night,' Jenny said. 'Who?'

'Butlin's Barry and Mrs Beige!' Amy announced sotto voce.

'Who?' James asked.

'You know, Barry the quizmaster from the Griffin and his wife,' Amy explained.

'Oh! Yes,' James laughed. 'Mrs Beige! Suits her.'

'Pauline to her friends, the other knitting nanas,' Jenny clarified.

'Small world. Did she remember you?' Finn asked Amy.

'Yeah. Apparently they've been doing this quiz for a while now. She said the ones to watch are the old boys over there – the late, great Norm was one of theirs and the star player by all accounts – and the ones called the Drinking Team or something. I think that's the team with the hecklers.'

After marking, Stoned Folke were two points behind Pauline's team, who were called Get Knitted.

'Well done,' Amy smiled, as she handed Pauline back the answer sheet.

'Right, people, round two is the chocolate question,' Kev announced.

'Ooh, Ames, this is right up your street,' Jenny declared.

'I doubt very much if it's actually questions about chocolate, Jenny,' Amy told her.

It turned out to be a single question and the team who guessed closest to the actual answer won a box of chocolates. Unfortunately for Amy, they were miles out with their answer and the prize went to the team of older men, who looked smug as Kev handed them the big box of Dairy Milk.

'I'll bring our own chocolates next time,' Amy announced, feeling aggrieved that they'd lost. She was only mildly mollified when the box got passed round the tables for everyone to share.

She took her favourite orange one, with only a brief panic about all the other fingers that had been in the box.

After the chocolate round, Kev announced a short break, during which he recommended they 'get a drink' or ''ave a fag'. After about ten minutes came a music round: 'Point for the artist, point for the title,' Kev informed them, only with fewer tees.

The music was a real mix and between them Stoned Folke did pretty well, with ten out of the twelve being sure things. Another general knowledge round of fifteen questions was followed by Amy's least favourite round: the wipeout. Kev explained that each correct answer was worth two points, but any wrong answer would cancel out the score for the round.

'Nooo! I hate wipeouts. They're bad for my blood pressure,' Amy groaned, not for the first time.

'Maybe that's what wiped old Norm out,' Jenny cackled.

'Not funny,' Amy groaned again. 'Let's be sensible.'

Jenny started a chant of 'Gamble, gamble …' and James joined in.

Amy, who was writing the answers, held up her pen. 'Don't encourage her, James. In fact, go to your room. Anyway, I have the power of the pen!'

There followed a small scuffle involving Jenny trying to wrestle the pen away from Amy. Failing that, Jenny tried to grab Amy's bag, which contained the three spare pens. 'Fuck's sake, Jenny,' Amy scolded as she wrapped her bag strap around her wrist and tucked the bag between her knees.

'Let's play it by ear, shall we?' Finn said sensibly, and Amy smiled gratefully at him.

'Teacher's pet,' Jenny said to Finn, folding her arms sulkily.

CHAPTER 13

Go big or go home

The wipeout was more of a whine-out in the end. Of the five questions, Amy's team were confident of three answers.

'A hundred per cent?' Amy asked, each time one of the others gave an answer. If they couldn't answer in the affirmative, she wouldn't write it on the answer sheet. 'I'll write it on a spare bit of paper and then we can decide at the end if we want to include it.'

Jenny grumbled and crossed her arms. She'd made the mistake of saying ninety-nine per cent.

James and Finn seemed to think that was reasonable.

After the five questions had been asked, Kev gave them a couple of minutes to finalise their answers.

'Go for all five!' Jenny said.

'Yeah, go big or go home!' James agreed.

'But think about it,' Amy tried to reason, 'we've got a safe six points here. Why risk losing them with two guesses?'

'Er ... because it makes it more exciting?' Jenny offered.

'What she said,' James agreed. 'Big risk, big reward.'

Finn was staying very quiet, clearly on the fence and not knowing which way to lean.

'That makes no sense,' Amy said, shaking her head and throwing up both hands in frustration.

Big mistake. Jenny reached over and grabbed the pen from Amy's right hand. 'James, get the paper!'

James whipped his hand out and dragged the answer sheet away from Amy, dragging it through a wet patch on the table as he did so, and smearing the answers in the process.

'For fuck's sake, you two!' Amy exclaimed.

Finn was trying not to laugh, but not doing anything to come to Amy's rescue.

Jenny and James were cackling as they quickly scribbled down the two missing guesses.

Amy sighed theatrically and sat back with folded arms. 'You are such dickheads. I give up.'

'We hadn't done enough to win without all five, to be fair,' Finn offered to try and make Amy feel better.

'S'pose,' Amy sighed. 'I just hate wiping out.'

'Clean-up in the orgasmic yoghurt aisle,' Jenny piped up, holding out the now decidedly soggy sheet for Amy to swap with the other team.

'I'm not taking *that* anywhere,' Amy declared.

Jenny shrugged and got up to make the exchange.

Get Knitted had answered four of the questions. If they were correct, then Stoned Folke had indeed wiped out. Amy pouted and sighed with resignation. She took some consolation in the fact that they weren't last, beating some of the younger teams by quite a margin. Everyone applauded politely after Kev announced each team's score. The losing team, or 'not quite first place' as Kev put it, were awarded some chocolates and 'crisps or nuts of their choosing'. Get Knitted took third place, with two teams vying for first. Nobody in the pub seemed surprised when Kev announced they were Forever Jung (the old boys minus the late Norm), and the British Supercross Drinking Team (the hecklers – apparently they changed their team name to something topical each week).

'Just half a point separates the teams, but ... in second place is ...' Kev waited a beat, 'the British Supercross Drinking Team! which means the winners, with forty-six points, are Forever Jung.'

A less than enthusiastic round of applause followed. It was obvious to the newbies that the other teams were tired of the same team winning week after week.

'They're as smug as the Scrambled Eggheads,' Amy said.

The others didn't disagree.

'Well, with any luck they'll all have followed Norm's example and carked it by Christmas,' Jenny said charitably. 'I mean, look at them. They must have the combined age of God.'

'Jenny! You can't say that!' Amy said.

'Can. Just did.'

'Well, even if they did all cark it by Christmas, you'd still have the small matter of the Drinking Team. They're obviously really strong. And they look to be in their thirties,' James said.

Jenny screwed up her face. 'Maybe we could poison their drinks?'

'That's the spirit, Jenny.'

'All's fair in love and quizzing.'

'Well, before you start bumping off other quizzers, what did we think of the quiz? Are we going to stick with this one or go back to the Merry Monk?'

'This one gets my vote,' Finn said.

'Mine too,' said James.

'Mine three,' from Jenny.

'Okay, that's settled then. The Old Town Bar on a Friday night it is,' Amy smiled round the table.

'Seriously though,' Jenny began, looking at Finn and James in turn, 'don't you young'uns have anything better to do on a Friday night?'

'Ah, Jenny, the night is still young! I'm going on to a party when we leave here,' James informed her.

Jenny looked surprised. And a bit envious.

'Oh to be young again,' Amy sighed. 'It's already past my bedtime.'

James looked at his watch. Nine forty-five. 'Bloody hell, is that what we've got to look forward to? In bed before the ten o'clock news? Jeez.'

'I'm afraid so. Mug of Horlicks and hair in rollers by nine most nights at Amy's house,' Jenny explained.

'Cocoa, actually, thank you very much,' Amy corrected.

James looked doubtfully at the pair of them, not quite sure if they were joking. 'Maybe we ought to ask if we can join the Drinking Team, Finn?' James said, lifting his still half-full glass in their direction.

'Only if you want to be bumped off by Jenny at some point in the near future,' Amy smiled sweetly at him.

'Hm, I s'pose we can put up with you oldies for now.'

'Cheeky fucker,' Jenny said, punching him on the arm holding the glass, and sending lager sloshing over the rim.

'Oy!' James exclaimed, as he lurched backwards.

'Oh dear, hope I haven't ruined your best party shirt?' Jenny smiled saccharinely.

'Thank goodness the answer sheet wasn't still on the table,' Amy said.

'If I wasn't a nice young man, I'd call you a right twat, Jenny,' James said, wiping at his sleeve.

'You wouldn't be the first,' Jenny smirked.

'That's true. I call her a right twat on a regular basis,' Amy said.

'She does,' Jenny agreed.

Finn was just smiling as he watched the exchange between his three quiz mates. He didn't like to admit in front of James that he was actually looking forward to an early night.

Before anyone else could call Jenny a twat, Pauline appeared from around the corner and came over. 'Did you enjoy the quiz then?'

The four nodded. 'Yes, it was good fun! We liked the heckling, and Kev seems like a good laugh,' Amy smiled.

'Oh, that's good. Yes, Kev is a sweetie.'

'Well done for coming third,' Finn said.

Pauline huffed. 'Oh, young Finn, it's a frustrating business. We come third most weeks, I'm afraid. Can't quite seem to knock those two teams off the top.'

'You won't have to worry for much longer,' James said. 'Jenny here's got a plan.'

'Oh?' Pauline said.

'Yeah, I'll knock them off. Permanently!' Jenny said menacingly.

'Oh!' Pauline exclaimed, her hands going to her face. 'Oh! You're joking of course, Jenny, dear. Oh, my goodness, what a thought! Of course, it was terribly sad about poor Norman. He was a dear old boy. Brilliant quizzer. I thought with him gone, we might be in with more of a chance, but no such luck.'

Jenny opened her mouth to speak again, but Amy stopped her by putting her hand on Jenny's arm. She wasn't sure Pauline was an appropriate audience for their gallows humour. 'What happened to Norm, do you know?'

'I'm not sure, dear. Possibly his heart? I did hear he had a bit of a weakness there,' Pauline said.

'Was he very old?'

'Mid-seventies I think. Lovely, lovely man,' Pauline added, shaking her head sadly.

'Well, better luck next time, Pauline. Surely those other teams must have an off-week one of these days,' Amy smiled.

'We can hope. Although that Drinking Team is very strong too. Perhaps Jenny could knock them off too?' Pauline chuckled.

Okay, Amy thought. *Maybe she can cope.*

Pauline left then, saying she hoped to see them on Wednesday at the Griffin.

'We'll be there,' Amy said. 'Unless Jenny's in prison,' she added under her breath.

'I wonder if they do pub quizzes in prison,' Jenny piped up. 'Minus the pub bit, of course.'

'Of course. You probably wouldn't win money though.'

'What is prison currency these days?' Jenny asked.

'Dunno. Cigarettes?'

'You might get shanked in the shower if you win,' James said helpfully.

'Best I don't get caught then,' Jenny nodded sagely.

'Good plan,' Finn agreed.

'I can't go to prison, anyway. Who'd look after my cats?'

'And how would you keep your hair pink?' Amy pointed out.

Jenny looked suitably horrified at the thought.

'What even is your natural hair colour?' Amy asked her friend.

'Buggered if I know anymore. Mousy with a hint of salt and pepper? I don't intend to find out.'

'Well, as fascinating as your hair colour is, Jenny, I'm off,' James announced.

'Have fun,' Amy said.

'Yeah, hope you win at pass the parcel,' Jenny said. 'And musical chairs. Don't eat too much jelly and ice cream.'

'You're a right twat, Jenny,' James grinned as he got up to leave. 'Laters, losers.' James was gone with a backwards wave of his hand.

Amy yawned. 'Time to go?'

The other two nodded and they made their way to the exit, thanking Kev as they went and smiling at the Drinking Team. Over in the corner, Forever Jung were counting their winnings. And still looking smug. Jenny gave them a hard stare and the three of them made their way out into the street. Finn said his goodbyes and Amy and Jenny set off on the walk home.

'That was fun,' Amy said, realising she hadn't thought of Willem all evening.

'In spite of wiping out?'

'Yes, in spite of that.'

'I think we need a better team name though. And a more permanent one.'

CHAPTER 14

Who is Sylvia? What is she ...

It was about nine o'clock the next morning, Saturday, when Amy got a call from Jenny. Amy was still languishing in bed, wondering if there was any point in getting up, and she stifled a yawn as she answered.

'Are you still in bed?' Jenny asked. 'Lazy arse,' she continued, not giving Amy a chance to confirm or deny.

'I'll have you know I'm very busy looking for something actually,' Amy protested.

'Yeah? Your marbles? The plot?'

'A reason to get out of bed, if you must know.'

'Knew it. I wouldn't bother mind you. It's raining out.'

'Is that why you phoned? To give me a weather report?' Amy said through another yawn.

'Nope. I phoned to give you a news report.'

'Is it good news? I'm only accepting good news stories today,' Amy sighed.

'Depends how you look at it,' Jenny informed her cryptically.

'Through squinty eyes at the moment. Why am I so tired?'

'Old age. Anyway, you don't need to open your eyes, just your lug holes.'

'I wonder what the origin of lug holes is?' Amy mused.

'Will you just shut up and listen! You can ask Alexa later.'

'Okay, I'm listening ...'

'Right, so, you know the Scrambled Eggheads from the Griffin?'

'Uh huh.'

'And remember one of them died recently?'

'Um ... Stanley, wasn't it?'

'Yeah, I think that was his name. Anyway, I just saw on Facebook that another one of them has died unexpectedly. Remember the woman with the Princess Anne hair and face to match?'

'The one you called horseface?'

'Don't speak ill of the dead, Amy,' Jenny reprimanded. 'But, yeah, horseface. Her real name was Sylvia apparently.'

'Vaguely. What did she die of? She wasn't that ancient.'

'Dunno, it doesn't say. Just says suddenly.'

'And it definitely wasn't you?' Amy joked.

'Nope. Looks like someone beat me to it,' Jenny laughed.

'We're bad people. We shouldn't be making light of this, Jenny. And she wasn't really all that much older than us, was she? I'm not ready to die yet.'

'You'd better bloody not die on me. I'll kill you if you do.'

Amy laughed. 'Well you seem to be getting plenty of practice. Could you target a couple of Saga Crews, Forever Jung, and the Drinking Team next. We might have half a chance of winning a quiz then.'

'Don't forget Pauline's team – Get Knitted – they're better than us too.'

'Oh yeah. Be a shame to bump off Barry and Pauline though.'

'Stabbed through the eye with a knitting needle.'

'Ouch! I reckon they'd kill each *other* off with the right provocation,' Amy went on.

'What … like Pauline spilling tomato sauce on his favourite yellow jacket?'

'Ha! Yeah, or Barry scratching her Burt Bacharach's *Greatest Hits* LP?'

'Both valid reasons to commit murder, methinks.'

'Kind of sad about Sylvia though. Makes you feel your own mortality, doesn't it?' Amy said.

'Yeah, s'pose. I'm actually going to live to be a hundred though.'

'Ugh, no, can you imagine? I dread getting old much more than dying,' Amy told her.

'Maybe Sylvia felt the same and took her own life?'

Amy sighed deeply. 'If you're going to live to be a hundred, who am I going to do a Thelma and Louise with when I start needing incontinence pants and forgetting where I live?'

'Well, if you're forgetting where you live, you're probably going to forget the Thelma-and-Louise-driving-off-a-cliff thing too, aren't you?'

'Oh yeah. You'll have to remind me,' Amy told her.

'Maybe we can go into the same old people's home?' Jenny suggested, trying to cheer up her friend.

'One where they have quizzes,' Amy smiled to herself.

'Probably wouldn't have to cull the other quizzers. Just let nature take its course.'

'Hm. A wipeout round really would be just that, wouldn't it?' Amy chuckled. 'They'd be on permanent standby with a defibrillator.'

Jenny laughed. 'Wipe-your-arse round. The shitty shots would probably be in those little medicine pots you get.'

Amy went quiet.

'You still there, Thelma?' Jenny asked.

'Yeah, just thinking, you know …'

'Chin up. You're not old yet.'

'Won't be long though. And I already need a defibrillator for this broken heart of mine.'

'Stop feeling sorry for yourself. It's a beautiful day and the world's your oyster.'

'You said it was raining.'

'Well, it's a beautiful day somewhere,' Jenny laughed. 'Chin up, chicken. Plenty more oysters in the sea.'

'What if Willem really was my oyster though?' Amy said sadly.

'Er … you don't even like oysters, dickhead. Remember when I made you try one in Whitstable? You nearly vommed on my shoes.'

'Ew. Yeah. Revolting. My lobster then?'

'Plenty more lobsters out there too.'

'No, no more seafood for me. If it's not Willem, it's nobody. There's no point, Jenny.'

'Being single's not so bad. Look at me,' Jenny said.

'Can't. Eyes closed.'

'What can I do to cheer you up? Do you wanna do something?'

'Um … yes. Please.' Amy thought for a moment or two. 'Actually, do you fancy a trip to Canterbury? Haven't been shopping over there in ages and I do need some new boots.'

'Canterbury it is then. Will you pick me up?'

'Yes. Give me an hour,' Amy replied.

Hanging up the phone, Amy stretched, yawned once more and then dragged herself out of bed and into the shower.

It was just over an hour later when she pulled up outside Jenny's. The rain had stopped thankfully and the autumn sun was doing its best to dry the streets, glinting off the road and making Amy reach for her sunglasses.

'Alright, Jackie,' Jenny said, as she got in beside her.

'Ahem. These definitely do not qualify as Jackie O sunglasses, thank you very much.'

'Want to borrow mine then?' Jenny grinned, pulling said article out of her bag.

Twenty-five minutes later and they were parking in the multi-storey car park in the centre of Canterbury. Amy was feeling much brighter at the prospect of a shopping trip and new boots. She linked arms with Jenny as they headed out through Marks and Spencer.

Canterbury was busy, as ever, the streets awash with tourists, students and locals. As much as Amy loved living in Folkestone now, it was nice to be somewhere that wasn't all about Willem or serial killers.

CHAPTER 15

May the Force be with you

Amy was wearing the new conker-coloured Chelsea boots she'd bought in Canterbury when she and Jenny set off for the Griffin Alehouse on Wednesday evening. It had been a quiet and rather reflective few days for Amy, the weather as grey as her mood, as she thought about her life without Willem and what the future might hold. Pulling on the shiny boots had put a smile on her face though and she was looking forward to another night of quizzing with the now reinforced team of six.

Amy had created a new Wednesday-night-quiz WhatsApp group which included the newer members (she didn't think Pippa would appreciate the often sweary content of the original one), and they had discussed team names going forward. After James's rather inspired 'Griffindor' the previous week, they'd decided to tailor the team name each week depending on the specialist subject. It was a little bit of light relief to join in the banter which ensued.

Urgh. Have you seen this week's topic? Amy began.

Yesss! Brilliant, eh? James was the first to respond.

No. Star Wars can fuck off. No surprise when this pinged in from Jenny.

Pippa added a polite, *Oh dear, I don't know much about Star Wars.*

Me neither, Amy agreed. *Only the main characters and a few bits. I've never actually watched a whole Star Wars film.*

You what?! How is that humanly possible, Amy?! James asked.

Amy sent the shrugging emoji.

I'll ask Dave, but I don't think he's much of a fan either, Pippa sent before disappearing.

You'll find all you need to know in Wookieepedia, James advised.

I'd rather Chewbacca my own arm off, Jenny typed.

That was quite good for you, Jenny.

Don't be a patronising twat, young man.

A message from Finn appeared then. *Looks like I've arrived just in time. I LOVE Star Wars, so I reckon me and James can come up with a cracker.*

Thank God for that, Amy said.

Rebel Scum.

Jenny! That's not very nice! Amy reprimanded.

Two laughing emojis appeared from Finn and James before a tennis match of suggestions began:

Sith Happens.

Qui-Gon Jinn & Tonic.

Boba Feta Cheese.

Alderaan Answers.

What does that even mean?

It's a planet.

Oh.

Looking for Love in Alderaan Places, Amy joined in with a crying emoji.

Livin' la Vida Yoda.

Kamino Acids.

You've lost me again. I quite like a couple of those though. Shall we take a vote after Pippa and Dave have seen them?

And so it was on Wednesday night, that Amy came to be

writing *Livin' la Vida Yoda* on the answer sheet as Barry was telling everyone the shocking news that another of the Scrambled Eggheads, Sylvia, had tragically died, and that the team had decided not to continue quizzing for the foreseeable future.

Finn and James both turned to look at Jenny, raising their eyebrows.

'What?!' she exclaimed, hands outstretched, palms up, to demonstrate her innocence. 'It wasn't me!'

When Pauline came round a minute later to collect their money, she too looked askance at Jenny.

'It wasn't me!' Jenny reiterated. Amy wasn't sure if Jenny was cross or secretly rather flattered to be considered an arch-villain.

'Still no Wilhelm?' Pauline asked.

Amy just shook her head and looked down at the table.

'Oh well, never mind, I'm sure you'll do just fine without him, and you might have a better chance of a win without the Scrambled Eggheads,' Pauline smiled, before moving on to the next table.

Amy was busy thinking that she wasn't fine without Willem when Barry asked the first question. Shaking thoughts of the absent South African away, she focused on the matter at hand. Finn and James did brilliantly on the *Star Wars* round and Amy was feeling much better when Barry began a music round of eighties one-hit wonders, and couldn't help but smile when she heard the likes of 'Funkytown' and 'Waiting for a Star to Fall'. James, who'd had his fingers in his ears for most of the music round, claimed he was bloody glad he'd missed the eighties.

'Best years of my life,' Amy sighed, flashbacks of bad perms and pixie boots appearing with the rosy glow of fond remembrance. She conveniently forgot all the accompanying teenage angst and heartbreak, and stuffing her terrible curls under a grey trilby. Her bubble didn't last long as Barry unceremoniously burst it with the picture round: African countries to be identified from shapes on a map. The only one she knew for sure was South Africa. 'Arse,' she said, with another sigh.

Amy was subdued for the remainder of the quiz, dutifully carrying out her task as team scribe, but not really engaging very much in the remaining rounds. She didn't even object when Jenny and James wanted to gamble on the wipeout. Thankfully, this time the gamble paid off and the team came second, with their highest score to date. The winning team, no surprise that it was Saga Crews, were celebrating on the other side of the pub.

'Doddery old smug gits,' Jenny said charitably.

'Well, Jenny, if you could target said smug gits before next Wednesday, that would be appreciated,' James said. 'We might actually win then.'

'What? Sink the Saga Crews ship? Yeah, sure. Get me a missile launcher and I'll see what I can do,' Jenny nodded, obviously having decided protesting her innocence was pointless.

'Not sure where you buy weapons from around here,' James said, screwing up his face.

Amy looked across at Jenny and their eyes met. They were both thinking *Spud*. But even Jenny's dodgy friend Spud wouldn't be able to help with obtaining anything bigger than a handgun.

'That's good 'coz I don't think I've got a Bag for Life big enough to fit one in anyway,' Jenny said sarcastically.

'And it definitely wouldn't fit in your bicycle basket. Like a baguette,' Amy giggled, the image of Jenny riding along with a missile launcher sticking out of the pannier cheering her up.

'What about using a drone?' James asked.

Pippa and Dave looked quite bemused by now.

'Willem's got one, hasn't he?' James continued.

Amy went quiet again. She could feel Finn's eyes on her, sympathy on his face.

'Are you proposing we drop a bomb on the Saga Crews from Willem's drone?' Jenny asked.

'Could work,' James shrugged.

'Apart from the fact that Willem's buggered off. And I don't reckon I could fly a drone, let alone build a bomb and some sort of dropping mechanism,' Jenny was shaking her head, completely caught up in the fiction.

'How hard can it be?' James persisted. 'There are YouTube videos for bloody everything.'

Jenny's head dropped to one side and she nodded slowly, pouting her lips, as she thought about James's proposal.

'Oh my God! You two! This isn't gambling on a wipeout round, you know,' Amy exclaimed. 'You're quite mad.'

'Calm down, Ames. We're only messing,' Jenny said. 'Besides, they're not actually a cruise ship, are they, stoopid.'

'Oh for fuck's sake!' Amy threw up her hands. Her sense of humour and perspective had rather deserted her this evening. 'Sorry, Pippa,' she added, for the swearing.

Before anyone could say anything else, Pauline sidled up to them. 'Very well done this evening. Second place! You'll be winners in no time, I'm sure. I don't think the Scrambled Eggheads will be coming back after losing two members, and Saga Crews must have an off-week or crew leave one of these days. Don't despair!' she smiled, squeezing Finn's shoulder as she turned away.

'Ow!' Finn mouthed, putting his hand to his shoulder. 'Bloody hell, that woman's got a grip like a vice!'

'No wonder Barry's always so red in the face,' Jenny grinned.

'Ew,' from Amy.

'Is that the time?' from Pippa.

James spat the remainder of his drink in Jenny's general direction.

Jenny punched him.

And with that, they all got up to leave, with promises to 'see you in the chat group'.

CHAPTER 16

Saga Crews

Of course, the Saga Crews were blissfully ignorant of the plotting taking place as they raised their glasses and counted their winnings. They were just jolly pleased to have finally won the quiz, even if it had taken a couple of deaths for it to happen. They were all pensioners and fourteen pounds each was not to be sniffed at. Nor was one of their members as it happened.

'What are you going to spend yours on then, Jean?' a lady called June, who was of the same ilk as Pauline, asked.

'Well,' Jean began, beaming, 'I do need a new hot water bottle now the nights are drawing in. My old one has started to perish.' She shook her head in disappointment. Her permed white hair didn't move. Nor did the old-fashioned spectacles perched on her powdered nose.

June nodded, clearly familiar with Jean's plight. 'Things don't last the way they used to, do they? I might treat myself to some goodies from Markses. Lidl's all very well, but every now and then I do like to splurge. Maybe some custard tarts.'

The old man sitting across the table from them, Jack, harrumphed. 'Well, I'll be spending mine on Scotch,' he said, with a firm nod of his balding, liver-spotted head. His bulbous red nose glowed like a beacon. Jack probably knew the correct term for this was rhinophyma.

'No surprise there, then,' June murmured to Jean, who

pursed her thin lips in disapproval. They really only tolerated the old sot because he was an absolute fount of knowledge.

'What about you, Terry?' Jean smiled at the gentle old man sitting next to Jack, whose attention seemed to have already sunk back into his glass.

Terry smiled, his rheumy blue eyes crinkling. 'Thought I'd book that world cruise, Jean. First class all the way!'

Jean tittered behind her hand. 'Oh, you are funny, Terry!'

'Get a feckin' room,' Jack muttered into his whisky.

June tutted at him. 'No need for your smut, thank you very much.' She privately thought that Jean's crush on Terry was embarrassing, but still, no need for anyone's feelings to get hurt.

Jack belched in her general direction.

The two other members of the Saga Crews team were Jeff, a seventy-four-year-old retired maths teacher with a selection of cardigans which may well have been knitted by Pauline, and Jerry, who at sixty-nine was the baby of the team and worked part-time on the checkout at Morrison's. He pretended he didn't notice the younger shoppers steering away from his rather slow-moving conveyor belt. Jeff said he was putting his winnings in a jar to see how much he could save in a year. This earned him a 'boring old fart' from Jack. Jerry informed them his share was going in the Macmillan Cancer Support charity bucket at work. A further belch from Jack enlightened the team as to what he thought of that, before he raised his now empty glass to 'Saint-fucking-Jerry'.

With all the team members' names beginning with the letter J, Terry had been a welcome addition and had prevented Jack from getting his way with calling them, in a broad Irish accent, 'Jaysus H. Christ, what a team'. It was Terry who'd come up with 'Saga Crews' in the end. Clearly cruising was on his mind a lot. Jack had pronounced it 'a shite name' but was outvoted five to one. To be frank, if June could have voted more than once, she would have.

With the winnings all dished out, the team began to disband. Jack announced he was going for a piss, earning more tuts from June, who turned to the others and said, 'I wouldn't be surprised to discover he'd had a hand in the deaths of Stan and Sylvia.'

'More like a mouth. He'd probably only have to breathe on someone with a weak disposition to finish them off,' Jeff chuckled.

'Odious man. I wish we didn't have to put up with him,' Jean said.

'I agree,' June nodded, 'but he certainly knows his stuff. I've never met anyone who has more facts at his fingertips than Jack. You'd think his brain would be pickled by now, but he's still as sharp as a tack.'

Terry sighed. 'Yes, I think we're stuck with him if we want to stand any chance of a repeat of tonight's win.'

The other four heads around the table nodded. Sadly, Jack wasn't going anywhere anytime soon.

When Jack returned from the gents, he didn't seem in the least put out that the rest of his teammates had left without saying goodbye. Returning to the table, he upended his glass, just to make sure, scooped up his winnings from the table and weaved his way out of the pub. Stumbling out the door, Jack turned to his left and headed down the narrow cobbled street. He was humming to himself as he went, a tune from the earlier music round which had annoyingly got stuck in his head: 'Don't Worry Be Happy'. Not a bad motto to live by, he thought. Then he thought about the nightcap he would have when he got home. Or maybe two. Probably before falling asleep on the sofa and sleeping a deep, dreamless sleep, but snoring loud enough to wake poor departed Stan and Sylvia.

He didn't hear the steps approaching from behind. And he didn't feel the person's breath just before they grabbed him. He did feel the knife sinking into his neck. And the hot blood running down to his collar, the life seeping from him as he sank to his knees and then to the cold, hard cobbles. He was vaguely aware of a figure moving quickly away. He wondered fleetingly if Jaysus Christ would claim him or send him somewhere hotter. Maybe a cruise would be nice after all. And then he wasn't aware of anything, and wondered no more.

Stopping very briefly to rifle through the man's pockets and remove his wallet, the killer quickly reached the bottom of the cobbled street and, turning sharp left, made their way up the hill and away from the scene. Resisting the urge to dump the bloody knife and wallet into the first available storm drain, they hurried onwards, fuelled by adrenaline, to the waiting car, and to home and safety. They'd deal with the knife and wallet tomorrow. The priority now was to get safely behind their own front door, check their clothes for any trace of the man's blood and establish an alibi which they would hopefully never need.

Lying in bed later that night, the adrenaline having well and truly worn off, leaving the killer exhausted but exhilarated, their thoughts turned to how it had felt to plunge the knife into the man's neck. Disgusting drunk probably hadn't even felt it, anaesthetised by whisky. But *they'd* felt it: the resistance of his flesh as the blade went in, the grunt of shock and surprise, the collapse. So satisfying. Much more so than the neat and tidy injections administered to previous victims. It was a revelation, a real thrill. And best of all, Saga Crews had lost their strongest player and the world had lost a useless drunk. Happy days, the killer thought as they drifted off to sleep. Happy days.

CHAPTER 17

The shrinking drinking team

When Amy, Jenny, Finn and James met two nights later for the quiz at the Old Town Bar, the hot topic of conversation was the murder. The victim had been named as Jack Huggett, and his photograph shown on the local news only that morning. They'd recognised him as one of the Saga Crews team, although they hadn't known his name prior to that.

'It must have happened pretty much straight after we left the Griffin,' Amy said.

'The police said it was a mugging, didn't they?' Finn looked around the table for confirmation.

Amy nodded. 'Sobering thought. Could have been one of us.'

'There but for the grace of God and all that,' Jenny added.

'I don't think anyone would be crazy enough to mug you, Jenny,' James said. 'You'd probably go full-Ninja on them.'

'Yeah, don't mess with the crazy cat lady,' Jenny agreed, making kung fu hands and matching noises.

'Seriously though, it's really scary. We mustn't walk home alone in the dark. Any of us, even you, James,' Amy said.

'Oy!' said Finn.

'No offence, Finn. I just meant James looks like he could take care of himself,' Amy explained.

Finn said 'oy' again.

'Stop digging, Amy,' Jenny laughed. 'We know what you mean.'

Amy blushed.

'He seemed like a bit of a character though, this Jack fella,' James said. 'I was at the bar with him once and he was swearing like a trooper and knocking back a double whisky while he waited for the rest of the drinks.'

'I passed him on the way to the loo once. Smelt like he'd poured a double whisky over himself,' Amy said.

'Stood *next* to him in the loo once. Smelt like he pissed neat whisky,' James said, screwing up his nose.

'Ew,' said Amy.

'My kind of man,' said Jenny.

'Well, whatever kind of man he was, it's still sad. We should have a toast to him. Hopefully he's propping up a bar somewhere and telling rude jokes to the angels.'

'I think he might be propping up a bar further south,' James winked.

'That's okay, I don't s'pose he took ice in his whisky,' Jenny grinned.

'It's a bit mad that another quizzer's dead though,' Finn said. 'He's the fourth one to die in as many weeks. And from one of the strongest teams.'

'Has to be a coincidence though, doesn't it? Nothing's been said about the other deaths being suspicious, has it?' James questioned. 'And they were all pretty old after all.'

'Yeah, I s'pose. It's just a bit odd that all the deaths kind of benefit us and the weaker teams, don't they?' Finn persisted.

Jenny snorted. 'Do you really think the quiz winnings are worth killing over?'

Finn shrugged and went quiet.

'Like Jenny said, I can't believe anyone would kill for a

measly few quid,' James said.

'Absolutely!' Amy agreed. 'Unless one of the youngsters on the Drinking Team pops their clogs, let's not give it another thought.'

Kev arrived then to collect their money and hand out paper. He looked much more serious than usual. ''Ello, you lot. Nice to see you again, fanks for comin',' he said, still without really smiling.

'Hello, Kev, it's our pleasure,' Amy smiled at their host. 'Everything okay?'

Kev lowered his gaze to the floor and shook his head. 'I'm afraid not. I'll be making a bit of an announcement before we start.' With that, Kev moved away to the next table.

'I wonder what that's all about,' Finn said, frowning.

They looked around the room. The pub was busy, as it always was on quiz night. Nothing looked amiss.

'Dunno,' James said. 'I s'pose we'll find out soon enough.'

Amy was feeling a little anxious, and not just at the prospect of another wipeout round. She'd focused her gaze on the table where the Drinking Team always sat, before allowing her eyes to wander to the bar and back. *Too early to panic*, she told herself, having not seen the heckler, Jon, at the table. Telling herself he could be late/ill/in the loo – any number of places he could be or reasons to be absent. Even so, Amy couldn't shake off the feeling that something bad had happened.

Just before eight, Kev tapped the head of the microphone to get everyone's attention.

'I can't believe I'm sayin' this,' he began, 'and I wish more than anything that I wasn't … but we've lost another of our regulars … I still can't believe it t' be honest.' There was a definite break in Kev's voice as he spoke and Amy felt a sympathetic lump in her throat. 'You'll all know Jon from the Drinking Team. He was a right dickhead, but we all loved 'im, and the quiz won't be the same without 'im. So, I'd like to ask you all to raise your glasses … to Jon.'

As they lifted their glasses and all murmured 'to Jon', Stoned Folke had stunned looks on their faces as their eyes met across the table.

'Holy flaming fuck,' Jenny loud-whispered, just as James uttered, 'What the actual fuck?'

'Oh my God,' Amy said quietly. 'That's terrible. How bad do I feel after my earlier comment?'

'Pretty bloody shit, I'd imagine,' Jenny said, eyebrows raised.

Amy nodded, and pressed her fingers into her eyes.

'It's really shocking news,' Finn said sadly. 'He was a funny guy.'

'It *is* incredibly sad, but let's not get carried away. We don't actually know what happened – it could've been a car crash or something for all we know. Let's hold off on any conspiracy theories until we have the facts,' James said.

The others nodded, but a shocked silence had descended on the pub. The two women on the Drinking Team were dabbing their eyes and holding back sobs.

'I'm surprised they came tonight,' Amy said. 'They must be in bits.'

'I reckon they thought Jon would want the show to go on, if you know what I mean,' Finn said.

'Maybe. God, I still can't believe it. I wonder what did happen?' Amy said.

'How can we find out?' Jenny asked. 'We can't exactly go up

to them and grill them about it.'

'Dunno,' James said.

'I wonder …' Amy began. 'I think I might know who to ask.'

The others frowned at her.

'Pauline,' Amy said. 'If anyone knows what happened, I reckon she will.'

'The knitting-nana grapevine,' Jenny nodded.

'If the opportunity arises, I'll speak to her tonight,' Amy said.

'If not, she's in the shop tomorrow, Amy,' Finn informed her.

'Okay, great.'

All thoughts of Jon's mysterious demise were pushed to one side then as Kev started the first round. It was a subdued affair, hearts clearly not in it and, when Kev announced that the music round featured all Jon's favourite bands, a few more tears were shed around the pub. Even Amy didn't care if they came last. She'd seen Pauline only briefly when they swapped papers, and hadn't had an opportunity to say much more than 'hello', but she'd already made up her mind to pop into the shop the following morning anyway.

Stoned Folke were all rather relieved when the quiz came to an end. Forever Jung, minus Norm of course, had taken third place, with the RIP-Jon-We-Love-You Drinking Team coming second. At the top, and with their first ever win, were Get Knitted, Pauline and Barry's team. They had the good sense not to celebrate too loudly, but Amy knew that Pauline would be absolutely delighted.

Stoned Folke parted company soon after, with Amy first making sure that Finn and James weren't walking home alone, and promising to let them know if she found anything out from Pauline. She and Jenny then took a slow walk together.

'This is kind of scary now,' Amy said, turning to look at Jenny to gauge her reaction.

'People die all the time, Ames. I'm sure there's nothing to worry about. Okay, the mugging isn't ideal, but shit like that happens all the time. Maybe Old Jack put up more of a fight than expected and things got out of hand. Who knows?' Jenny shrugged.

'I s'pose ... but it is kind of mad. That's ...' Amy counted up the deaths on her fingers, 'five people from the best quiz teams in town all dead in a very short time period.'

'Yeah, I know, but like I said, who'd kill for quiz winnings?'

'I know, and you're probably right of course. I just can't shake the feeling that there's more to this.'

'Like what?'

'Like ... I don't know ... maybe it's not the money, maybe it's the ... glory ... the kudos, of winning.' Amy heard her own words and realised they sounded ridiculous.

Jenny clearly agreed and she snorted. 'The *kudos*? Can you hear yourself?'

Amy felt herself blush and she sighed, deciding not to say any more on the subject. 'So, what are you up to this weekend?'

'Bugger all currently. Depends on the weather. Might go for a walk if it's nice. Or a bike ride.'

'With a missile sticking out of your basket?' Amy smiled.

'Is that a euphemism?' Jenny elbowed her. 'No such luck I'm afraid. Not had a missile in my basket for longer than I care to remember.'

'TMI, thank you very much,' Amy said, while thinking much the same thing. Willem's face popped, unbidden, into her mind and she sighed again, before linking her arm through Jenny's.

'Never mind, we can be spinsters of the parish together.'

'Er ... I'm no lonely old maid, thank you very much,' Jenny said.

'You're absolutely right. And we're in our prime. Apparently. Although prime what I don't know. Prime suspect in your case,' Amy joked.

When Amy unlocked her front door a short while later, having waved Jenny off at the bottom of the road, she was out of breath. She'd fast-walked to her house, nervous in spite of Jenny's reassurance. She made a mental note to dig out the old rape alarm she had stashed somewhere. There may not be a serial killer on the loose, but there was definitely a mugger, and they had definitely killed someone. Amy thought of poor Jack Huggett, and how inapt his surname was.

Hanging up her coat on the hooks in the hall, Amy padded through to the kitchen, turning lights on as she went. Flicking on the kettle, she found a box of chamomile tea and waited for the water to boil. Her thoughts kept drifting to Willem, in spite of her best efforts to drag them in a different direction.

Tea made, she walked slowly upstairs to her bedroom. The night was dark, the moon only a sliver, and she sat on her bed, hoiking the pillows up to make herself comfortable. The curtains were open and Amy sat there in the semi-darkness, waiting for her tea to cool and trying to analyse how she felt. Was she a lonely old maid? If she was completely honest, she was certainly lonely. Sometimes, anyway. Finally giving in to them, she let her thoughts turn to Willem, and her eyes to the house across the valley. Was she imagining it, or was there a light on in his bedroom?

CHAPTER 18

The wanderer returns

Amy woke from a restless sleep early the next morning, her head pounding with a tension headache that she knew was a result of her clenching her jaw all night. A tired, pallid face looked back at her from the bathroom mirror.

'Morning, old maid,' she said, sticking her tongue out at her reflection. 'Don't you look like shit?'

Taking a cup of tea back to bed, Amy opened the curtains in her bedroom, and picked up the binoculars from where they sat, unused for some weeks, on the windowsill. She paused, wondering what the hell she was thinking. Even if he was home, there was no way Willem would have put a message in the window after the way things had ended between them. Would he?

She couldn't resist though, and put the binoculars to her eyes.

'Idiot,' she muttered a few moments later, replacing the binoculars on the sill and turning back to her bed. 'Stupid, stupid idiot.'

Tea finished a short while later, Amy was contemplating the day ahead and trying to muster enough enthusiasm to get up and face it, when a message from Jenny arrived.

Are you sitting down?
Yes, still in bed, why?
Willem's back.

Oh.

You OK?

Um. Yeah. No. I don't know.

Soz.

I did wonder if he was. I thought I saw a light on at his house last night. How did you find out?

Finn told me. He didn't want to be the one to tell you. Thought it would be better coming from me, what with me being Miss Tact and Diplomacy.

Amy couldn't help smiling. *Thanks for telling me. Did Finn say anything else?*

Nah.

OK. Thanks, Jenny.

De nada. What are you up to for the rest of the day?

Popping in at the shop. Food shopping. Not a lot.

Want me to meet you?

Sure. Shop at 11?

See you then.

'Bugger,' Amy said. She knew she'd run into Willem at some point and she was dreading it. It was definitely going to be awkward. She couldn't hide away forever though, much as she might like to, so Amy dragged herself off to the shower and to face the day.

Amy arrived at the shop just before eleven, and waited for Jenny to appear. It wasn't long before the familiar pink head bobbed into view and Jenny waved.

'Alright?' Jenny said, pulling Amy into a hug.

'Yeah. You?'

'Fine and dandy, thank you very much.'

Amy smiled at her friend before pushing the door to the

Coastal Creatives shop open. Pauline looked up from where she was dusting a shelf at the back of the shop.

'Well, isn't this a lovely surprise?' she beamed at Amy. Her broad smile waned somewhat as she turned to Jenny.

'Hello, Pauline,' Amy returned the smile.

Jenny lifted a hand in greeting.

'What brings you in today then?' Pauline asked, tucking the feather duster behind the counter.

'I've ... um ... brought a few more books in,' Amy said, holding out a bag.

'Oh, I thought you were still fully stocked, dear?'

'Oh, silly me, I thought there was space. Must have been wishful thinking on my part,' Amy laughed. The books had simply been an excuse to call in at the shop.

'Not to worry, I'm sure we can squeeze them in. Or just keep them out the back for when they're needed,' Pauline smiled at her.

'Oh, that would be great, thank you.' Amy passed the books to Pauline. 'Congratulations on your win last night,' Amy continued, looking around for Jenny, who was on the other side of the shop, idly flipping through greetings cards on the spinner. *So much for the moral support*, Amy thought.

Pauline beamed again. 'Thank you! Yes, our first win at the Old Town. Obviously we were very sad about Jon and would have preferred to win under different circumstances, but still, a win's a win, isn't it?'

'Um ... yes, of course,' Amy laughed nervously, thinking a win really wasn't a win if people had to die in order for you to get it.

Jenny stopped spinning at that point, apparently having

picked up on Amy's silent cry for help.

'So, what's the gossip then? How did Jon die?' Jenny asked.

Miss Tact and Diplomacy, Amy thought, cringing inwardly.

If Pauline was surprised by Jenny's question, she didn't show it.

'Well, dear ...' Pauline began.

Before Pauline could say any more, the door of the shop opened and three heads turned to see who was coming in.

Amy felt colour rush to her cheeks and a small 'oh' escape her lips as her eyes met those of the new arrival. 'Willem,' she said.

'Hello, Amy. Jenny. Pauline,' he nodded at them in turn.

'Oh! Wilhelm! How lovely to see you!' Pauline gushed. 'Come in, come in, what a nice surprise. I hear you've been away photographing ... lighthouses ... was it?'

Jenny sniggered.

Amy looked at her feet.

'Yes, I have been away for a while,' Willem confirmed. 'But I'm back now, and I don't plan on going away again anytime soon.'

When Amy lifted her eyes from the floor, it was to find Willem looking directly at her. She smiled shyly.

'Well, that's good to hear. Hopefully you'll be coming back to the quiz?' Pauline continued, oblivious to the frisson in the air.

'We'll see,' Willem said tactfully.

Amy felt a moment of panic, as their Wednesday quiz team was now at the maximum six.

Jenny was obviously thinking the same thing. 'You'll have to wait for one of us to get bumped off by the mysterious Folkestone quizzer killer, I'm afraid,' she informed Willem, who looked confused.

'Ooh, yes, you've probably missed all the excitement while you've been away!' Pauline said.

'I'm not sure excitement is the right word,' Amy said, finally finding her voice. She briefly outlined the events of the past few weeks to Willem, culminating in the shocking news of Jon's death which they'd received at last night's quiz.

'Well, I definitely won't be going away again if this is what happens in my absence,' he said, shock registering on his face. Amy thought he looked even more rugged than he had when she'd last seen him.

'Pauline was just about to tell us what happened to Jon when you arrived,' Jenny told him.

'Oh yes! Well, don't take this as gospel, but I heard it from Thelma, who heard it from Joyce, who lives next door to one of Jon's friend's mums, that it was an *overdose*.' She lowered her voice when she mouthed the word 'overdose', the way some people do when they say 'cancer' or 'gay'.

'An overdose of what?' Jenny asked. 'Was he on drugs? Didn't seem the type.'

Pauline shook her head. 'Well, you never know, do you? Not really. I mean, I don't like to speak ill of the dead, but his generation, they're all on something, aren't they?'

Amy could feel Jenny bristling next to her, and put out her arm to stop her before she spoke her mind to Pauline.

'No, well, whatever the case, it's desperately sad,' Amy said. 'Um ... anyway, we have to get on, don't we, Jenny? We'll see you soon, Pauline.' Taking Jenny by the arm, Amy pulled her away before her tact and diplomacy could get the better of her. 'Willem,' Amy added as they passed him. 'It's good to see you.'

'Amy,' he said, his eyes locking on hers, making her face burn once more. 'Good to see you too. Let's talk soon.'

'Um, yes, okay,' Amy mumbled, breathing a sigh of relief as the door closed behind them.

'Well, that wasn't awkward at all,' Jenny said, as they made their way down the road. 'And Pauline can fuck off. *Over ... dose*,' she mimicked.

'Mm ... I've gone off Pauline a bit. Sadly, I can't say the same about Willem,' Amy said.

'A blind person could have seen that, you sad cow.'

'Thanks for the sympathy. What am I going to do?'

'Carry on doing what you're doing. One foot in front of the other, one day at a time, and all that bollocks.'

'Couldn't I just go home, lock the door, put my pyjamas on and watch daytime telly for the foreseeable future?'

'Nope. No way, no how. Head up, chin up, chest out ... Actually, scrap that last one, you'll knock people out.'

Amy laughed and the mood was lightened once more.

'I am glad I've seen him though. You know, got that first awkward meeting out the way.'

'Yep, now you can look forward to the second awkward meeting,' Jenny grinned.

CHAPTER 19

To be or not to be

It was the next day, Sunday, when Amy heard from Willem. Her heart gave a little flip when she saw his name flash up on a message on her mobile. She was sitting at the kitchen table having breakfast, and brushed the toast crumbs from her fingers before picking up her phone.

Hi, Amy. Hope you're OK. It really was good to see you yesterday. How would you feel about me coming back to the Wednesday quiz? I've missed it. And you.

Amy was wondering how to tell him that there was no longer a space for him on the team, when another message arrived.

Sorry, I should have said, James has offered to step back from Wednesdays. He says he prefers the Friday quiz.

How did she feel? She had missed Willem, terribly at times, but nothing had changed. She still couldn't be honest with him. But surely she could cope with the quiz, couldn't she? It hardly seemed fair that Willem should miss out.

Of course you should come back to the quiz, it's fine by me.

She wondered briefly if she should offer to leave, instead of James, but decided that wouldn't be fair on Jenny, so she sent the message.

Thank you, Willem replied.

Don't thank me. It's my fault you were forced to go away after all.

Nobody forced me. My choice.

Well, I'm sorry anyway. For everything.

No apology needed. Let's just go back to the way things were before.

Amy wasn't sure what he meant. Reading her mind, as he always seemed to, Willem sent a single word: *Friends*.

Friends, she wrote back, a huge weight lifting from her horribly tense shoulders. As an afterthought she sent, *Thank you for making it not awkward!*

Feeling much better about things, Amy finished her breakfast and faced the day with much more optimism than she had for a while. There was pruning to be done in the garden before the frosts came, and she tackled it with gusto, all thoughts of dead quizzers supplanted by happier ones of Willem's return.

Feeling much better about things lasted until Wednesday when they arrived at the Griffin for the quiz. After introductions had been made between Willem and Pippa and Dave, they realised there were now two empty tables. Not only were the Scrambled Eggheads missing, but the Saga Crews team appeared to have sunk without a trace.

'It wasn't bloody me,' Jenny said, before the looks started.

It wasn't long before Pauline appeared, a spectre in beige, and informed them in a loud whisper that the rest of the Saga Crews team had been so shaken by what happened to Jack that they no longer felt safe coming out after dark. 'If you ask me, it's because they know they don't stand a chance without the old drunk. He was by far their strongest member.' She smiled knowingly at them, adding, 'You'll really be in with a chance of winning now,' and tipping them a wink before moving away.

'Is she a psychopath, or what?' Jenny asked.

Any discussion of whether or not Pauline was actually a

psychopath was prevented as Barry's dulcet tones filled the room.

'Welcome, lads and lasses, ladies and germs!' he began.

Willem chuckled. 'I've missed Butlin's Barry. It's good to see some things haven't changed in my absence.'

'His jacket,' Amy quipped.

'Probably his undies,' Jenny added.

'Do you think Pauline knits his undies?' Pippa joined in.

'I really don't want to think about Barry's underwear, knitted or otherwise,' Willem said, pulling a face.

'That's a shame, it's tonight's specialist subject,' Jenny quipped.

'Yep, our team name's either going to be Butlin's Barry's Beige Boxers or … um …' Amy began.

'The Banana Hammocks,' Jenny supplied.

'Or the Manhole Covers,' from Finn.

Willem was laughing, and realising how much he'd missed the banter and his friends. If he couldn't be in a relationship with Amy, so be it. The friendship was more important, although he'd be lying if he didn't admit that deep down a part of him still hoped it might be more one day.

'Being serious for a minute,' Amy said, 'am I right in thinking we settled on the Merchants of Menace for tonight's team name?'

The others nodded.

'Yeah, the others were all too rude,' Jenny said. 'Apparently.'

'They'd have been alright for the Merry Monk or Old Town, but not here,' Amy said.

'Yeah, we don't want any more of the old codgers shuffling off this mortal coil from the shock, do we?' Jenny said.

With Willem back, the team was the strongest it had ever been, and even the Shakespeare round didn't faze them. Amy's background in literature and everyone else's good general knowledge saw them get all but one question right. The music round was rock and heavy metal, which was right up Willem's street, and the picture round was brand logos, which were a piece of cake, especially the Betty Crocker one.

The Merchants of Menace were feeling quietly confident going into the wipeout round and hoped that answering seven of the ten questions confidently would be enough to give them their first win at the Griffin.

When Barry announced the placings a short while later, they held their collective breaths.

'And the winners are ... drum roll, please ... The Merchants of Menace!'

'Yesss!' Jenny said, punching the air.

'Maybe keep the celebration down to a dull roar, Jenny,' Pippa shushed.

'Yeah, people have died so we could win this,' Amy said, grimacing, but secretly as delighted as Jenny.

'My bad,' Jenny said. 'Although, it's actually bloody selfish of them because their absence means less moolah for us in the way of winnings.'

'I thought we were in it for the glory?' Willem said.

'You might be. I've got two hungry cats to feed at home,' Jenny informed him. 'Cat food doesn't grow on trees, I'll have you know.'

Willem chuckled.

'Speaking of cats, how is Cat? Happy to have you home, I bet,' Amy asked him.

'Ach, not so much. Cat is still very much giving me the silent treatment to punish me for going away.'

'Cats are dickheads,' Jenny said. 'That's why I get on so well with them.'

Everyone was laughing when Barry came over with the pint glass containing their winnings. 'Congratulations,' he beamed at them. 'The first of many wins, I'm sure. Now that those pesky old people are out of the way,' he added sotto voce, giving a conspiratorial wink.

'It wasn't me,' Jenny said, as Barry moved away from their table. 'Also, is Barry actually a psychopath too?'

'I think so,' Amy nodded, looking as serious as she could.

Pippa counted out the money and they'd won just over a tenner each, the winning pot down by two teams' entry fees. 'Hopefully some new teams will fill the empty tables,' she said, as she doled the piles of money out round the table.

Pippa's husband, Dave, who rarely spoke, said, 'I feel bad taking the money tonight, I barely contributed anything. Shakespeare and heavy metal are *not* my strong suits.'

'Hand it over then, I'll donate it to charity. It's a cat charity,' Jenny winked at Dave, holding out her hand.

Dave looked as though he was actually thinking of doing just that, so Amy intervened. 'She's only joking, Dave. I think.'

'Totally not joking,' Jenny shook her head. 'It's a very worthy, underfunded cause, I'll have you know.'

Amy laughed. 'Ignore her. Anyway, everybody contributes, and even one point can make the difference between winning and losing.'

'I'm blaming you if my cats starve, Amy.'

'You can feed them the bodies of all the quizzers you keep bumping off, Jenny,' Finn chuckled.

'For the last time,' Jenny huffed, 'IT'S NOT ME.'

'Ooh, the lady doth protest too much, methinks,' Amy said.

Everyone laughed and agreed it had been a really good night. They said their goodbyes, with reminders from Amy not to walk home alone, and Finn left with Pippa and Dave, leaving Amy, Jenny and Willem standing outside the pub. Jenny, belying her usual lack of tact, actually started walking slowly up the hill, leaving Amy and Willem alone.

Amy called after Jenny, 'I'll catch you up,' before turning to Willem. 'That was fun.'

'It was,' he nodded.

'It's good to have you back.'

'Good to be back. I just needed some time to reset.'

'I understand. Did it work?'

Willem nodded again. 'It did. Now, catch up with Jenny before she mugs someone.'

Amy laughed. 'Um ... would you like to join us at the Friday quiz? It's just me, the mugger, Finn and James. It's usually a giggle. You'd be very welcome.'

'Thank you, yes, I'd like that,' Willem smiled.

'Um ... do you want to walk up with us?'

'Thanks, but I've got my bike at the bottom of the hill,' Willem informed her.

'Oh, okay, goodnight then.'

'Goodnight, Amy.'

Amy turned to jog after Jenny, catching up with her before they rounded the corner at the top of the street.

'Okay?' Jenny asked.

'Yes. Okay. He's making it easy for me, could've been really awkward.'

'That's because he's a very nice man,' Jenny nodded sagely.

'He is. It would be much easier if he was a twat.'

'If it's a twat you're after, I can introduce you to one of my exes,' Jenny offered.

'Thanks, but I'll pass if that's okay.'

'Wise choice.'

The friends made their way slowly on, until their paths diverged, with promises to catch up tomorrow, and Amy made the short remainder of the walk to her house alone. She walked fast, her hand curled around the rape alarm in her coat pocket, and closed the front door behind her with a huge sigh of relief. She admitted to herself that she was pretty pissed off at feeling unsafe in the town again. She also admitted to herself that she'd always felt very safe with Willem.

CHAPTER 20

The Mutineers

The following Wednesday saw a new team turn up at the Griffin. Jenny gave them a traditionally warm welcome by giving them the evil eye. Amy had a vague feeling she'd seen them somewhere before. And she was right.

The new team was called the Mutineers and had previously quizzed at the Merry Monk in Canterbury. Unfortunately, that quiz had been cancelled indefinitely due to Gemma offending too many people with her colourful language. Clearly, blue wasn't everyone's favourite colour. As some of their team actually lived in Folkestone, the Mutineers had decided to give the Griffin a try.

Their reputation had apparently preceded them as Pauline was quick to inform Amy's team that they were 'the ones to beat' in Canterbury, and regularly won or were a close second.

'The ones to beat, eh?' Jenny said. 'With a shitty stick if necessary.'

'Now, now, Jenny,' Pippa admonished. 'Play nicely. They look like nice people.'

'There's no *nice* in quizzing, Pip,' Jenny responded mutinously. 'This is war!' A little of Jenny's drink sloshed over the edge of her glass as she thumped it down onto the table.

Pippa simply raised her eyebrows and chuckled.

Over on their table, the Mutineers were settling into their new quiz environment, and sussing out the opposition.

'That woman over there keeps glaring at us,' Jo said. 'The one with the pink hair.'

'Yeah, I noticed that,' Gwynne said, pulling a face.

'Probably stunned by our good looks and obvious intelligence,' Paul commented, flicking his hair and trying to look more like a male model than the fifty-nine-year-old, balding man he actually was.

'She's still doing it,' Jo said. 'What is her problem?'

'Take no notice,' Janice said, as she put her two pounds entry fee on the growing tower of coins on the table.

Jo sighed, and turned her attention back to her team. 'Who's writing?' she asked, producing a red and a black biro from her handbag. Jo was the team's Amy: organiser and provider of pens. It was really a rhetorical question as Janice was the team's regular scribe. Only occasionally did she declare herself in need of a rest from writing. On one particularly memorable – not necessarily for all the right reasons – night, Janice had decided to write all the answers using her non-dominant hand. Apparently it was good brain training for her, but it was a frustrating business for the others as she painstakingly penned her way through the first round of twenty questions.

The tepid welcome continued when Pauline, bristling in beige, arrived at the Mutineers' table to collect their entry fee.

'Welcome to the Griffin quiz,' she said, with a cool smile that most definitely did not reach her eyes. 'I understand you're over from *Canterbury* tonight?' She pronounced 'Canterbury' as though it put a nasty taste in her mouth.

'Um ... yes, that's right,' Jo said, smiling much more genuinely at the spectre in beige, even though she was picking up the decidedly hostile vibe. 'Thought we'd give it a go.'

Pauline harrumphed, and bristled some more.

'Yes, we've heard good things about your quiz,' Dirk said, hoping to thaw the *yskoningin* in front of them. (That's ice queen for those of us who don't speak Afrikaans. Dirk was a German South African, who sometimes lapsed into the language of his home country.)

Pauline seemed to bristle a little less, and smiled slightly more warmly at him, thinking he reminded her a little of Wilhelm. 'Well, we certainly try to make it an enjoyable evening for everyone. Barry puts his all into his quizzes.'

Dirk smiled at Pauline again as he scooped up the coins from the table and handed them to her.

'Thank you. Do you need a pen?' Pauline asked, holding out a mugful after she'd doled out answer sheets.

'No, thank you,' Jo said, indicating the two biros in front of Janice.

'Well, I'd wish you good luck, but from what I hear, you won't need it,' Pauline said, trying to make light of it, but clearly wholly insincere, before turning to move on to the next team.

'Thanks very much,' Jo said, pulling a face at Pauline's departing back. 'Bloody hell, what was all that about?'

Chris, who was Janice's brother, said, 'I was worried we might all be turned to stone for a minute.'

The others laughed.

'I reckon that perm of hers could easily contain a snake's nest,' Janice added.

'I definitely wouldn't want to meet her in a dark alley,' Gwynne said.

'I wouldn't want to meet her in a *light* one. There's a definite feeling of "this is a *local* quiz, for *local* people" isn't there?' Jo said, shuddering a little. 'She gave me the willies.'

'You should be so lucky,' Paul threw out.

Jo ignored him.

'Well, let's reserve judgement,' Dirk suggested. 'It might be a good quiz once we all thaw out from that encounter.'

'The rum's helping,' Chris said, holding up his glass.

'Arrrrrrr!' Gwynne said.

Further discussion of Pauline and her death stare was halted by the arrival of Barry, resplendent in a red sequinned jacket.

'Holy shit,' Paul remarked. 'It's Elton John and Dame Edna's lovechild.'

The others giggled. Barry was certainly a sight. If your eyes weren't sore before you clapped eyes on him …

'Good evening, ladies and germs,' Barry began his usual, over-the-top introduction, much to the bemusement of the Mutineers. 'Welcome to the Griffin for your Wednesday-night quiz, hosted by yours truly, and more than ably assisted by my glamorous assistant, my lovely wife, Pauline.'

The Mutineers were stunned when Barry pointed at the beige ice queen as he said this.

'Someone pass me a dictionary,' Paul hissed. 'I need to look up "glamorous".' Paul was basically Jenny in male form, with an acerbic wit and sarcastic tendencies. The only real difference, apart from genitalia, was that Paul needed no help from alcohol.

'I see we have a new team here tonight,' Barry continued, waving his arm theatrically at the Mutineers. 'All the way from Canterbury, as I understand it.'

'Yeah, all of about eighteen miles,' Chris chortled.

Janice looked up from the sheet she was doodling on. 'Are we actually at Butlin's?' she asked. 'I honestly feel like I've slipped into a time warp and I'm back at Bognor with the parents.'

'I don't remember the Redcoats being quite that sparkly,' Chris added.

Janice returned to her doodling. She had picked up Jo's red pen and was adding colour to a red-jacketed, Billy Bunter-style cartoon drawing. Jo brought the red biro specifically for Janice to doodle with, and also for aggressive marking of other teams' answer sheets if the urge took her. As a secondary-school physics teacher, she wasn't allowed to mark students' work in red any longer as it was considered to be 'too aggressive' for the little darlings. Next to the drawing that was obviously Barry, Janice had drawn a female figure that was clearly Pauline, with a headful of snakes, and lasers coming out of her eyes.

'I hope Barry doesn't collect the answer sheets in, Janice,' Jo said, a slightly worried expression on her face.

Janice shrugged. She didn't much care what other people thought. You couldn't be a teacher for as long as she had and not develop a thick skin.

'Yeah, Janice, we might not be able to come back. Ever,' Paul said, the implication clear that that would be absolutely fine with him. Paul definitely preferred blue over red.

Janice ignored him again, as was her wont, and continued scribbling.

Unlike the regular, *local*, teams, the Mutineers had no idea what subjects the rounds would be on. They got a bit of a clue to one when they discovered that the team which included the woman with the pink hair was called Flowery Twats.

'What do you reckon, then? Seventies sitcoms?' Chris asked.

The others nodded.

'Did you know that Flowery Twats was actually the only time they used all the letters from Fawlty Towers on the hotel sign?' Paul asked them.

Dirk was just looking lost, having spent the seventies in South Africa. 'Sorry, guys, I might not be too much help on this one.'

'Too busy chasing lions?' Jo asked him.

Dirk nodded. 'Yep, with the stick I got to play with for ten minutes every other Wednesday.'

'Don't worry,' Jo smiled at him. 'I reckon we've got this covered.'

CHAPTER 21

The slipped discos

By the time the music round came around, the Mutineers were absolutely flying, with full marks on British sitcoms of the seventies, and a picture round of characters from shows such as *Fawlty Towers*, *Dad's Army*, *Are You Being Served?* and *It Ain't Half Hot Mum*.

Paul, who was also a keen member of the local am-dram society, said, in his best Young Mr Grace voice, 'You've all done very well.'

Dirk was feeling useless, but also quite grateful to have grown up on a different continent.

Over on Amy's table, where they were also doing extremely well, Jenny had remarked that the new team were looking like smug bastards. 'Where's that stick?' she'd asked, more than once.

The music round, unsurprisingly, was hits of the seventies, and included such delights as 'Tie a Yellow Ribbon Round the Ole Oak Tree' and 'Tiger Feet'. Janice came into her own with the disco tracks from Earth, Wind & Fire and The Trammps, singing along to 'Disco Inferno'.

'I can't sing either,' had been Paul's response.

Janice ignored him and sang a bit louder.

Discovering the final round was a ten-question wipeout wasn't the best news.

Chris, the gambler of the team, was already chanting, 'Gamble, gamble!'

Jo, the more risk-averse one, was trying to control her blood pressure, and to rein him in. 'Let's see what comes up first.' She was of the Amy school of thought where wipeout rounds were concerned: better to have some guaranteed points than take a needless chance.

Unfortunately for Jo, she was outvoted on one of the answers and the Mutineers wiped out.

Jenny didn't even try and conceal her delight at this from across the room, punching the air, and saying, 'Yesss!' none too quietly.

'That's not very sporting, is it?' Jo said, under her breath.

The Mutineers came second to Flowery Twats after Amy's team had a better wipeout round, and Jenny's celebration was none too subtle.

'It's probably best that we didn't win,' Gwynne chuckled. 'I'm not sure we'd have made it out alive if we had.'

'Jeez! I think you might be right. Between knitted-nightmare-woman and pink-hair, we haven't exactly been made welcome, have we?' Jo said.

Heads shook around the table.

'Do you think we should give it a miss in future?' Chris asked.

'Um ... not sure. I don't like being forced out by bullies,' Janice said.

'I'm with Janice,' Paul agreed, earning a surprised look from everyone. 'Sod 'em. I think we should come back and thrash the living daylights out of them!' (He couldn't have known how prophetic this was, the next week's specialist round being the James Bond books and films.)

'I'll go with the majority,' Jo said, ever the diplomat.

'Yeah, I don't mind either way,' Gwynne agreed. 'Shame to be forced out though.'

'I think, until we can find a good replacement in Canterbury, we should stick with it then,' Janice suggested.

There was general agreement from around the table.

With that settled, the Mutineers sat back to finish their drinks and watch as the prize money was delivered to the Flowery Twats.

Just as they were about to make their departure, the brunette from the Flowery Twats came past on the way to the Ladies, stopping briefly to say, 'Bad luck! You'd have beaten us if you hadn't wiped out. You certainly gave us a run for our money though!'

Jo smiled and said thank you, adding, 'Well done! You're obviously the team to watch.'

'We have our moments,' Amy smiled. She hesitated then, before pulling a face and adding, 'Sorry about Jenny – my friend with the pink hair. She's lovely really, honest.'

'We believe you,' Jo said. 'Although between … er … Jenny … and um … Pauline, we were wondering if we'd arrived in Royston Vasey,' she laughed.

'Oh God! A *local* pub for *local* people?!' Amy laughed, pushing the tip of her nose up. 'It's not like that really, I promise. I'm sorry we haven't made a very good first impression. I hope it won't put you off coming again. It's been a bit quiet since … Well, it's been a bit quiet lately, so it's nice to have some new blood.' Amy cursed herself mentally for the expression, and added hurriedly, 'Well, anyway, I hope we'll see you next week.' She gave the Mutineers one last smile before moving away.

'She seems alright,' Gwynne said.

'Yeah, relatively normal,' Paul agreed.

'Maybe we misjudged them after all,' Dirk added. 'I guess we'll find out next time.'

With that, the Mutineers made their way to the exit, passing the Flowery Twats as they went. Everyone smiled at them in a friendly fashion, except Jenny who looked decidedly smug.

'Congratulations,' Jo said, ignoring Jenny and smiling back at the others.

'Thanks! Better luck next time,' Pippa said, filling in for Amy who was still in the loo.

'Thanks, see you next week.' With that, the Mutineers were gone.

'They seem really nice,' Amy said to the rest of the team when she came back from the loo.

Everyone agreed except Jenny, who sort of harrumphed.

'They did. I think they're coming back next week too,' Pippa informed her.

'Oh good. Nice to have the place a bit fuller again.'

'At least it's more money for us to win,' Jenny relented.

'We were very lucky to get the win tonight,' Amy reminded her. 'They were only one answer away from beating us.'

'I'm not worried,' Jenny told her. 'If they get too big for their boots, the phantom killer of Old Folkestone Town will just have to strike again. Mwah ha ha!' she finished menacingly.

CHAPTER 22

Team Bonding

When Wednesday rolled around again, the Mutineers were indeed all present and correct at the Griffin when Amy and co arrived. Smiles and waves were exchanged, two fingers and a grimace in Jenny's case.

With a specialist round on James Bond, Amy's team had had the usual exchange of messages on WhatsApp to decide on that week's team name. It had been an unusually tame exchange, once they'd got past the pussy galore.

From Folkestone, With Love
Quiz and Let Die
The Quizzing Daylights
Quiz Another Day
Dr No It All
How about no. They're all boring. From Jenny.
What about Goldeneye Ointment? Amy put in.
That got a few maybes.
What about one of the female characters? They had some pretty bonkers names, didn't they? Pippa suggested.
I'll google them, hang on, Amy sent. *Here you go ... Pussy Galore, Holly Goodhead, Octopussy, Plenty O'Toole, Chew Mee, Honey Rider, Mary Goodnight, Agent Strawberry Fields, Dr Molly Warmflash, Penelope Smallbone, Jenny Flex...*
Penelope Smallboner?
No, Jenny.

Agent Strawberry Fields Forever? From Willem.
Boring. Holly Gives Goodhead?
No, Jenny.
Bite Mee? Dr Molly Warmflesh?
Jenny, you're barred from this chat.

They'd finally settled on Dr No It All. While they had prepared as much as possible for the quiz, they weren't prepared for Barry turning up dressed as Blofeld, forgoing his usual bright blazer for a Mao suit and a facial scar.

'Oh my Jesus H. Christ,' Jenny said.

Amy was giggling. 'Let's hope Mrs Slocombe's pussy isn't still hanging around from last week.'

'Yuck. Nobody wants to see Butlin's Bazzer stroking a pussy,' Jenny said, pretending to throw up.

Willem was looking lost as he didn't understand the *Are You Being Served?* references. He'd spent the seventies in South Africa.

'Please tell me Pauline's not going to appear as Ursula Andress in *that* bikini,' Finn said, pulling a face.

'Ursula *Un*dress, you mean,' Amy chuckled.

'I will be asking for my two pounds back if that happens,' Finn added.

'You haven't paid yet,' Pippa pointed out.

Right on cue, Pauline arrived to collect their entry fees. A sigh of relief went round the table when she was dressed in her usual beige knitted uniform. Amy couldn't stifle her giggles though.

'Something funny, dear?' Pauline asked, smiling a smile that would have done any Bond villain proud.

'What? Oh, no. Er … just something Jenny said … about … er … something,' she explained, weakly.

Pauline raised her eyebrows, took their money, and doled out the picture round and answer sheets. She gave Willem a squeeze on the shoulder and a 'good luck, dear', before bustling away.

'Oops!' Jenny said to Amy. 'Someone's in her bad books now. Be afraid!'

Amy pulled a scared face. 'Trust me, I am! Don't leave me alone with her, whatever you do!'

Any more thoughts of Pauline were pushed aside as they turned their collective attention to the picture round, which was Bond villains. Amy's team did pretty well, although they did stumble on a few of the more recent ones. Thankfully, the youth of the team, Finn, managed to have a stab at all but one.

Over on the Mutineers' table, they were having a similar problem with the picture round. Unfortunately for them, the 'youth' of their team, Gwynne, while he still thought of himself as one of the lads, was actually fifty-two. To give him his dues, he was pretty good on current music, which would otherwise have been the Mutineers' Achilles heel. Along with US presidents, kings and queens, and Marvel characters.

After about ten minutes, Barry got the ball – make that *Thunderball* – rolling with the first general knowledge round. Amy got the giggles again at the sight of him.

'Do you expect me to quiz?' she asked, in a loud whisper. 'No, Mr Bond, I expect you to die.'

'Wrong villain, Amy,' Willem pointed out. 'I think that was Goldfinger.'

'Also … Tut tut. Dead quizzers,' Jenny added. 'Very bad taste indeed, Amy,' Jenny said, mock seriously.

Amy looked suitably chastised for the briefest of moments, before turning back to Barry.

The specialist James Bond round was surprisingly hard, with many of the questions seeming quite obscure to Dr No It All.

'Roger Moore apparently suffers from hoplophobia. What is hoplophobia the fear of?' Barry asked.

Blank faces around the table.

'Fear of hopscotch?' Pippa suggested.

'Fear of running out of beer?' Finn put forward, making the others laugh.

'Where did Ian Fleming get the name James Bond from?' was question five.

Jenny groaned. 'Buggered if I know. Or care.'

They were saved on this one by Dave, who'd read that it was actually taken from a birdwatching book Ian Fleming had handy when he was looking for a name as mundane as possible. James Bond was named after an ornithologist.

'Who knew?' Amy said in surprise.

'Dave, thankfully,' Pippa said, smiling at her husband.

When they marked the Bond round, and learned that hoplophobia was the fear of weapons or firearms, Amy experienced a slight shudder as she had a momentary flashback to the time she had fired a gun in anger. She blinked the memory away as fast as it had appeared.

After the break, the music round was, naturally, Bond themes: point for the artist, point for the title as usual.

'Got to love a bit of Burly Chassis,' Jenny said, when they played 'Moonraker'.

They were only stumped by the theme for *Quantum of Solace*, when no one could remember the title or who performed it.

'Oh! Yes, of course!' Amy said, bouncing the heel of her hand off her temple, when Barry read out the answer as 'Another

Way to Die' by Jack White and Alicia Keys.

The last round before the wipeout was on Marvel characters. The women round the table all groaned, but Willem and Finn were able to have a good stab at the answers. Over on the Mutineers' table, it wasn't only the women who groaned. Thankfully, Chris and Dirk had a smattering of knowledge and the round wasn't a complete disaster. As with every time Marvel questions came up, the Mutineers agreed that someone needed to mug up on it. Nobody ever did though.

By the end of the quiz, Dr No It All had no idea at all if they'd done enough to beat the Mutineers. As it turned out, they'd beaten them by one point, their slightly superior Marvel knowledge winning the day.

'Bugger,' Jo said, over on the Mutineers' table. 'They're good, aren't they?'

'Never fear, our time will come,' Paul said, steepling his fingers like many a Bond villain, but looking more like Montgomery Burns from *The Simpsons*.

CHAPTER 23

When Amy met Jo

It was the following Monday when Amy bumped into Jo from the Mutineers. She'd taken herself off to Steep Street Coffee House to write, hoping for warmth and inspiration. And possibly cake. Jenny had said she might join her later for a catch-up over cake, and Amy was already eying up a rather delicious-looking lemon and blueberry one, gluten free of course.

She was staring into space when the door opened, letting in a blast of cold air, and making Amy shudder. When she focused on the person who'd come in, Amy realised it was Jo, and smiled and waved at her. Jo smiled and waved back and came over to Amy's table.

'Hello!' Jo said brightly.

'Hi,' Amy said. 'Nice to see you.'

'Do you mind if I join you? Or are you working?' Jo asked, indicating Amy's laptop open on the table in front of her.

'Please, do. Supposed to be working, but my muse has other ideas,' Amy groaned.

'Your muse?' Jo looked puzzled.

'Oh, I'm a writer.'

'Ooh! Let me get a drink and you can tell me all about it. Can I get you anything?'

'No, I'm good thanks,' Amy said, indicating the frothy coffee on the table in front of her.

Jo joined the queue and was back at Amy's table a few minutes later, carefully carrying a mug of hot chocolate. She shrugged out of her coat, placed it on the back of the chair opposite Amy and settled herself down.

'What brings you to Folkestone?' Amy asked.

'Oh, I actually live here,' Jo told her.

Amy was surprised she'd never seen her around, and said as much. Jo explained that she hadn't been living in the town for very long and that her social life was still very much centred on Canterbury.

'What brought you to the town?'

'I missed being by the sea, to be honest. I did wonder if I'd done the right thing when I heard about the killings here over the last couple of years,' Jo said, pulling a face.

Amy felt her own face flush. She didn't really want to admit how closely connected to both serial killers she was. 'Well, that's all behind us now, hopefully,' she said, holding up crossed fingers. She didn't mention the recent deaths of several quiz-team members.

'So, tell me about your writing,' Jo said. 'What sort of thing do you write?'

'Novels. Crime these days. I used to write women's fiction, but people seem to want a juicy murder or six.'

'That's so cool!' Jo looked impressed.

Amy smiled, gratified. 'It would be if I really made a decent living from it. These are a couple of mine,' she said, pointing to the shelf behind her. (Steep Street was a literary café inspired by the famous book cafés of Paris, and its walls were stacked floor to ceiling with books. Amy had actually snuck hers on the shelf when no one was looking.)

'Amazing! I always wanted to be a writer. Life kind of got in the way though.'

'Tell me about it! I came to writing late in life. It's never *too* late though.'

Jo screwed up her face. 'I think it might be for me.'

'Never say never. What do you do to pay the bills?'

'Oh God, don't ask, it's too boring for words.'

Amy persisted.

'I work in the pharmaceutical industry – quality assurance,' Jo told her, pulling a face. 'Not my dream job, just something I kind of fell into.'

Amy nodded. 'I used to have one of those. I don't think I could do a "proper" job anymore. As Jenny will tell you, I'm unemployable.'

Jo laughed. 'Jenny's your friend with the pink hair? From the quiz?'

Amy nodded.

'She seems like a … um … character,' Jo said tactfully.

Amy laughed. 'She's alright really. Just a bit competitive. When you get to know her she's very funny. And loyal.'

'I'll take your word for it. She terrifies me!' Jo said, only half joking.

'What about your team? How do you all know each other?'

'We actually met through a Meetup group in Canterbury. All started going to the same pub quiz over the course of a few months. Eventually got a bit fed up with never knowing who'd turn up each week, and how annoying or weird they'd be. So I suggested a few of us break away and form our own team.'

'Ah!' Amy said. 'Hence the team name? You actually did mutiny!'

Jo grinned. 'We did. And we've been quizzing together ever since.'

'They seem like a nice bunch.'

'They really are. Paul's got a razor-sharp wit and doesn't hold back. If he's thinking something, his face says it even before he can get the words out. I think he's probably won awards for eye-rolling.'

'Sounds a bit like Jenny!'

'I suspect you might be right! Janice is lovely, very funny too. She's a physics teacher and we hear lots of horror stories about her pupils – what the Head Girl's been up to in the boys' loos! She's always counting the days until the next school holidays.'

'Another "proper" job I wouldn't want,' Amy shuddered.

'It's not the vocation it once was, I reckon.'

'Hats off to her for sticking it,' Amy said.

'Janice and Gwynne are hilarious together. They always compete to see who can keep clapping the longest at the end of the quiz. And every time Gwynne gets up to go to the bar or to the gents, she leans back and stretches her arms out, pretending to yawn, so he can't get by.' Jo was smiling as she talked about her team. She was clearly very fond of them. 'How did you guys all meet?'

Amy filled Jo in on the writing group and Coastal Creatives, including a broad-strokes account of her link to the serial killers Robert Seymour and Jeff Teller.

'Oh my God!' was Jo's shocked reaction. 'I can't believe Seymour was in your writing group! What was he like?' Jo looked intrigued.

Amy squirmed uncomfortably and Jo, being the observant type, noticed.

'Oh, sorry, Amy! You don't have to tell me. Forget I asked. Just ghoulish curiosity on my part,' she apologised, reaching over and giving her new friend's arm a squeeze.

Amy shook her head. 'No, it's fine. It's perfectly natural to be curious. And, after all, I write books which appeal to the ghoul in us all, so I can hardly complain when someone asks about a real-life killer.' She paused. 'Robert was ... Well, at first he was kind of sweet and humble. He seemed so thrilled to be accepted into the writing group. Then, as time went by, we started to see another side of him – he'd make tactless remarks, things which normal people would keep to themselves.' Amy shuddered as she thought back to a difficult period of her life in Folkestone.

Jo was quiet, giving Amy her full attention.

'It was really when we wrote our short stories that everyone began to think he was more than a little depraved,' Amy continued.

'Short stories?'

Amy nodded. 'We arrived at the pub we used to meet in one day, and our booth was taped off – you now, a bit like a crime scene – and I joked there'd been a murder. Not very funny now, looking back. But anyway, I suggested we should all have a go at writing our perfect murders, more as a writing challenge than anything else, and the others were all up for it. It was only when we read Robert's story that we really started to think he was pretty warped. Some of the stuff he wrote was really quite disturbing, even for a crime writer like me!'

'And then the real murders started happening?'

'Mm hm,' Amy nodded, lowering her gaze. It wasn't easy to recount the horrors of two summers previously, even with the distance of time. She picked up her coffee and took a sip, unable to make eye contact with the woman sitting opposite.

'And is it true he killed himself?' Jo asked.

Amy sighed deeply. 'Do you mind if we don't talk about it anymore?'

'Oh! Of course not! Sorry, Amy, I didn't mean to make you feel uncomfortable. Tell me more about the shop,' Jo said, trying to move the subject to safer ground.

Amy put her head in her hands, and gave a sort of strangled laugh.

Jo frowned. 'Oh God, what have I said now?'

Amy dropped her hands from her face, and shook her head. 'It's not you, Jo … it's just, well, the shop is kind of tied up with the second serial killer.'

'Jeff Teller?'

'Yep. He murdered one of the members of the shop collective. Gloria.'

'Oh Jesus! Amy, I'm so sorry! You don't need to say another word,' Jo apologised again.

Amy scratched her head. 'Yeah, it's been quite a couple of years one way and another.' She paused, wondering whether to continue. 'Teller also murdered a friend of Jenny's …'

Jo's hand flew to her mouth. 'Oh no! Oh how awful. Poor Jenny.'

Amy smiled sadly. 'She's had a rough time coming to terms with what happened. She … um … she saw photos of what he did to Bella.' Amy looked at Jo and saw tears forming in the corners of her eyes. 'It's why Jenny's been a bit more … well, a bit more Jenny, lately. She's been so angry about it all.' Amy hoped she wasn't being disloyal to her best friend. She simply felt the need to explain Jenny's recent behaviour, and make Jo understand that it didn't define her friend.

'I'm not surprised. Poor thing. I'd be in absolute bits.'

'It's been tough. I'm trying my best to help her through it. She's always there for me, and always so strong. I honestly don't know what I'd do without her.'

'You're very lucky to have each other,' Jo smiled, squeezing Amy's hand. 'Now, let's change the subject. Politics? War? Religion? Take your pick!'

Amy couldn't help laughing, and the tension evaporated.

Jo took a sip of hot chocolate. 'You're lucky to have Finn on your team. I often think we could do with someone younger on ours. We'll have to wait until somebody pops their clogs though, I reckon,' Jo joked.

Amy cringed inwardly as Jo unwittingly steered the conversation straight back into dangerous waters. *Don't joke about something like that*, she thought to herself. *Might just become a self-fulfilling prophecy.*

Jo continued. 'We do actually have a seventh team member these days. Russ used to be on an opposing team called the Vagabonds. They were older – in their sixties and seventies, I think – and you could tell from the longing looks in our direction that Russ *really* wanted to be a Mutineer. We always had the most laughs out of any team in the pub, and won the most too. Then, two of the Vagabonds died in quick succession, and another just kind of disappeared, so we took pity on Russ and adopted him. The quiz we used to do in Canterbury allowed teams of eight, otherwise we wouldn't have been able to. Russ is a really great guy. Ex-military and police. Quite deaf, which makes sharing answers a bit tricky, but good fun and he fits into the team really well.

Rum drinker too, so always destined to be a Mutineer!'

Jo paused to take another sip of her hot chocolate, before continuing.

'Anyway, we naturally starting joking that Russ had actually bumped off the others so he could join us. It became a bit of a running joke,' Jo continued.

Amy's brain was going nineteen to the dozen. She hoped her thoughts weren't showing on her face. 'That's funny!' she said, laughing rather unconvincingly. She couldn't believe the turn the conversation had taken.

Jo frowned at her, as if picking up on Amy's discomfort. 'Oh God, there I go again, putting my size nines in it! He didn't really kill them!' she assured Amy.

'Oh no, of course not! Who'd kill for quiz winnings?' Amy pooh-poohed.

'Exactly! Although I think Russ wanted to be a Mutineer more than he wanted to win.'

Eager to change the subject from dead quizzers, Amy asked Jo what they thought of the quiz at the Griffin.

'It's okay,' Jo said. 'To be honest, it's a bit tame for us. We prefer more heckling and something a bit more sweary.'

'Ah! You'd probably enjoy the other quiz we go to. It's on a Friday night at the Old Town Bar. It's much more relaxed and usually a right laugh.'

'That does sound more like our sort of quiz. I might see if the others are up for it. What's the quizmaster like?'

'Kev? He's brilliant. Gives as good as he gets. Regularly tells us all to fuck off. And absolutely nothing like Barry.'

'Oh my God! Barry! He is hilarious, but for all the wrong reasons.'

'Right?!' Amy nodded, laughing. 'Butlin's Barry we call him.'

Jo laughed. 'He definitely has a holiday-camp vibe. Not sure what to make of Pauline. Is it just us she hates? She really gives me the creeps.'

'I'm so happy you said that! We think she's a certified psychopath, and all agree we wouldn't want to meet her in a dark alley.'

'Or even a light one!' Jo said, and not for the first time. 'Glad it's not just us. What's her problem with my team specifically though?'

'Don't take it personally. I think she just has a thing about outsiders thinking they can come in and rock the boat, steal the winnings, you know.'

'Well, we've hardly done that!' Jo laughed. 'Always the bridesmaids lately. We might have to change our team name, although I can't imagine Paul being very happy to be called a bridesmaid.'

Both women laughed, and Amy thought she may just have made a new friend. She'd have to be careful, or Jenny might get jealous and bump Jo off.

CHAPTER 24

Go big or go Homer

Amy half expected to see the Mutineers at the Old Town Bar on Friday, but she didn't see Jo and the others until the following Wednesday night at the Griffin. She earned a hard stare from Jenny when she smiled and waved enthusiastically at them.

'Er ... excuse me?' Jenny said.

'You're excused,' Amy responded.

Jenny raised her eyebrows.

'What? I'm just being friendly. Trying to make up for the decidedly *cool* welcome they've been getting from *some* people,' Amy said, raising her own eyebrows right back at Jenny. She hadn't told Jenny about her chance meeting and conversation with Jo.

Jenny huffed.

'What's up with you two?' Willem asked them.

'We have a traitor in our midst,' Jenny said theatrically, nodding first at Amy and then at the Mutineers.

Amy laughed. If she only knew! 'Take no notice, Willem. She's cross with me for being friendly.'

'To the opposition!' Jenny felt the need to clarify. 'Next thing you know, she'll be going full Fletcher Christian.'

Willem couldn't help chuckling at her. 'Ach! I don't think you need to worry about that, Jenny.'

'Oh, I don't know; if she carries on being a dickhead, I just might!' Amy joined in with his laughter. 'And I am rather partial to a Bounty,' she winked. 'You know, *Mutiny on the Bounty*,' she was forced to explain, when Willem and Jenny looked at her blankly.

Willem had the good grace to laugh.

Jenny simply shook her head slowly and uttered a single, damning word, 'Shocking.'

Any further bickering was prevented by Barry's arrival. They were relieved to see him back in his regular blazer, all traces of Blofeld removed. With the specialist subject being Greek and Roman mythology, they'd had serious concerns he might turn up wearing a toga.

The team name they'd chosen was the Dis-Graces, which had been Finn's rather clever suggestion. Everyone had naturally thought of Jenny when he'd suggested it. They'd ruled out Herpes, Juno What I Mean? and the Gorgon-zolas.

Amy had half-heartedly tried mugging up on the subject, but found it rather boring and was counting on the others having done better.

'I wonder what the music round will be?' Pippa asked.

'The greatest hits of Nana Mouskouri and Demis Roussos?' Amy suggested, jokingly.

'That'll be a short round,' Jenny added.

Finn looked at them blankly.

'Don't knock Nana. She's one of the biggest-selling female artists of all time, apparently,' Pippa enlightened them.

'Huh! Who knew?' Amy said.

'Pippa, apparently,' Jenny said.

'What was that really well-known song Demis Roussos sang?' Amy asked, screwing up her face as she tried to remember back to her childhood.

'"Forever and ever",' Pippa obliged.

'Yes!' Amy exclaimed, before launching into the chorus. 'Oh, Finn, you don't know what you were missing, not being a child of the seventies.'

'Oh yeah,' Jenny said sarcastically, 'I treasure my memories of a hairy Greek bloke in a kaftan warbling about loving you 'til the cows come home, or some such shit.'

Amy giggled. Finn looked relieved to be a child of the nineties.

'We used to call Nana Mouskouri, *Banana* Mouskouri,' Amy chuckled.

'All sounds pretty wild and crazy,' Finn said sarcastically.

'Oh yeah, one long acid trip, the seventies,' Jenny nodded. 'All those crazy orange-and-brown patterns. You'd have to be on drugs to think they were a good idea.'

They were saved any more reminiscing on the groovy decade by Pauline's arrival. Amy groaned when she saw the picture round, which consisted of twelve sculptures of Greek gods and goddesses.

She held up her hands, declaring it 'all Greek to me'.

'Don't give up your day job,' Jenny told her, in response to Amy's feeble attempt at humour.

The others made a pretty good fist – and just about every other body part – of the picture round though, along with the general knowledge and specialist rounds, and Amy was relieved when they were only a point behind the Mutineers going in to the music round. She'd caught Jo's eye a couple of times, and smiled at her new friend. (Making sure Jenny was looking the other way first.)

The music round turned out to be on the Eurovision Song Contest.

Finn screwed up his nose. 'I've never seen it.'

'Lucky you,' Jenny said.

The others all admitted they used to watch it 'back in the day', but nobody had much of a clue about more recent years. Luckily for them, Barry was stuck in a similar time warp and there were plenty of songs they all – except Finn – recognised.

'If we know them, you can bet they do too,' Jenny moaned, nodding over at the Mutineers, as Amy wrote down *Johnny Logan* on the answer sheet.

The final song almost stumped them. It was a female singer and she was singing in French.

'I don't know any French singers,' was the general consensus around a table of blank faces.

'That's because they're all shite,' Jenny said, constructively.

'Didn't Céline Dion do Eurovision?' Amy asked the others. 'Did she sing in French?'

'Mm ... she sang for Switzerland, I think,' Pippa answered. 'But I don't think it's her.'

They listened again.

Amy shook her head.

Jenny yawned.

Pippa looked thoughtful. 'Do you know ... I think that's Nana Mouskouri!'

'Really?' Jenny asked.

Pippa nodded.

'But wasn't she Greek?' Willem asked.

'Yes, but she was well known for being fluent in several

languages. I think she might have performed for a country other than Greece at Eurovision. Don't quote me on that though,' Pippa told them.

'Totally gonna quote you on that,' Jenny said.

Amy wrote *Nana Mouskouri* on the answer page, and sat back. 'Not too shabby,' she said.

Amy redeemed herself a little with a food-and-drink round, and they were one point in front going into the wipeout round. Luckily for the Dis-Graces, the Mutineers matched them with just two correct answers, making Jo's team runners-up for the third week in a row.

'Always the bridesmaids,' Jo mouthed, nodding in Paul's direction and pulling a face, when Amy looked over to commiserate with her.

Amy chuckled.

'What's so funny?' Jenny asked.

'You are, my friend. You're bloody hilarious,' Amy informed her, shoulder-bumping her friend.

Jenny looked a little mollified. 'That is true,' she agreed, nodding.

'That's three wins on the trot, now,' Finn said, looking round the table.

Pippa looked up from where she was counting out the winnings. 'Goodness, we'd better watch our backs!' she said, chuckling.

'It's not funny,' Amy said. 'We genuinely could have put a target on our backs by winning all the time.'

'Do you honestly believe that?' Finn asked.

Amy nodded. 'I really do.'

'Maybe we'd better throw it next week then?' Jenny joked.

'That's not a bad idea actually,' Amy said. 'Just to be on the safe side.'

'Don't be a lemon,' Jenny told her. 'I'm not chucking the quiz on purpose. Letting those interlopers win. No way, no how.'

Amy didn't say anything else, but she told herself she would withhold answers the following week. That's if she actually knew any of course.

CHAPTER 25

Close Encounters of the Quiz Kind

When the Mutineers and Amy's team met for a fourth time, the specialist subject was Steven Spielberg films, hence the name Raiders of the Lost Quiz. Willem had suggested Don't Feed Jenny After Midnight, which made everyone laugh, but they thought not everyone would get the *Gremlins* reference. Nobody had wanted to go with the obvious Saving Ryan's Privates.

'Maybe if we had a Ryan on the team …' Finn had said.

'Well, it's too late to start a recruitment drive now,' Willem said.

'Besides, we're a full squad … we'd have to discharge someone first.'

'The Dishonourable Discharges. That would be a great team name,' Jenny laughed.

That had led to Amy suggesting The Goolies, and Willem, E.T. The Extra-Testicle, but fear of Pauline's disapproving face had put the kibosh on them. And so, in the absence of any other brilliant flashes of inspiration, they had settled on Raiders of the Lost Quiz. They all agreed with Jenny that it was a bit boring.

As they waited for Pauline to arrive to collect their money and hand out picture rounds, Amy looked over at the Mutineers. She knew them all by name now, following her chat with Jo. It was, of course, Jo's face she was seeking out as she looked around the Mutineers' table. She wasn't there. In Jo's usual seat sat a trim man with a neat and tidy haircut, who Amy assumed was Russ, the most recent addition to the team following the deaths of his previous teammates. Amy experienced a heart-stopping moment when it occurred to her that Russ might have killed Jo to get a regular, permanent place on his dream team. Telling herself she was being ridiculous, Amy turned her attention back to her own team.

As Barry appeared to start proceedings, Amy was still trying not to panic. She knew deep down there was probably a perfectly reasonable explanation for Jo's absence, but Amy couldn't quite shake the worry that something terrible had happened. She didn't really engage with the picture round, which was stills taken from Spielberg movies (name the film and the year), and she let the others focus on it as she tried to rationalise her thoughts.

Surely the Mutineers wouldn't have come if anything bad had happened to Jo?

'Are you okay, Amy?' Willem asked, sensing her attention was elsewhere.

'What? Oh yes, fine. I was just wondering where Jo is tonight,' she said.

'Who?' Willem asked.

'Jo. You know, from the Mutineers,' Amy enlightened him, nodding in the direction of the other team.

'Oh,' Willem said, looking over at the opposing team. 'There are six of them still,' he observed.

'Mm hm, that's Russ in Jo's seat. He fills in when one of them can't make it.'

If Willem was surprised at Amy's knowledge of the other

team, he didn't mention it. 'Well, then presumably Jo couldn't make it,' he shrugged, not really seeing what the problem was.

'Yeah, I guess,' Amy said, still not quite convinced.

Willem frowned at her. 'You don't think there's a reason to worry about her absence, do you?'

Amy hesitated just a beat before she answered. 'No, of course not,' she said, smiling at Willem.

Willem, as tuned in to Amy as ever, knew she was still worried. 'I'm sure Jo simply had another engagement,' he tried to reassure her. 'Or she could be ill? Or maybe she just wanted to give … er … Russ, was it, a chance.'

Amy nodded. 'I'm sure you're right. Anyway, how are we getting on with the picture round?'

Jenny piped up at that. 'Pretty well, no thanks to you. Where's your head at? You've been absolutely useless so far.'

'Sorry, my bad,' Amy apologised. 'Back in the room now.'

'Well, thank you so much for gracing us with your presence,' Jenny said sarcastically.

Amy screwed up her face at her friend, and they braced themselves for Barry and the opening round.

'Round one, ding ding,' Barry began.

'Oh Jesus, please tell me Pauline isn't going to reappear dressed like one of those bimbos who prance round the boxing ring with a board showing the round number on it?' Jenny pulled a throwing-up face.

'Dressed in a beige knitted bikini and high heels,' Pippa chuckled.

'Oh my God, can you imagine?' Amy asked them, trying to be fully present once more.

'I'd rather not,' Finn said, with a face to match Jenny's.

Willem laughed. 'Don't those bikinis sometimes have advertising on them? You know, the sponsor's logo or something?'

'Who would sponsor Barry and Pauline?' Pippa wondered.

'Goodyear?' Dave suggested, in one of his rare vocal moments.

The others were slow to catch on.

'Tyres, blimp ...' Dave explained.

'Oh! Yes, good one,' Willem laughed, along with everyone else.

'How about Shreddies?' Jenny said.

'Ah! Yes, the knitting nanas. Nice one.'

'Isn't shreddies slang for undies too?'

Further discussion of hypothetical sponsors was halted by Barry calling out the first question.

'Which company's logo features the winged foot of Mercury?' Barry asked.

'No! What are the chances?' Dave said, in an unusually animated display.

'What?' the others asked.

'The answer's Goodyear!' Dave enlightened them.

'Huh! That is a spooky little coincidence. I do love a spooky little coincidence,' Amy said, as she wrote down the answer.

'I think that question was left over from last week,' Jenny added, thinking back to the previous torturous mythology round. 'I wouldn't have known the answer then either.'

'Well, thank goodness for Dave,' Pippa smiled at her husband.

'Thank God-ness for Dave,' Jenny said.

At the end of the general knowledge round, Amy's team were behind the Mutineers by a couple of points.

'Obviously that Jo woman is their weakest link,' Jenny pointed out.

Amy said nothing, but huffed inwardly at the slight against her new friend.

The specialist round was a bit hit and miss, with the more obscure Spielberg film answers eluding them. Over on the Mutineers' table, film buff Paul was doing rather better.

By the break, Raiders of the Lost Quiz were trailing by five points, and Amy took advantage of the time to congratulate the Mutineers on their performance thus far, and also ask about Jo's absence.

'She's not well,' Dirk informed her.

'Oh, nothing serious I hope?'

'Just a bout of food poisoning or something. I'm sure she'll be fine in a couple of days.'

'Oh, that's good,' Amy smiled in relief, earning herself some puzzled looks from the rest of the Mutineers. 'Well, anyway, well done so far and good luck with the remaining rounds.' With that, Amy took herself off to the loo. Couldn't have Jenny accusing her of fraternising with the enemy.

The music round, unsurprisingly, was theme songs from Spielberg films, and both teams dropped only one point. By the end of the quiz, however, Amy's team hadn't managed to claw back the points they were behind by, and the Mutineers took their first scalp at the Griffin.

'Arse,' Jenny announced.

'Now, now, Jenny, let's be gracious in defeat,' Willem chuckled at her.

'No. And also, fuck off,' Jenny glared at him.

Willem laughed. He knew not to take Jenny's abuse to heart.

Amy was secretly pleased to have lost. And nobody needed to know that she'd deliberately given a couple of wrong answers along the way. 'Oh! Damn, sorry!'

When the winning team filed past them on the way out, Amy made a point of congratulating them. 'Jo will be sorry to have missed your first win here,' she added.

The one called Dirk nodded and thanked her. 'She will, but she'll be happy for Russ.'

'Will we see you next week?'

'Probably.' With that, the Mutineers were gone.

CHAPTER 26

Pauline who?

After a few pretty uneventful weeks with no more 'sudden' deaths and no more muggings or stabbings, Amy began to feel a bit safer again, especially as Willem now walked her and Jenny home after the Wednesday and Friday quizzes, but she still carried her rape alarm. She'd heard from Jo that the Mutineers had decided to return to Canterbury for future quizzing, but Jo had promised to keep in touch.

Willem seemed content with life – it might have had something to do with the new motorbike he'd bought, Amy thought. When he'd said 'bike', she'd initially thought he meant bicycle, but it was actually a BMW touring motorbike, a big black beast of a machine, and Willem couldn't mention it without grinning. 'At least he's got something he can ride now,' Jenny had cackled when she found out.

They still hadn't managed a win at the Old Town Bar. Forever Jung and the Drinking Team had not bounced back from their losses, and Get Knitted had won five quizzes in a row.

Christmas was just around the corner, and Amy had been mugging up on Christmas trivia just in case Kev asked any seasonal questions. When Friday rolled around again, she was determined they'd knock Pauline and Barry's team off their perch, or die trying. *Shouldn't joke about that, Amy Archer*, she grimaced.

Pauline had already 'popped' round to their table to wish

them luck, sounding, to be frank, smug and insincere.

'You can really go off people, can't you?' Finn said.

'Yep,' Amy agreed. 'We need to take them down!'

'Steady on there, Amy,' James chimed up. 'Have to think about your blood pressure at your age.'

'Off you fuck, James,' Amy glared at the younger man, who laughed and said, 'You know I'm only joking, love you really.'

Amy blushed at his words and couldn't make eye contact with Willem.

'Maybe it's time for Jenny to do her thing,' Finn suggested, winking at her across the table.

'Isn't it someone else's turn? Killing people is so last season,' Jenny sighed dramatically.

'But you're so good at it,' Finn persisted. He'd definitely become more at ease with Jenny over the months.

'Plenty of practice,' Amy said, laughing nervously. Conversations like this always made her a bit uncomfortable, bearing in mind her own history.

'I'm surprised no one's bumped off a member or two already, with their winning streak,' James said.

'I wouldn't want to go up against Pauline,' Finn said. 'She's scary.'

'Yeah, I reckon she's head of the knitting-nanas' mafia,' Jenny said, nodding knowingly.

Willem laughed. 'If you cross her you might wake up with a knitted horse's head beside you in the bed.'

They all laughed, except Amy. She was thinking that actually it *was* a bit strange that all the other big winning teams had lost members in recent weeks.

'You alright, Amy?' Trust Willem to notice.

'What? Oh. Yes, just thinking, you know ...' she smiled at him. He always made her feel as though he was reading her mind. *Abandon hope all ye who enter there*, she thought with a grimace.

Any more discussion of Pauline being the Godmother of the knitting brigade was halted as Kev was getting the quiz underway.

There was indeed a Christmas round and Amy's homework paid off, but even that couldn't prevent another loss to Get Knitted, and a disappointing second place. Forever Jung were third, and the We Miss Jon Drinking Team took fourth. The applause for Get Knitted was noticeably lacklustre. The other teams clearly felt the same as Stoned Folke.

'Bugger,' Amy said as Kev delivered the prize to Pauline's team. 'I thought we might've done enough.'

'Sadly not,' Willem said.

'Well, that's it then. Either the phantom killer of Old Folkestone Town needs to strike again, or we will,' Jenny announced in mock seriousness, banging her fists on the table.

Amy had a brief vision of a surreptitious meeting taking place between Jenny and Spud, and a gun changing hands, which she shook away.

A week later and the quiz yielded the same result. Get Knitted were all present and definitely not dead, and Amy's spidey senses were still tingling. She couldn't shake the feeling that something was off, other than the contents of the salad boxes in her fridge.

'Does anyone know any of the other members of Pauline's team?' Amy asked when they were waiting for the quiz to start.

'Nope,' Jenny said immediately.

Willem and James shook their heads.

'I've seen a couple of them around, I think,' Finn said. 'And I recognise the woman with the purple hair – she's been in the shop a couple of times. I think she's an artist. I can probably find out, my dad's bound to know.' Finn's dad, Brian, had a reputation for knowing everyone and their business.

'Yes, do that, Finn, please, and let me know,' Amy nodded.

'You don't seriously think what I think you're thinking, do you, Amy?' Willem asked her.

'I know, it's silly. Humour me,' she said.

'She can't help it,' Jenny informed Willem. 'Overactive imagination of a writer and all that. Take no notice.'

Amy shrugged with her shoulders and hands. 'Guilty as charged,' she smiled, making light of it.

It was the last quiz until after Christmas, and the team disbanded, wishing each other a happy one as they went their separate ways. James was off to another party and Finn for an early night as he was in the shop the next day. Willem walked Amy and Jenny home.

'So, what are you two doing for Christmas?' he asked the friends.

'Not a lot,' Amy said. 'Mum's going to my sister's and I'm planning a quiet one this year. I want to try and finish the book.'

'I'm actually going to stay with a friend from uni in Edinburgh,' Jenny said. 'Quite excited actually. You haven't forgotten you're looking after the cats, have you, Amy?'

'Of course not. The cats will be well looked after. As will the plants. How about you, Willem? Heading to family?'

'No, not this year. I'm also planning a low-key holiday. I plan to eat too much, watch rubbish TV, and maybe get out on the bike with my camera.'

'That sounds perfect,' Amy smiled at him.

'Perhaps we can catch up sometime?' Willem said. 'No pressure though.'

'That would be nice,' Amy said.

Jenny nudged her friend and grinned.

Amy glared at her and hoped Willem hadn't noticed. She and Willem were just good friends, and that was how it was going to stay.

Back at home a short time later, Amy made herself a cup of tea and settled down on the sofa. It was almost ten thirty, but she wasn't ready for bed yet. She still couldn't shake off the feeling that something was amiss.

Firing up her laptop, she opened Facebook. 'Bugger,' she said a moment later. She didn't know what Pauline's surname was. Finn would know, she thought, and she sent a quick message asking him.

Bulmer, Finn replied quickly. *Why's that?*

Just being nosy. Amy didn't want to admit that she was about to stalk Pauline on the internet. *Thanks, Finn*.

A search for Pauline Bulmer brought up too many hits, but when Amy typed in *Barry Bulmer* she struck lucky, with far fewer to look through, and a short scroll soon revealed Barry's beaming mugshot. A quick look at Barry's Facebook friends and there was Pauline. Amy wasted no time in having a nose at Pauline's page, but it was clear that Pauline had set her security settings to friends only. Before she could chicken out, Amy sent her a friend request. After all, they were in the shop together and sort of friends, so it wasn't an odd thing to do.

While she waited to see if Pauline accepted her request, Amy did a bit more googling. She had an assortment of memberships to ancestry sites and the like and could usually turn up something on people if she tried. The surname Bulmer had its roots in Yorkshire and the North East, and Amy wasn't too surprised to track down a marriage certificate for a Barry Bulmer and a Pauline Wilkinson dated 29th April 1987 in York Registry Office. Amy thought she'd detected a slight Yorkshire accent in the pair's voices, almost gone, but not quite. Amy thought they must have moved down south quite some years back. She wondered what had made them leave God's own country in favour of the south-east corner of England.

While she was mulling this over, Pauline had accepted her friend request and Amy wasted no time in trawling through the other woman's content. Her photographs were largely things she'd knitted over the years. There were quite a few of Pauline and Barry taken on holiday in Spain – it looked like they were creatures of habit and went to Spain every year, with the only exception being the Covid years. Mental images of Pauline in a beige knitted bikini and Barry in a matching mankini popped unbidden into Amy's head. 'You can bugger off,' she told them, with a shudder. Finding nothing remarkable on Pauline's account, Amy went back to revisit Barry's.

'Right, Bazzer, what have you got to show me then?' she mused.

Barry's Facebook page had lots of quiz-related stuff and pics of him looking Butlin's-ready, along with some on-the-smutty-side jokes and cartoons. There were similar holiday photos to those Pauline had posted, although many more of Barry's focused on food and drink, and selfies which revealed his face to be even more red than normal. Clearly Barry didn't bother with sunscreen. Amy was close to giving up when she spotted a photo of Barry standing with a group of men outside what looked like a pub or club. When Amy looked more closely she could make out the name of the place: TANG HALL WM CLUB. Before she could look it up, another message pinged in from Finn.

I asked my Dad about the woman with the purple hair. Her name's Esme Hudson. I was right, she is an artist – got a studio on Tontine Street.

Thanks, Finn, Amy sent back.

She then went down another rabbit hole as she googled *Esme Hudson artist*, and it was gone midnight when Amy finally closed her laptop with a yawn and took herself off to bed.

CHAPTER 27

Amy in Wonderland

Christmas came. And went. Jenny went to Edinburgh. And came home. Amy and Willem met for coffee and a couple of walks, just as friends. And then it was January.

'New year, new you,' Amy said to herself as she wrapped a warm scarf around her neck and rummaged in the hall closet for the woolly hat which matched it. She hated the winter, but had vowed to get outside and get moving every day. Or maybe every other day ...

On this particular day – glossing over the fact that she'd been hibernating for a week – she was, of course, meeting Jenny who was much better at being active than Amy and was happy to get out of the house. Thankfully it was one of those cold-but-blue-sky days, rather than the damp, grey mizzle they'd had to put up with for the past week.

The two friends met where the paths from their houses converged and hugged each other.

'Bloody hell, it's like hugging the Michelin Man,' Jenny grinned at her friend.

'I wish I could say it was layers of clothes,' Amy pulled a face, only half joking.

'Layers of blubber, eh?' Jenny chuckled. She'd never carried an ounce of fat in her life.

Amy did her best seal bark and clapped her arms together like flippers. A man walking on the other side of the street looked round in surprise and the two friends laughed, linking arms as they continued on their way.

'I've missed you,' Amy said, squeezing Jenny's arm. 'Did you have a lovely time in Edinburgh?'

'Ah! Soppy cow. Missed you too,' Jenny bumped shoulders with Amy. 'I did, thank you. It was lovely to see Hannah but kind of strange after all these years. And, honestly, I was glad to come home to Folkestone.'

'And to me!' Amy added.

'Yeah, and to you, you needy person you.'

'Rude. I thought I demonstrated remarkable self-control not messaging you every day while you were away,' Amy pouted.

'Yeah, I thought you must've died,' Jenny said.

Neither of their faces stayed straight for long.

'So, did you and Willem spend Christmas together?'

Amy shook her head. 'No, we met up, but just as friends. Nothing's changed there. Nothing can,' Amy said sadly.

'So, what else did you get up to while I was away then?' Jenny asked, keen to change the subject.

'Not a lot. Some writing. Mainly ate chocolate and watched Netflix.'

'How's the new book coming along?' Jenny asked.

'Pretty good, actually, although it's pretty grisly in places – definitely darker than the last one. I think everything that happened last year has had a knock-on effect on my writing.'

'That's not a bad thing, is it? People love a good murder.'

'Well, that's the problem, Jenny, I think. Is there such a thing as a good murder? From what I'm seeing in the bookshops and on TV, it feels like there's been a shift towards cosy crime – you know, all the crime, but none of the gruesome bits.'

'Well, can't you just do that then? I thought you were a big fan of the Agatha Christie school of murder.'

'I am. I was. I don't know,' Amy sighed. 'I grew up reading Agatha Christie and I still love a good adaptation, but that's not real life, is it? Murder is meant to be abhorrent. Setting something in the Cotswolds or a sleepy seaside town, and having some doddery old dear investigate is hardly true to life, is it?'

'I hope you're not insinuating that I'm a doddery old dear?' Jenny said, mock-frowning.

Amy managed a smile. 'You know what I mean. Murder isn't cosy. I don't know, maybe it's me that's changed, but watching *Midsomer Murders* now makes me want to throw something at the television. And don't get me started on those *Agatha Raisin* books!'

'Calm down,' Jenny grinned. 'Think of your blood pressure, old girl.'

'Sod off!' Amy retorted, but she couldn't help laughing. 'I just think that crime shouldn't be sanitised and presented with a pretty pink ribbon around it. It should be raw, and real, and ... I don't know ... brutal ... because that's what it is,' Amy shrugged.

'Noted. I'll return those Richard Osman books I got for you,' Jenny winked.

Amy groaned. She had a bit of a bee in her bonnet about those.

'Get up to anything else?' Jenny enquired, eager to change the subject.

'I did fall down a bit of a rabbit hole actually ...' Amy began.

'Oh God!' Jenny groaned. 'Alright, spill, Alice.'

Amy obliged with an 'Alice, who the fuck is Alice?' before

continuing. 'Admit it, you've missed me and my suspicious mind.'

Jenny responded with an Elvis-style 'uh-huh-huh', and they both launched loudly into the lyrics: 'We can't go on together/With suspicious minds/And we can't build our dreams/On suspicious minds,' and then giggled.

'Good to see that Elvis round at the quiz wasn't completely wasted on us,' Jenny said.

'Yep. Anyway, as I was saying … the rabbit hole …' Amy began again, at which point Jenny stuck her fingers in her ears and began singing again.

'Listen!' Amy said exasperatedly. 'You know how we have our suspicions about all these sudden deaths?'

'Er … *you* have all the suspicions, Ames; the rest of us just think a few people sadly died and some of them happened to be quizzers. Think of all the people who died in the same period who weren't quizzers.'

Amy ignored that. 'So, I was thinking about Pauline's team Get Knitted, and how we don't know anything about the other members of the team.'

'Nor do we want to. Do we?' Jenny looked round at Amy. 'Oh, we do don't we.'

'So, Finn got a name for the lady with the purple hair and I googled her. She is an artist as Finn thought and her art is … well, dark to say the least.'

'Dark how?' Jenny asked.

'Um … imagine if Millais and Hieronymus Bosch had a lovechild who became an artist,' Amy began.

'You've lost me,' Jenny said. 'Somewhere between "um" and "lovechild".'

'You know, the Pre-Raphaelite painter Millais ... famous for that painting "Ophelia" where she's floating with the flowers ...'

'Oh, yeah, I know who you mean,' Jenny nodded. 'And thingy Bosch – wasn't he that Dutch dude who painted really disturbing stuff?'

Amy laughed at Jenny's description. 'Yes, he was the disturbing Dutch dude.'

'So ... their lovechild would paint, what? Beautiful redheads being spit-roasted by a four-legged bird while a giant nose sneezes on them?'

'Something like that, yeah.'

'Interesting. I like her already.'

They lapsed into silence as they walked the rest of the way to the harbour and made their way to the aptly named Harbour Coffee which, thankfully, was open all year round. Hot chocolates ordered, they slipped into a booth looking out to sea.

'What's this woman's name again? This artist woman,' Jenny asked, getting her phone out.

'Esme Hudson.'

'Okay,' Jenny said, after scrolling through several pages of Esme Hudson's paintings. 'I can see what you mean, a bit weird, but what's that got to do with the price of fish-with-legs?'

'Well, don't you see, what sort of a mind must she have to produce work like that? Demons torturing women, for heaven's sake. That's not normal, is it?'

'Doesn't mean she goes around killing people, Amy, though, does it? I mean, look at you, you're always bumping off people in stories but you're not a serial killer in real life, are you?'

Amy was silent.

'Well, are you?'

'No,' Amy said finally, ignoring the little flashback of the gun in her hand and Robert's head flying back as the bullet penetrated his skull.

'Can I also point out that if your theory is that someone from the quizzes is going round killing other quizzers, then it can't be this Esme woman, can it?'

'Why not?' Amy asked, not ready to admit defeat just yet.

'Well, I've never seen her at the Griffin on a Wednesday, have you?'

Amy stopped to think. 'Bugger,' she said.

'That concludes the case for the defence, m'lud.'

Amy sipped her drink and stared out at the sea, her thoughts of a killer still bobbing about in her mind. Something was still nagging away at her. 'Can you picture the other people on Pauline and Barry's team?'

'Vaguely,' Jenny said, screwing up her eyes as she tried to visualise them.

'Now, do you recognise them from the Griffin quiz?'

'Um ... no, I don't think so,' Jenny shook her head. 'Can't be a hundred per cent though.'

'Hm ... I don't either.'

'Come on, out with it, what's going on in that brain of yours?'

'Just a feeling, a hunch. Take no notice, you know what I'm like,' Amy smiled at her friend.

'Yeah, you and your writer's brain.'

Amy was letting it go for now. 'Shall we head out again?'

Jenny nodded and they headed back out, pulling on hats as they went. Jenny was wearing the black beanie which always reminded Amy of the night they'd stalked Jeff Teller and staked out the art installations together last summer. This time, it was Amy who had the hunch and she knew she couldn't just ignore it, but she needed more evidence before bringing Jenny on board.

They walked up the Arm towards the lighthouse, pausing briefly to admire the cast-iron Gormley figure halfway down. Amy couldn't help thinking of Willem, who had recently added a stunning photograph of the sculpture to his display at the shop. It was nice to be reminded of something happy and positive, when so many of the art installations around the town brought back such shocking memories of the past two years. Two years, two serial killers. Amy really hoped she was wrong about there being a third.

Rounding the lighthouse, they made their way back along the upper walkway and began the trek home. Amy was warm now and regretting the thermal undies she'd donned under her jeans and jumper. By the time she got home, having hugged Jenny goodbye where their paths diverged, she was red in the face and glad to be able to remove her outer layers. She wasted no time in plonking herself down on the sofa with her laptop. She had another rabbit hole to fall down.

CHAPTER 28

The knitty-gritty

The rabbit hole took Amy to the local obituaries from the past few months, but there was little to be gleaned from them regarding causes of death for Stan, Sylvia or Norm. She knew, obviously, how Jack had died at the hands of a supposed mugger, but the death she was most curious about was Jon's.

Pauline had said the young man from the Drinking Team had died due to a drug overdose, but Amy wasn't convinced. He'd seemed like a pretty clean-cut guy to her. Amy knew better than anyone that you couldn't always judge a book by its cover, but her instincts were screaming that foul play was involved in Jon's death. The trouble was, she had no idea how to find out more.

The niggle she couldn't shake was Pauline's assertion that it was drugs. Why would she say that if it wasn't true? Was it purely gossip she'd picked up? Or was she dangling a red herring in front of Amy's nose? Amy had a brief Hieronymus Bosch-style image pop into her mind, which she shook away.

Back on her laptop, Amy typed in the following: *Pauline Wilkinson York*. She scrolled past the usual social media, LinkedIn and 192 entries and kept going. It was a few pages in that she was struck by a headline from the Yorkshire Evening Press: *Charges dropped against local woman in mysterious hospital deaths.*

Clicking on the link, Amy was taken to a newspaper archive

and an article regarding a spate of deaths in a Yorkshire hospital in the early eighties. The patients who had died had all been terminally ill, but their deaths actually brought about by an overdose of end-of-life drugs. Police investigating the deaths had arrested a nurse, but charges had subsequently been dropped due to lack of evidence. The nurse had been named as Pauline Wilkinson of Millfield Lane, Clifton. There was a rather grainy and poor-quality photo of the suspect which was disappointingly inconclusive.

Amy's heart was beating out of her chest as she read though. Could it be? Could this be the same Pauline Wilkinson who'd married Barry Bulmer and moved to Folkestone? *Calm down*, she told herself. It was a pretty common name, after all. No sense getting all worked up if it wasn't the same woman. But Amy's gut was telling her it was the same woman. It would certainly explain a move down south. Mud sticks, after all.

Amy considered herself a bit of an expert at research and she lost herself for the next couple of hours, tracing Pauline and Barry's muddy trail south as much as was possible on the internet. She also did a search for deaths involving end-of-life drugs since the eighties and her interest was piqued by a story about a care home in Suffolk which had several deaths that had been put down to a lethal dose of midazolam, which Amy had already learned was one of the four main end-of-life drugs. From what Amy read, no one had been charged in connection with the deaths.

When Amy finally closed her laptop, stretching out her aching neck muscles, she had confirmed that Pauline Wilkinson of Millfield Lane, Clifton, had indeed married one Barry Bulmer. She'd also found a record for them living in the village of Martlesham in Suffolk, which wasn't a million miles away from the Ipswich care home whose residents had died.

'Pauline, Pauline, Pauline ... what have you done?' Amy said to herself. 'And, more to the point, what are you doing now?' After nipping off to the loo, Amy opened her laptop once more. 'Bum,' she said a short time later, having confirmed that coroner's reports were not available online. For the moment she was stuck, but Amy was more sure than ever that Pauline was fishier than one of Hieronymus Bosch's fishy paintings.

Amy was more confused than ever though, when she heard from Finn, who'd heard it from his dad, that Esme Hudson, the artist from Pauline's quiz team, had died. She rang Jenny at once.

'You'll never guess what?'

'I think we've established that's the case, Amy, so maybe just tell me?' Jenny said dryly.

'Spoilsport. Well, I just heard from Finn who heard it from—' Amy began.

'Get to the point,' Jenny interrupted.

'Esme Hudson's dead!' Amy announced, wishing she could see Jenny's face.

'Who?'

'For fuck's sake. We were only just talking about her! The woman from Get Knitted who paints all that dark stuff.'

'Oh, her. Master of the Dark Arts and painter of weird shit.'

'Yes, her.'

'So?'

'Well, don't you see?'

'Clearly not.'

Amy made a sort of strangled noise of frustration. 'Think about it,' she said.

'Nope. Still nothing,' Jenny said. 'And by the way, I can tell you're raising your eyebrows at me.'

'I'm not,' Amy said, lowering her eyebrows. 'If Pauline is the killer, why would she kill someone on her own team? Especially when they're on a massive winning streak.'

Jenny sighed. 'We're going there are we? Again?'

'I never left.'

'Do you know how she died?'

'Yes!' Amy exclaimed.

'Well? Are you going to enlighten me? Or do I have to guess?'

'She was killed by a car – hit and run.'

'Nasty. Maybe someone didn't like their portrait? She probably painted them being swallowed by a giant mussel shell while someone rammed a giant woodwind instrument up their arse.'

'Jenny!' Amy reprimanded, while trying not to giggle.

'What? Okay, it's very sad, but people get run over every day.'

'Yeah, but ...' Amy began.

'Yeah but, no but, Amy,' Jenny said, in her best Vicky Pollard voice.

'But it could ...'

'La la la la la.'

Amy could picture Jenny with her fingers in her ears. She sighed. 'I was just going to say it could have been deliberate.'

'Well that I *did* guess. Were there any witnesses?'

'I don't know. That's all Finn told me. But you can't rule out it being deliberate, can you?'

'Well, no, but even if it was, like you said, why would Pauline kill someone on her own team?'

Amy was silent for a few moments, thinking.

'You still there, Miss Marple?' Jenny prompted.

'Mm ... just thinking.'

'Wondered what the strange noise was.'

'Rude. What if Pauline killed Esme to put us off the scent?' Amy persisted.

'I didn't know we were on the scent.'

Amy ignored her. 'She might have thought it would divert attention away from her and Barry if one of their own team died in questionable circumstances.'

'If we're talking conspiracy theories, then it could have been a member of Esme's family. You should check her Will. Maybe they thought her paintings would be worth more if she was dead. It's always money or passion of some sort, isn't it? Murder, I mean.'

'Don't be daft,' Amy said.

'*I'm* being daft?' Jenny said, snorting with laughter. 'It was just a terrible, tragic accident, Amy. Don't turn it into something it's not. Besides, killers have an M.O. don't they? They normally stick to the same method of killing. They can't help themselves. That's how the police catch them.'

'But ...'

'No buts.'

Amy sighed. She knew she was wasting her time.

'Have you got any more harebrained ideas, or can I go now?' Jenny asked.

'You can go,' Amy said resignedly. 'Catch you later.'

'Later tater.'

Not for the first time, Amy wished Jenny shared her suspicions. For now, she was on her own. She needed to find out more about Pauline. And where better to start than the horse's mouth? This time she didn't mean Sylvia, the Princess Anne lookalike from the quiz. Because Sylvia was dead. And her horsey mouth wasn't going to confirm anything. Not a yay or a neigh. And not the knitted horse's mouth Amy might find in her bed if she upset the Godmother of knitting.

It was Pauline's shift in the shop the following day so, before she could chicken out, Amy headed out as soon as the shop was open. She'd had a moment of panic just as she'd arrived, palpitations in her chest and a catch in her throat which she coughed away. Sticking a smile on her face, Amy pushed open the door to the shop and went in, making sure she closed the door behind her. It was bloody freezing out and she didn't want to get off on the wrong foot with Pauline.

Pauline looked up from where she was arranging some brightly coloured knitted socks, and smiled when she saw it was Amy.

'Well, isn't this a nice surprise. You must have known I was about to put the kettle on.'

'Hello,' Amy said brightly. 'Just passing and thought I'd pop in. Writer's block, you now, sometimes it helps to get out for a walk and a chat with people to get the flow going again,' she rambled, before mentally telling herself to *shut up, you gibbering idiot*.

'That's nice, dear. Tea?'

'Um, yes, please, tea would be lovely. Freezing out.'

'You just mind the shop for a minute then,' Pauline said, before disappearing out the back.

Amy hadn't realised anyone actually used the tea-making facilities at the shop, preferring decent coffee-shop drinks. She'd looked in the fridge once and all she'd found was a dead fly.

A few minutes later Pauline reappeared with two mugs. They were shaped like balls of wool, and when Amy looked closer, she could see that the white label around the middle of one said *Knit Happens*.

'Milk and sugar?' Pauline asked.

Amy thought about the fridge. 'Just sugar, please.'

Pauline put a spoonful of sugar in the second mug, stirred it and passed it to Amy, where she'd taken up residence on the stool on the shop side of the counter. Amy lifted the light-blue mug and read aloud: 'I Like Big Balls and I Cannot Lie', before bursting out laughing. 'Oh, Pauline, that's hilarious!'

Pauline just smiled at her, a wicked little glint in her eyes.

Amy sighed.

'Penny for them?' Pauline enquired.

'Oh, just feeling frustrated. My characters aren't behaving as I'd like them to.'

'Well, that won't do. How can I help? I don't know much about writing, but I know quite a lot about people,' Pauline smiled encouragingly at Amy.

Amy wondered briefly if she'd got Pauline wrong; she was being so lovely. Deciding to press on, she said, 'I'm trying to come up with a back story for someone in my latest book and nothing feels right. You know, where they come from, what their life looks like, stuff like that.'

Pauline took a sip of tea. 'Maybe I can be a sounding board then?'

'Oh yes, that would be great! But only if I'm not holding you up?' Amy said enthusiastically.

Pauline gestured around the empty shop. 'Fire away, dear.'

'Okay,' Amy began, 'so, this man – he's called … um … Vince … for now anyway, and he's a bit of a mystery man. He's joined this … um …' – *for fuck's sake, Amy, stop umming!* – 'this amateur dramatic group, and nobody really knows anything about him. He's got a slight accent – I'm not sure where from yet, maybe Cornwall – and I'm trying to pad him out a bit … you know, why he moved to Kent …' Amy glanced at Pauline who was listening intently. 'Just nothing feels right, you know? Did he move for … um … love, for instance? Or a job? Or … was he running away from something?' Amy paused and took a sip of her tea. She was feeling anxious and Pauline's eyes on her weren't helping.

Pauline didn't speak straight away and Amy's disquiet increased. She sipped her tea to give her hands, mouth and eyes something to do.

Finally, Pauline spoke up. 'Well, it seems to me you need to decide if this … Vince character is a goodie or a baddie, don't you? Do you like him?'

'Er … I'm not sure. I think I want him to have a bit of a dark side. You know, maybe something in his past that he's running away from?'

'Well then, what might that be, d'you think?' Pauline asked, her face giving nothing away. 'Sometimes good people do bad things, you know. Or think they're doing them for the right reason, don't you agree?'

'Um, yes, yes, of course, absolutely,' Amy babbled. She could feel a flush starting to creep up from her chest towards her face. She would have liked to gulp down her revolting milk-less tea and make her escape, but she didn't want to make Pauline suspicious. Besides, she needed to steer Pauline away from her non-existent fictional character, Vince, and onto herself and Barry. 'I like my characters to have more interesting back stories than my own. I've never lived outside Kent. I have travelled a bit, of course, actually made it to Australia in my twenties, but my roots have kept me here. How about you? And Barry? There's definitely a hint of an accent there, if I'm not mistaken?' Amy asked, hoping her face wasn't giving away the fact that she knew exactly where Pauline and Barry hailed from.

Pauline smiled at her, her own face definitely not giving anything away. 'Oh, we've lived all over, me and Barry. I expect my accent's a little bit of a lot of places now,' she smiled.

Amy felt an involuntary shiver, and Jenny's face popped into her head saying, 'Is Pauline a psychopath, or what?' She knew she should stop pushing and get out, but she kept pushing. 'Sounds like a little bit of Yorkshire in there,' Amy said, forcing herself to make eye contact with the other woman.

Amy wasn't sure if she imagined a split second when Pauline's face changed, a flash of something like anger in her eyes. But it was gone as fast as it came. 'Well spotted,' Pauline said. 'We are originally from Yorkshire, but not for many, many years.'

Amy nodded. 'I knew it. I'm usually pretty good at accents.' *Keep going, Amy, just a little push.* 'I don't suppose that's a hint of East Anglian there too? Every now and then, I can hear a little bit of ... maybe Suffolk? I've got family in Ipswich so I'm quite tuned in to it. Come on, you Tractor Boys!' Amy chanted, before laughing nervously.

Pauline smiled again, but it definitely didn't reach her eyes. 'No, dear, we never lived in East Anglia. Perhaps you've got it mixed up with Bristol – we lived there for some time and that's quite a similar dialect.' Pauline got up and reached across for Amy's half-empty mug. 'Now, I really must make myself useful,' she said, clearly dismissing Amy.

Only too happy to take the hint, Amy got up to go. 'Thank you for the tea. And the chat. I do think it's helped clear things up in my mind a bit.'

As she watched Amy leave, Pauline reached for her mobile. *We've got a problem*, she typed. *I think you'd better get the room ready.*

CHAPTER 29
Missing

Willem was at his desk, yawning after another early morning shoot, when the message arrived. His first thought was that he hoped it was from Amy. He hadn't heard from her for a couple of days and, while he had no right to feel aggrieved since they weren't an item any longer, he still looked forward to any contact with her.

Picking up his mobile, he saw that the WhatsApp was actually from Jenny. Frowning, Willem read it: *Yo, dodgy Dutch dude. Have you heard from Amy?*

Hello, and no I haven't. Should I be worried? And why the dodgy Dutch dude? I'm offended.

Private joke, you're not really all that dodgy. Or that Dutch, come to think about it. I don't know if you should be worried. But I am.

Hm. Now I'm worried too. Presumably you've tried phoning etc?

Dur. Yeah. Her phone's out of service and no answer at her house.

That's not like Amy. She knows you'd worry.

Will you help me look for her?

Yes, of course, but where do we start?

Can you meet me now? Steep Street?

Be there in twenty mins.

Willem saved his work on the computer and got ready to go and meet Jenny, his face reflecting the worry he felt about

Amy. He couldn't bear it if something had happened to her.

Just under twenty minutes later and Willem was sitting in the coffee shop with an equally worried-looking Jenny. The windows of the place were steamed up, and Willem shed layers as he thawed out.

'So, when did you last see her?' Willem asked.

'Not since the quiz on Friday,' Jenny said. 'You?'

'Same. What about speaking to her or messaging?'

'Briefly on Saturday. She said she was working on something.'

'Do you know what?'

Jenny shrugged. 'Just assumed it was her latest book. Sometimes when she's on a roll she doesn't come up for air.'

Willem didn't like the image that flashed into his head of Amy without air. 'And you've been to her house?'

'Yep. No answer. Peered in the windows and checked around the back.'

'Hm. Could she have been called away? A family emergency or something?'

Jenny shook her head. 'She'd have told me. She'd never go away without telling me.'

They sat in silence for a few moments.

'Where the bloody hell is she?' Jenny asked finally.

'I don't know, Jenny, but let's not panic just yet. There's bound to be an innocent explanation.'

'That's what we said when Bella disappeared, and look how that ended,' Jenny said, thinking of the fate of her friend at the hands of Jeff Teller. Tears prickled her eyes and she brushed them roughly away with her fingers. She wasn't going to fall apart in public.

'She'll be okay. Teller's behind bars and nobody's out to get

Amy. It'll be okay.'

'I can't lose another friend, Willem. I just can't. Not Amy.' The tears were winning now, and Jenny rummaged in her pocket for a tissue. She dabbed at her eyes and blew her nose.

'You're not going to lose Amy. Come on, let's put our heads together and I'm sure we can work out what's happened.'

'You think something *has* happened to her then?' Jenny said, terror showing on her pale face.

'No, no, sorry, bad choice of words. Work out where she is,' Willem tried to reassure.

Jenny sighed. 'I've wracked my brains and come up with nothing.'

'Okay, let's go about this logically. Right, family: you're confident she'd have told you if something came up?'

'Yes, absolutely. We tell each other everything.'

'Could she be ill?'

'Maybe, but why would she not have her mobile on? Or let me know? Like I said, we …'

'Yes, you tell each other everything,' Willem sighed. 'Did you speak to the neighbours when you went to her house?'

Jenny shook her head. 'Do you think we should go round and speak to them?'

'I think it would be a good idea. Don't you have a key to Amy's place?'

'Shit! Yes, I do. God, I'm an idiot. Let's go.'

Willem didn't disagree with Jenny's self-diagnosis, but downed his Americano and followed her out onto the street, struggling back into his coat as he went.

'We'll have to go via mine to pick up the key,' Jenny said, as they walked briskly up the Old High Street.

Just over half an hour later and Jenny was unlocking Amy's front door. She called out to her friend as she stepped into the hall. Willem followed her in and closed the door.

The house was silent.

'I'll check upstairs,' Jenny said, jogging up the stairs and leaving Willem to look around downstairs.

Willem could see nothing untoward downstairs, and soon heard Jenny calling out: 'Nothing upstairs. Everything looks normal,' she finished, finding Willem standing in the lounge.

'Nothing here either. Her laptop's here,' he said, pointing to the machine on the coffee table. 'Have you seen her mobile anywhere?'

Jenny shook her head. 'No, but her handbag's gone. And I think her big coat. Let me double-check.'

Willem waited in the lounge while Jenny checked.

'Coat's definitely missing.'

'Okay, so we know she went out somewhere …'

'But why hasn't she come back? And why's her phone off?' Jenny added.

'I don't know, Jenny, I just don't know.' Willem's eye was drawn to a notebook next to Amy's laptop. Picking it up, he saw, amongst doodles of flowers and stars, Pauline's name circled several times, along with some other names and dates. 'Look at this. Amy seems to have been looking into something,' he said, holding out the pad to Jenny.

'Christ, Amy, what have you been up to? I know she had a bee in her bonnet about someone bumping off quizzers, said she'd been down a rabbit hole … You don't think …?'

Willem cut her off. 'No, I don't think she's been bumped off, Jenny.'

'What's all this about then?' Jenny asked, looking more closely at the notes. *1980s York Hospital deaths?? End-of-life meds. Ipswich care home – midazolam. Coincidence??* <u>*How did Jon really die?*</u>

Willem shook his head, at a loss.

'I think she found something scarier than a rabbit,' Jenny pronounced.

'If you're right, then what? What do we do?' Willem asked.

'Then we follow her into the rabbit hole,' Jenny said firmly. Willem could hear the resolve back in her voice. This was the Jenny he needed right now, the one who had been known to keep a gun in her breakfast cereal.

'Okay. Where do we start?' he asked.

Jenny pointed to the notebook, where Amy had ringed Pauline's name.

Willem sighed. 'You don't think we should contact the police now? Report her missing?'

Jenny screwed up her face. 'I don't know. Amy's not a big fan of the police …'

'But surely they'd have a better chance of finding her than us? And besides, it's the right thing to do. It's what normal people would do,' Willem persisted.

'Exactly. Normal people,' Jenny echoed.

Willem thought again of the gun in the cereal box, and the scene in Jenny's kitchen a few short months ago.

The pair lapsed into silence as thoughts of their missing friend and what to do next filled their heads.

'Bloody hell, is it Wednesday?' Jenny asked suddenly.

'Yes,' Willem said. 'Oh, quiz night. What do we do? Cancel? We surely can't carry on as if nothing's happened?'

'That's exactly what we should do,' Jenny told him. 'We go to the quiz and we carry on as normal.'

'But you just said …'

'I never said whose normal,' Jenny said.

'What do we say about Amy? If anyone asks.'

'Just say she's ill or something. Doesn't matter. The important thing is we can suss Pauline and Barry out.'

They left Amy's house soon afterwards. Jenny had torn the page out of Amy's notebook and pocketed it.

'Meet me at the bottom of the Old High Street at seven. Drive down and park your car in Tram Road car park,' she instructed Willem.

Willem simply nodded and turned to walk away, relieved that Jenny seemed to be in control once more.

'Oh, and Willem, wear dark clothes,' Jenny called after his departing back.

'What …? Why …? Oh God,' he said, as the penny dropped. *They were going stalking.*

CHAPTER 30

I shouldn't have said that

When Willem and Jenny arrived at the Griffin later that night, they found Pippa, Dave and Finn already seated at their regular table.

'No Amy?' Pippa asked.

'Um ... no ... she's not well,' Willem said.

'Oh, that's a shame. Poor Amy. Hope it's nothing serious.'

'Migraine,' Willem said.

'Food poisoning,' Jenny said, at the exact same moment.

Pippa and the others looked bemused.

'Oh ... yeah ... um ... food poisoning gave her a migraine,' Willem said.

'From all the retching I expect,' Jenny added.

Pippa pulled a face that said TMI. 'Well, it won't be the same without her, will it?'

'Nope. For starters, someone else will have to write,' Finn pointed out.

Thankfully, Pippa volunteered, leaving Jenny and Willem free to observe Pauline. They didn't have to wait long before Pauline bustled over, a vision in beige, and an extra-wide smile on her face.

'Hello, hello,' she said. 'Lovely to see you all!'

They all smiled at her. 'Hello, Pauline.'

'Now then, there's an empty chair. Who are we missing?' Pauline asked, looking round the table.

'As if you don't know,' Jenny muttered under her breath.

'What was that, dear? Didn't quite catch it,' Pauline addressed Jenny.

'I said, Amy's laid low. Not well,' Jenny improvised.

'Well, I'm very sorry to hear that. Nothing serious, I hope?'

When nobody responded, Pauline said, 'Well, I'm sure you'll do just fine without her anyway,' and trotted off to the next table.

'She reminds me of that horrible Dolores Umbridge from *Harry Potter*,' Jenny said, sticking her tongue out at Pauline's departing back.

'Reckon she's got an office with tacky kitten plates all round the walls?' Finn chuckled.

'Er ... please don't use tacky and kittens in the same sentence, Finn,' Jenny reprimanded.

'My bad,' Finn held up his hands.

Jenny leaned over to Willem. 'If she's got anything to do with Amy's disappearance then she's one cool customer,' she hissed in his ear.

Willem nodded.

Both Jenny and Willem found it virtually impossible to concentrate on the quiz and were, frankly, relieved when it was over. Neither had contributed much at all in the way of answers, and had felt quizzical eyes on them from around the table.

'Right, bye then,' Jenny said, pushing her chair back as soon as the applause had died down and the winnings handed over. She grabbed Willem's arm.

'Er ... yes ... bye. See you next week,' he said with a wave of his hand, ignoring the puzzled looks on everyone's faces.

He followed Jenny away from the pub and down the hill

to his car.

'Are we doing what I think we're doing?' he asked Jenny, once they were seated in the two front seats.

'That depends. What do you think we're doing?'

'Er ... following Pauline and Barry.'

'Ladies and germs, we have a winner.'

Willem groaned. 'Can't we just go to the police?'

'Well, you can, but I'm following Pauline and Barry. And I don't have a car. And I can't actually drive ...'

'In other words, I'm coming too.'

Jenny nodded. 'Yep.'

'Great.' Willem sounded resigned, but he'd already made up his mind to go to the police the next day, with or without Jenny's blessing.

They sat in silence and waited. It was about another twenty minutes before they saw the portly figures of Barry and Pauline come into view and head for the car park. Jenny ducked down and hissed at Willem to do the same, but he sat very still and watched as the couple got into a silver Skoda Octavia parked on the other side of the car park.

Jenny slid back up in her seat when Willem started the engine. She'd pulled her black beanie over her pink hair. Giving the Skoda a head start, Willem pulled out of the parking lot and followed at a distance.

'Tell me again why we're following them?' he asked.

'To see where they live, for starters. And if there's anywhere they could be keeping Amy.'

'This is nuts, Jenny.'

Jenny harrumphed. 'Have you forgotten the past two years? Nuts is my middle name.'

'I think I might be allergic,' Willem said under his breath.

They drove on in silence, keeping well back. The Skoda took the New Dover Road to Capel and wound slowly up the hill out of the town, headed through Capel and almost out the other side, before turning left into Winehouse Lane. Willem dropped back a bit as they were now on a quiet country lane and more likely to be spotted. They turned right into Satmar Lane, drove past a campsite and holiday park, and watched as Barry pulled the car onto a property through a gap between two hedges.

'We can't risk getting any closer,' Willem said.

'Can we find somewhere to park the car and go and have a shufty?' Jenny asked.

Willem reversed the car and pulled into a lay-by near the holiday park. He was wondering how he'd let himself get dragged into this.

'Well?' he said.

'Well what? Now we wait. Can't go rushing in like absolute amateurs now, can we?'

Willem snorted. 'No, of course not. Silly me.'

They waited.

'What's the optimum waiting time for professionals?' Willem asked eventually.

'Do I detect a hint of sarcasm there, Mr. de Groot?' Jenny asked, arching her eyebrows at him.

'Perish the thought.'

Jenny huffed. 'You have to put yourself in their shoes,' she said, nodding in the general direction Pauline and Barry had gone in. 'Think like them. What would their routine be when they get home after a quiz?'

'I'm not sure I want to imagine what those two get up to behind closed doors,' Willem shuddered.

'I know what you mean,' Jenny agreed. 'Reckon they've got a sex dungeon?'

'With kitsch kitties on the walls?' Willem added.

'Er ... dangerous ground there, as I told Finn.'

'Actually, as much as I don't want to, I can imagine Barry on all fours with a ball-gag in his mouth,' Willem said.

'And Pauline standing over him dressed head to toe in beige leather and wielding a knitted whip.'

'Ew,' Willem said.

Jenny smiled sadly. 'That's just what Amy would have said.'

The mention of Amy brought them both to their senses once more.

'What do you think? Leave it an hour or so and then take a look?' Willem suggested.

'Yeah, sounds good,' Jenny agreed.

They didn't talk for a while but eventually it was Jenny who broke the silence.

'I hope Amy's alright. I genuinely couldn't bear it if anything happened to her,' she said quietly, turning to face Willem.

'I know, Jenny. Me too.'

'She really cares about you, you know.'

Willem didn't reply.

'I know she fucked it up, but it wasn't her fault, not really,' Jenny continued. 'It's complicated.'

Willem sighed. 'I can do complicated, Jenny. But she was holding something back. All the time. Not being honest with me. She could've trusted me. She could've trusted me, Jenny,' he repeated sadly.

'She thought if she told you everything you'd hate her. Or worse,' Jenny said. She knew she should stop talking.

'What could she possibly have told me that could've made me hate her? Hey? It's not like she killed anybody.'

Jenny didn't need to answer. The look on her face in the moonlit car spoke volumes.

'What?! No. Jenny, what are you not telling me? For Christ's sake, woman, tell me the fucking truth!' Willem sounded angry now.

Jenny flinched. 'Don't fucking swear at me!' she threw back at him. 'For fuck's sake.'

Willem closed his eyes and put his face in his hands. When he looked up again he apologised for his outburst. 'I'm sorry, Jenny. I just can't bear this. Whatever it is Amy's done, I'm sure she had a damn good reason. Please just tell me.'

'It's not my secret to tell. Amy would never forgive me. If she's even still alive to forgive me.' It was Jenny's turn to put her face in her hands.

Willem reached over and squeezed her shoulder. 'Let's just focus all our efforts on finding Amy,' he said. He was feeling shaken to his core, but now was not the time to lose sight of the goal.

There was still no sight or sound of Amy when Willem arrived at Jenny's house early the next morning. She led him into the kitchen and he couldn't help remembering the events that had taken place in the small room the previous summer, when he and Amy had found Jenny tied to a chair, wearing what looked like a suicide vest, with the serial killer, Jeff Teller, standing behind her holding a dead man's switch. He shook the images away and forced himself back to the present, pulling out a chair at the table and sitting down.

'Any chance of a cup of tea?' he asked Jenny, who looked as though she hadn't slept a wink, and was still wearing the black beanie.

Jenny set about making tea and soon they were both hugging steaming mugs and going over the events of the previous night.

'It's fairly isolated, their house, isn't it?' Jenny began. 'Then there are those outhouse/shed things round the back too.'

'I was wondering if the house had a cellar,' Willem said. 'I don't think the outhouses we saw would keep people out and noises in very well, from what I could make out in the dark anyway.'

'What's our next step?'

'I'm going to report Amy missing,' Willem said firmly. Jenny made to speak, but he held up his hand, 'I'm not saying we stop looking for her, but I think it's the right thing to do.'

Jenny huffed a bit but didn't object. 'Fine, but I'm not coming with you.'

'Fair enough. After I've been to the police station, I thought I might head back to Capel with the drone. Just get a better look at the lay of the land in daylight.'

'Good idea. Then what?'

'Then I don't know, Jenny.'

CHAPTER 31

Best cellar

Amy was starting to lose track of the days. There was a tiny, barred window, green with age and algae, which was obviously below ground level, and let in very little of the gloomy winter light. Was it Wednesday? Or maybe Thursday? By now she would definitely have been missed, by Jenny at least. She would have been missed at the quiz and, if it *was* Thursday, she would soon be missed at the shop.

She was cold and stiff after another night on the camp bed. She'd asked Barry if she could have her coat and hat what felt like days ago, but he'd just laughed and told her cryptically they had 'gone on a little jaunt'. Her exhausted brain couldn't even begin to fathom what he'd meant by that. The oil-filled radiator in the corner of the room helped take the edge off the chill, but the cold of the damp cellar had leached into Amy's bones. Glancing at the radiator she wondered, not for the first time, if she could throttle someone with the cable. Did she have the strength? Mental or physical?

In the opposite corner from the heater was a camping-style portable loo and Amy's heart sank at the thought of using it again. Getting stiffly to her feet, she switched on the light and padded over to the portable toilet and reluctantly lifted the lid. She wrinkled her nose at the smell which was released, from both the blue liquid in the bottom and last night's dinner which she had thrown up. Hopefully it would be emptied today.

Having no idea what time it was, Amy got back under the blankets on the bed and tried to get warm. There was nothing to do except wait for breakfast. Which she'd probably throw up anyway. Amy didn't know if she had a stomach bug or was simply reacting to the stress of the situation and the type of food she was being given. At least she'd stopped crying. The tears had finally run out the previous day and a kind of resigned acceptance had overtaken her. She'd screamed and shouted at first too. But it was clear that no one could hear her. Except *them*.

A short while later, Amy heard the key being put in the lock and turned. They'd learned not to leave it in the door after Amy had pushed a piece of paper under the door and used a teaspoon handle to push the key out of the lock so it dropped onto the paper, a trick she'd learned as a girl. Unfortunately for Amy, there wasn't enough clearance under the door for the key to fit through when she pulled the paper back to her side.

Holding her breath now, Amy waited. She was wondering if she could rush them and make her escape.

'Right, no funny business now, please,' a male voice said, a second before a round face leaned in and was followed into the room by a round body. Barry came in carrying a tray. Next to the plastic plate of toast and plastic mug of tea was what Amy knew to be a Taser, and she had no desire to find out what it felt like to be on the receiving end of it. 'Breakfast is served,' Barry said, setting the tray down on the small table which sat under the window.

Amy let out the breath she'd been holding. She wasn't as intimidated by Barry.

'What day is it?' Amy asked him.

'Thursday, all day,' Barry said brightly, as if all was normal with the world.

'I ... I'll be missed, I should be in the shop ...' Amy began.

'Don't you worry about that,' Barry informed her. 'Pauline has very kindly offered to fill in for you, having heard that you're otherwise ... uh ... detained,' Barry said, chuckling.

'Well, I'll still be missed ... I'll still have been missed by now.' Amy could hear how pathetic she sounded, and she hated herself for it. What had happened to rushing Barry, or strangling him with the electrical cord?

'No doubt,' Barry smiled at her, 'but they won't be looking for you here, will they?'

Amy said nothing, simply looked down at her hands.

'Anyway, after you've had your breakfast, there's another tape for you which Pauline recorded last night. She didn't want you getting bored.'

'Very considerate of her,' Amy mumbled.

Barry nodded to the tray. 'Have your brekkie and then I'll bring the bits.' With that, Barry picked up the Taser and moved to the door. 'Bzzzzzzz,' he sounded, holding the Taser out towards Amy, and laughing as he closed and locked the door.

Amy put her face in her hands. Her head ached, her stomach hurt and she could feel herself staring into an abyss which was threatening to stare back at her. She knew she needed to eat to keep her strength up, but her cow's-milk-and-wheat intolerance meant her stomach would soon reject the tea and toast, one way or another. Her other meals had consisted mainly of soup and scrambled eggs and her delicate digestive system was making its feelings known in all too unpleasant ways. She'd tried telling Barry and Pauline that she needed something else to eat, but they didn't listen. Or they didn't care.

'Food intolerances,' Pauline had harrumphed. 'Stuff and nonsense.' And Barry clearly just did as he was told.

With a sigh, Amy reached for a bottle of water by her bed and swallowed a few mouthfuls, deciding she'd skip breakfast altogether and give her insides a break. She was desperate for a cup of coffee and she was also feeling the effects of a few days without the many supplements she took normally, her joints stiffening up without turmeric and collagen for one.

'Bugger,' she said, as she screwed the lid back on the water. She'd forgotten to ask Barry to empty the loo.

It must have been about twenty minutes later when Barry returned. He picked up the tray and took in the uneaten toast and undrunk tea. 'You haven't eaten your breakfast. You'll waste away. Pauline won't be happy,' he tutted.

'I can't eat it. I told you, it makes me ill,' Amy pleaded. In desperation she had licked the jam off the toast.

Barry ignored her. 'Right, I'll get the machine,' he said, leaving the room briefly. Moments later he was back with a word processor, some paper and a small Dictaphone. 'Here you are then,' he said. 'Time to start work. You'll want to get this typed up before Pauline gets home.'

Barry made to leave and Amy remembered the loo.

'Barry! Before you go, please can you empty that?' she asked, nodding at the offending article in the corner, embarrassment showing on her face.

Barry made a gagging noise. 'Sorry, lass, no can do. Have to wait for the missus. Weak stomach,' he gagged again, holding his considerable belly.

'You and me both,' Amy said through gritted teeth.

With Amy locked in once more, she sighed again. What the hell was she going to do? Closing her eyes, she let her thoughts drift back to Saturday when she'd left Pauline at the shop.

She'd known she was onto something and was convinced that Pauline was indeed the nurse who'd been suspected of killing those patients in York, and was pretty sure the Ipswich deaths had been down to her too. Why else would Pauline have lied about living in Suffolk? Amy hadn't had the chance to take her suspicions to Jenny though before Pauline and Barry had grabbed her. She thought back to earlier on the day she'd been taken.

She'd planned to spend the rest of that Saturday writing, but hadn't been able to concentrate, unable to still the suspicions about Pauline pinballing around her head. The question she most needed an answer to was how did Jon die? His cause of death could, Amy believed, make or break her case. If he'd died of natural causes, then maybe the other deaths really were simply age-related. She knew full well that she wouldn't be able to rest until she had the answers which could lead her out of the warren. God knows, she could get lost in a straight line. But how did she get those answers?

Looking at the time on her mobile and realising that a) she'd missed lunch, and b) she wasn't actually hungry, Amy decided she had to be proactive. But where to start?

Half an hour or so later, and Amy found herself pushing open the door to the Old Town Bar. The pub was busy, the throng of people adding heat to an already overheated room; the tables were all occupied, and a string of people hung around the bar, either waiting to order drinks or simply occupying the backless wooden stools along its length.

Amy was gratified to see Kev, the Friday-night quizmaster, on his regular stool. She couldn't believe her luck. Making a beeline for him, Amy shrugged off her bulky coat, already feeling flushed.

'Hello!' she said brightly.

'Oh, 'ello ... it's Amy, isn't it?' Kev smiled.

Amy nodded, slightly surprised that he remembered her name.

'What brings you in 'ere on a Saturday then?' Kev asked. 'We normally only see you on quiz nigh'.'

'Oh, you know, spur of the moment ... was passing and it looked so warm and inviting ...' Amy gestured vaguely around the noisy pub. 'Can I get you another?' she asked, pointing at Kev's pint.

'Fanks very much,' Kev said.

Amy looked around for someone to serve them. She'd never had much of a bar presence. Kev stepped in and lifted his pint mug, and a young barman appeared in front of them.

'Same again, please, Keiron, an' ... Amy?' Kev said.

'Oh, a ginger ale, please, no ice.'

As Keiron turned away to get their drinks, the couple next to them at the bar got up to leave, and Amy bagsied a stool, pulling it a little closer to Kev, and shuffling herself up onto it. She hated stools. Never felt very safe on them, but needs must, and it was better than standing.

'We love your quiz,' Amy said, as she paid for the drinks.

'Fanks very much. I love doin' it.'

'It's the highlight of our week. We do the quiz at the Griffin on a Wednesday too, but it's not nearly as much fun.'

'Ah! So you'll know Barry and Pauline then?'

'Yes! They're quite a pair, aren't they?'

Kev nodded. 'Funny buggers, if you ask me.'

Amy paused, processing Kev's comment. 'Funny ha ha? Or funny peculiar?' she pressed.

'Peculiar, definitely.'

'You think?'

'Yeah, I get a weird vibe off 'em. Might be me imagination,' he shrugged.

'No, I think you're right, there is something a bit off about them.'

''Armless enough though, I reckon.'

Amy had a brief flash of Pauline and Barry with no arms. 'Mm.' Amy wanted to swing the conversation around to Jon. 'I really love the banter and heckling at your quiz. We have such a laugh.'

Kev smiled, gratified.

'Such a terrible tragedy – losing Jon I mean. He was so funny. He used to give us the evil eye ... you know, that thing where you point your fingers in a V at your own eyes and then at the other person,' Amy said, demonstrating what she meant.

'Yeah, it's not the same wivvout 'im, that's for sure. A real tragedy.'

Amy nodded sombrely, and took a small sip of her drink. 'It's always extra sad when someone dies young. I mean, any death is sad, obviously, like old Norm, but at least he'd lived a long life.'

'Poor old Norm. It was still unexpected. He was as fit as a fiddle as far as I know.'

Amy made a mental note of that. 'Do you know how he died? Norm, I mean.'

''Eart attack, I 'eard, but don't quote me on that.'

'Um … what happened to Jon? If you don't mind me asking.'

'Epileptic fit. So fuckin' sad.'

'Oh!' Amy screwed up her face. She wasn't expecting that and it threw a big old spanner in her working theory. She wasn't sure if she felt surprised, confused, or even a little disappointed. 'That really is sad.'

Kev nodded. 'Made all the sadder by the fact that 'e'd just been given the all-clear to start learning to drive.'

Amy frowned at Kev.

'Three years with no fits,' Kev explained.

'Oh my God, that really does suck.' Amy's brain was going nineteen to the dozen as she tried to work out what this meant in the bigger picture. 'Do they know why he had another fit out of the blue like that, after all this time?'

Kev shook his head. 'Just one o' those fings, I s'pose.'

'Life can be a real bitch.'

'Amen to that,' Kev agreed, raising his glass.

They were both quiet for a few moments, lost in thoughts of the unfairness of it all. Amy was also wondering if she should say what she was thinking of saying. She did.

'Honestly, Kev, I was starting to wonder if someone was going round bumping off quizzers!' As she spoke, Amy could hear how bonkers her words sounded, and she blushed.

Kev raised his eyebrows, all the more obvious due to his completely bald head, and said, 'You weren't the only one!'

'Really?!'

'Yeah, for about a split second. Then I realised that was barmy.'

Amy laughed self-consciously. 'Yeah, right, barmy!' Maybe

she was barking up the wrong tree? Maybe there wasn't even a tree. And she was a cat. After all, Jenny really liked her a lot. Realising she was starting to feel uncomfortable in the busy pub, with the football showing on the big screens, and people getting steadily pissed, Amy channelled her inner white rabbit, checked the time, downed the rest of her drink and made her excuses.

'Well, lovely to see you, Kev. Must be off, I'm late for a ... er ... thing. See you next Friday. Enjoy the rest of your weekend.'

'Fanks, Amy, you too. And fanks for the drink.'

'Bye.' Amy struggled back into her coat and made her way back out into the cold January afternoon. She hurried home, eager to take a different turn in the rabbit warren. She was really hoping it would lead to the way out.

Back at home, Amy wasted no time in opening her laptop and doing a quick search: *Is it possible to induce a seizure in a person with epilepsy?*

The search seemed to suggest that visual stimuli such as flickering or flashing lights, waving a hand in front of your eyes, or slow closure and forced upward deviation of your eyes could do it. As could stress, hot water, sleep deprivation, and alcohol.

It didn't seem likely from this that Pauline, or anyone else, could have triggered an epileptic seizure in Jon, especially in light of the fact that he hadn't had one for three years. Unless Pauline and Barry had kept him up late drinking alcohol, stuck him in a hot bath in a room with flickering lights, it seemed wholly implausible. Besides, even if they had somehow caused a seizure, there was no reason to think it would be fatal.

Amy added the words *using drugs* to the Google search, and

things got a bit more interesting. Antidepressants, antipsychotics, anaesthetics, could possibly do it. And either overdosing on or discontinuing antiepileptic drugs. It still seemed too unlikely though. For starters, where would Pauline have got hold of any of the drugs mentioned, and even if she had, how would she have administered them? And again, how could you guarantee a fatal seizure?

Amy was really starting to think that she was, after all, entirely mistaken that foul play was afoot. Maybe a foot really was just twelve inches. And killing healthy people, whose only crime was being a better than average pub quizzer, was very different to taking the lives of people who were at the end of theirs or suffering horribly.

Any further thoughts on the matter were halted by her mobile ringing. Surprised to see Pauline's name on the display, she'd experienced a flutter of anxiety. Frowning, she answered the call.

'Oh, Amy dear, thank goodness!' a flustered-sounding Pauline began. 'I couldn't get hold of young Finn and I'm having trouble with the lock on the shop door. I simply can't get it to lock. I don't suppose … oh dear … I don't suppose you could come, could you, dear?'

'Um …' Amy began. Pauline sounded genuinely stressed. Besides, what could she do to Amy in the middle of the Old High Street at five o'clock on a Saturday afternoon? 'Um … yes, of course. Be about twenty minutes though.'

'Oh! Thank you, you're a lifesaver. I'll wait inside,' Pauline said, and ended the call.

Amy stared at her phone for a few seconds, frowning still. Her instincts were niggling. She knew the lock at the shop was stiff though. Shaking her head, Amy got up and pulled on boots, coat and hat, tossed her mobile and spare shop keys in her handbag – sometimes one key worked better than another – and set off at a brisk pace to the shop. No point driving as parking was a nightmare and it was almost as quick to walk.

When she arrived at the shop, cheeks flushed from the cold, she found Pauline waiting behind the counter.

'Ah! Amy, you're a sight for sore eyes,' Pauline gushed. 'Thank you for coming to my rescue.'

'Er ... that's okay, no problem. Shall we give it a go then?' Amy nodded to the door and reached out a hand to take the key.

Just as Amy turned towards the shop's front door, the side door opened from the little storeroom, and Amy exclaimed when she saw Barry appear. Before she had a chance to really work out what was going on, why Pauline had called her when Barry could have helped with the sticky lock, Barry had grabbed her arm and was brandishing a rather large kitchen knife at her.

'What the hell? Oh! Get off me!' Amy exclaimed.

'Now, now, dear, there's no need for blasphemy, is there?' Pauline said, coming round from the counter, switching off lights as she went. 'We're going to leave now, walk down the street together and you're not going to make a fuss.'

Amy struggled against Barry's grip, and he pushed the tip of the knife against her side.

'As I said, you're not going to make a fuss. Because if you do, well, I'm sure you can imagine, you being a writer and all,' Pauline smiled.

Barry shoved Amy out of the door and into the street while Pauline made short work of locking up. The street was quiet, all the other shops having closed already and shoppers headed home on a cold January Saturday.

Amy looked around frantically as they walked down the cobbled hill, wondering what the hell to do, but Barry's grip on her arm was vicelike and she could feel the tip of the knife pressing into her back. It was only a short walk to the car park at the bottom of the hill, and Amy was soon being bundled into the back of a silver Skoda. Barry got in beside her and Pauline got behind the wheel.

'What ... why ...' Amy began. 'Where are you taking me?'

Neither Barry nor Pauline answered and they drove on in silence. Amy could feel her heart beating in her ears and she felt nauseous. Barry kept the knife to her side and didn't take his eyes off her. Amy wondered if she could get the car door open and throw herself out.

As if reading her mind, Pauline said, 'The child locks are on.'

Tears prickled Amy's eyes. *Why couldn't she have left well alone?*

They drove on and Amy soon realised they were heading out of town and up the hill to Capel. An unwelcome thought popped into her head – they didn't care that she could see where they were going. Amy had seen enough crime shows to know that couldn't be a good thing. They weren't worried about her giving their location away as they didn't plan on her leaving it alive. Tears were now streaming down Amy's face unchecked. She knew she was being driven towards her death.

CHAPTER 32

Skeletons

'Who's in the shop today?' Jenny suddenly asked, frowning at Willem.

They were still sitting at Jenny's kitchen table. Willem had been lost in thought, staring unseeing at the picture of a cat's bum on his mug.

'What?' he asked, looking up.

'The shop,' Jenny repeated. 'It's Thursday. Amy should be in the shop.'

'Oh, you're right. I'll ask Finn.' Willem fired off a message and waited.

Pauline's covering – I hear Amy's still not well, Willem read aloud when Finn's reply came after a minute or two.

'What the actual fuck?!' Jenny exclaimed. 'The gall of the woman!'

'We don't actually know that Pauline has got Amy,' Willem said.

'She bloody has, I know it. Why else would she be covering for her at the shop?' Jenny insisted. 'We need to go out there! Right now!'

'Calm down, Jenny. We can't go round accusing people of kidnap. Anyway, it's preposterous. This sort of stuff doesn't happen to normal people.'

Jenny started to protest, but Willem held up his hand. 'I know, I know, you're not normal, but we need to tread carefully.'

'Treading carefully won't save Amy!' Jenny protested.

'Nor will rushing in like 'n bul in 'n porseleinwinkel,' Willem said, stress making him lapse into Afrikaans.

Jenny stared at him as if he was mad.

'Oh!' Willem said, realising what he'd done. 'Sorry, like a bull in a china shop.'

'Well, what are we going to do then?' Jenny asked. She could feel tears of fear and frustration building and didn't want to break down in front of Willem.

'I'm going to the police,' Willem said. 'Now.'

'What are you going to say? Are you going to tell them our suspicions about Pauline and Barry?'

'I'm going to tell them that Amy hasn't been heard from since Saturday and that it's very out of character for her not to have told anyone if she was going away or something.'

'But …' Jenny began.

'Jenny, I can't go round accusing people of kidnapping. What if we're wrong? Can you imagine? The police would think I was mad anyway.'

'I don't really fucking care if the police think you're mad! I care about my friend!' With Jenny's outburst came the tears. 'Fuck it!' she exclaimed. 'What if we're too late? What if she's already dead?!'

The same thought had already crossed Willem's mind, more than once, and he had pushed it firmly to one side. He had to believe Amy was okay. The alternative was simply unthinkable and he knew he wouldn't be able to function if he gave it headspace.

'I'm going to the police station. Can I trust you not to do anything stupid while I'm gone?' Willem asked.

Jenny wiped her face roughly on her sleeves. She closed her eyes for a moment, and then nodded.

Willem reached over and squeezed both her hands before getting up to leave.

When Jenny heard the front door close, she gave in to hot, angry tears, indulging them for only a couple of minutes before getting up, blowing her nose loudly and splashing cold water on her face. She needed a plan.

Back in the cellar, Amy was now sitting at the word processor, a blanket from the bed wrapped tightly around her, blowing on her fingers to try and get enough feeling in them to type. The cold and damp of the cellar were playing havoc with her one arthritic finger, which ached like mad and cracked loudly when she bent it.

Rubbing her tired eyes, and flexing her fingers, Amy sighed deeply and pressed play on the Dictaphone, waiting for Pauline's voice to begin speaking. She was getting to grips with the old-fashioned typing machine, but it would have been a darn sight easier using her beloved MacBook Air. Her dried-out contact lenses had removed themselves on the second day, and her eyes were feeling the strain as she tried to focus on the keys in front of her. She wished she'd had her glasses in her handbag the day she'd been snatched. And maybe a gun. As she began to type, Amy wondered what horrors today's tape would reveal. It seemed that Pauline was writing her autobiography and using Amy as free labour to type and edit it. She was seriously worried what would happen to her when the book was finished. For now though, she tried not to think about it as she began to type, hearing the more pronounced Yorkshire accent which Pauline seemed to develop when talking about her past. The previous tapes had covered Pauline's early life growing up in a small village outside York called Nether Poppleton, with her mother and father and three younger brothers. In normal circumstances, the name Nether Poppleton would have put a smile on Amy's face, but these were most definitely not normal circumstances, and wouldn't be even by Jenny's slightly warped standards.

From what Pauline described, she had basically been a bit of a skivvy, looking after her brothers, doing chores and running errands. She said she hadn't resented it at the time; after all, it was all she knew, but later, when she was in her teens, she'd begun to realise that her friends had had very different childhoods. As the resentment grew, so did Pauline's desire to be rid of the cause of it.

When Amy had typed the words *they all died in an electrical fire when I was seventeen*, her blood ran cold. She pressed pause on the Dictaphone. Had Pauline's career as a killer started with her murdering her parents and brothers? The answer had come soon enough as Amy listened on:

```
Nobody suspected a thing. Nice girl like me, wouldn't
hurt a fly, would I? People are basically stupid and
so wrapped up in themselves, they don't have a clue
what's really going on in the world around them. It
was the easiest thing in the world to start a fire by
the cooker in the kitchen when they were all tucked
up in bed. Made sure I legged it off to meet my best
friends, Julie and Pearl. Dressed up to the nines,
we were - 'Look at those three all clarted up' - and
```

off to the fair in a nearby town. Made sure we got
noticed – I was quite a looker in those days you know.
Flirted with those good-looking, dark-skinned gypsy
boys who spun the cars on the Waltzers. The more we
screamed, the faster they spun us.

Got the last bus home. Wasn't easy to calm myself
down and wipe the grin off my face when I got to
the house to find the police and fire brigade there
still. Proper mess it was, still smoke everywhere,
the neighbours all out in their nightclothes, gawping.

'Oh, Pauline!' the old girl from across the road
said when she saw me. 'Oh you poor, poor dear.' Told
the emergency services where I'd be and took me into
hers. Made me a cuppa, extra sweet, and wrapped a
blanket round my shoulders. A couple of times, I
remember, I had to look at the floor for fear my face
would give me away.

Then some policeman came to speak to me – I can't
remember his name now, nice enough fella though – and
he had a WPC with him who sat down next to me while
her boss broke the tragic news: no survivors. Well,
could I fathom up any tears? No, I could not. Deary
me, eyes as dry as a menopausal nun's gusset, I tell
you, Amy.

Pauline had laughed on the tape then and Amy had shuddered.

So, this WPC had her arm around me and I'm trying
not to giggle. In the end, I just sort of moaned and
shook my head a bit. 'Spect they just thought I was

in shock, couldn't take in what they were saying.

Anyway, of course I got taken into care after that, but it was only a couple of months 'til I turned eighteen, and then I could do what I wanted. Got the insurance from the house then too. Enough to get myself a little place in York and treat myself, Julie and Pearl to a holiday in Spain. Benidorm, it was. Well, what a time we had, I can tell you! Didn't want to come back to grey old Yorkshire, did we?

Anyway, after that I started my nurse's training. Not sure why I chose nursing, not really. Didn't know what else to do I s'pose, and I didn't fancy being stuck behind a desk typing for some stuffy old bugger in a stuffy old office. I think I thought it would be like those *Carry On* films, you know, *Carry On Nurse* and *Carry On Doctor*, all giggling and bottom-pinching. To be fair, there was plenty of both! It was fun being surrounded by all those dishy doctors, but they did think they were God's gift, some of them. Still, I'll always have a bit of a thing for a man in a white coat.

Amy, dear, I'm just going to pause to make a cuppa. Makes your mouth dry, all this talking.

Amy heard the Dictaphone click off and she hit the pause button herself. Pressing her fingertips into her tired eyes again, she tried to process what she'd just listened to. Pauline had been getting away with murder since the sixties. How she could have no conscience about killing her three young brothers was completely beyond her comprehension. Amy supposed they'd have been dead from smoke inhalation before the fire got to them, but even so ... it was unimaginable.

Getting stiffly up from the chair, Amy shrugged off the blanket and attempted some star jumps to try and get her circulation going and warm herself up a bit. All that did though was make her a bit dizzy and out of breath. Flopping forward, Amy put her hands on her knees and tried to regain her breath. Before she could stop them, big fat tears plopped onto the floor.

'Pull yourself together!' Amy reprimanded herself, straightening up and wiping her sleeve across her face. But cold, tired, hungry and scared, Amy couldn't halt the tears she thought had dried up, and she let them come once more. She had to find a way out of her predicament, but currently couldn't see any hope. With nothing else to do, and worried about repercussions otherwise, she returned to Pauline's tape. As awful as the story was, at least it would take her mind off her own problems for a while.

```
That's better. Can't beat a nice brew, eh, Amy, me
duck? What's better than a cup of tea? A cup of tea
and a biscuit. And what's better than a cup of tea
and a biscuit? A cup of tea and a biscuit and a nice
sit down!
```

Pauline cackled. Then she slurped a mouthful of tea, before crunching on what Amy assumed to be a biscuit. Amy's stomach growled.

```
Right, where was I? Oh, yes, York Hospital. Well,
that's when everything changed for me, Amy. This fella
```

came in with a particularly nasty ingrown toenail and it was love at first sight!

More cackling. Amy wrinkled up her nose and shook her head.

Have you guessed? Yes, it was my Barry. Oh, he did make me laugh. Even though he was in pain. Never met anyone so funny. He asked me out to the pictures the next weekend and we never looked back. Courting for six months and married within a year. I knew I'd found my soulmate. Imagine if I hadn't opted for nursing? I might never have met the love of my life. Or he his. He used to love me dressing up in my uniform for him back then. Still got it somewhere … course I wouldn't get into it now: too much good living!

As if to prove her point, Pauline munched noisily on another biscuit. Amy thought she might actually be sick. But Pauline wasn't finished.

CHAPTER 33

Police

While Amy was typing up Pauline's dictation and trying not to either cry or vomit, Willem was also feeling tearful and a little nauseous as he waited in a room at the police station. He hadn't had many dealings with the police in the past and that had suited him just fine. Until now. Now he would do anything and everything he could to get Amy back safely. They'd deal with whatever bombshell Jenny had started to drop once Amy was safe. Willem didn't let himself consider the possibility that she wouldn't be coming back. He had to hold it together.

It wasn't many minutes before a young plainclothes officer came in and sat himself opposite Willem.

'Hello, Mr ... de Groot,' he said, after looking at a Post-it note stuck on the front of an A4 folder he was holding.

Willem nodded at him.

'I understand you'd like to report someone missing.'

'Yes,' Willem nodded again. 'Amy. Amy Archer.'

The officer opened the file and took out a form. He proceeded to enter Amy's name at the top, before asking for Amy's personal details: phone number, address and so on. 'Right, that's great,' he said. 'Now, if you can give me a description of Amy – as much detail as possible please, sir. If you know what she might have been wearing, that would help.'

Willem pictured Amy in his mind's eye as he described her.

As he spoke, a lump filled his throat and he had to pause to swallow it back down.

'Take your time, sir,' the officer said.

'Sorry,' Willem said, clearing his throat before he continued. 'She may have been wearing a big, padded coat. I think it was a sort of olive green. Oh ... wait ... I have a photo on my phone.' Willem pulled out his phone and scrolled through until he found the image he was looking for: Amy smiling on the Harbour Arm, wearing her big puffy coat, the wind turning her cheeks rosy as she hung on to her woollen hat. 'Here,' he said, holding the mobile out to show the other man. 'And here, this is a close-up of her face,' he continued, scrolling some more until he found a portrait he'd taken of Amy.

The detective forwarded the photos from Willem's phone to his own, and handed it back to him. 'Now, tell me, when was the last time you saw Amy? Or that you know anyone else did?'

'Um ... it was on Friday evening, at the Old Town Bar. We do a quiz there. And I know her friend heard from her on Saturday morning. By WhatsApp, I believe. But nothing since.' Willem swallowed again. 'It's not like Amy. She'd never go off without telling someone.'

'And you've tried her phone and been to her house, I assume?'

'Yes, of course. Her phone is dead and there's no sign of her at the house.'

'Did you gain entrance to the house?'

'Yes, yes, Amy's friend, Jenny, has a key. Amy's coat and bag were gone.'

'Okay, and was there any sign of a disturbance at all? Anything that made you think there might have been someone else in the house?'

Willem shook his head. 'No, nothing like that. It just looked as though she'd gone out.' Willem was starting to grow impatient now. He simply wanted the police to get out there and look for her.

As if sensing this, the young officer said, 'Not much more now, sir. Did Amy have any ... er ... health issues we should know about? Is she vulnerable in any way?'

Willem screwed up his face. 'What? No. Well, no more vulnerable than any woman these days, it would seem,' he said, thinking back to the horrific events of the past couple of years.

'I understand. So, no ... mental illness or anything? No ... um ... violent exes who might still be hanging about?'

Willem shook his head. 'No, nothing like that,' he insisted, while thinking that actually he didn't really know the answers. How well did he really know Amy, especially in light of what had passed between him and Jenny? 'She's just a normal woman. She writes books and does pub quizzes. Just normal.'

'Of course. You understand we have to ask these things. Well, if I can just have your contact details, please, and those of the friend who was in contact with Miss Archer on Saturday, and any other close friends or family you might have, and I'll get on and file the report. And try not to worry, most missing persons turn up just fine.' He smiled what was supposed to be a reassuring smile, as Willem agonised over whether to hand over Jenny's details. He knew she wouldn't thank him, but what choice did he have?

'This is Jenny, Amy best friend – the one she messaged on Saturday morning,' he said, as he passed over his mobile with Jenny's mobile number on the screen. 'I'm afraid I don't have details of anyone else, sorry.'

'That's fine, sir, thank you,' the detective said as he took a note of the phone number. 'If you could tell ... um ... Jenny that we may need to speak to her, and also get Miss Archer's house key from her, please. We'll call you if we have any further questions, and if you think of anything else that might help us, you can contact me on my direct line,' he said, handing over a business card.

Willem took the card, muttered a thank you, and got up to leave. As he exited the police station, he felt a tight band of pressure around his head. He was sick with worry about Amy. It had now been almost a week since she disappeared and he didn't need a policeman to tell him that the longer someone one missing, the less likely they were to be found alive.

He phoned Jenny as he walked back to his car.

'Any news?' she blurted, before he could speak.

'No, nothing, Jenny, I'm sorry,' he sighed. 'I just phoned to warn you that you might get a call from the police.'

'Oh great,' she groaned.

'I'm sorry, but it was unavoidable. You were the last person to have any contact with her.'

It was Jenny's turn to sigh. 'It's okay, I know you're right. Did they take you seriously?'

'Yes, I think so, although they asked if she had any ... you know ... mental health problems or anything.'

Jenny harrumphed. 'I hope you told them she's remarkably sane. For a writer.' She managed a weak smile. 'Sorry I'm so shit about the police. You did the right thing. The more eyes out there looking for her, the better,' Jenny acknowledged.

'It feels good to have done something at least.'

Jenny just nodded, her pink hair bobbing around her pale face.

'Just make sure you haven't got a gun stashed anywhere in case the police do come round, eh? I can't have you getting locked up at the moment.'

'I'll bury my weapons cache in a dirty litter tray, promise. So, what next? Did you mention Pauline and Barry?'

'No, I didn't. I wasn't comfortable doing that. They might be completely innocent.'

'Pretty sure they're a couple of psychos, but take your point.'

'I'm going to send the drone up over that property in Capel. Just try and get a better picture of the buildings and stuff.'

'Can I come with you?' Jenny asked.

Willem paused. 'Best not, I think. I'll stand out less on my own.'

'Yeah, s'pose. I'm going round the bend though. I don't know what to do.'

'Sorry, Jenny, I feel the same. Helpless.'

'Will you let me know what you find later, please?' Jenny asked.

'Yes, of course.'

'Thanks,' Jenny said.

'And Jenny,' Willem began.

'What?'

'Don't do anything stupid.'

'Who? Me? As if.'

They hung up then, and Willem made his way quickly home to pick up his drone.

Jenny still hadn't come up with a plan and was feeling useless.

CHAPTER 34

A good yarn

Barry returned to the cellar with a plastic mug of soup and a cheese roll at lunchtime.

'I told Pauline you're not eating. She's none too happy, I can tell you. Doesn't want you wasting away before you finish writing her book now, does she?' he laughed, his considerable belly going up and down under his too-tight red sweater, reminding Amy of a giant red beach ball she'd had as a girl. 'She said if you don't eat your lunch, she'll have to force-feed you.'

Amy gasped.

Barry was nodding sagely, 'She'll do it too, you know. When my Pauline says she'll do something, she bloody well does it. Don't mess with a Yorkshire lass.'

'I'm not messing with anyone,' Amy said quietly. 'I want to eat, I'm starving, but bread and cheese upset my stomach. I'm not trying to be difficult, I promise,' she pleaded, meeting Barry's eyes.

Barry seemed to hesitate for a moment before he spoke. 'Pauline says those food intolerance things are a load of yuppy nonsense – just attention-seeking, trendy fads. And a cheese roll never did anyone any harm. If you don't eat it, you know what'll happen, now, don't you?'

Amy nodded her head, despair roiling in her empty stomach.

'That's good then, glad we understand each other. Now, how's the typing coming along? Bloody good yarn, eh?' Barry laughed again, his beach-ball belly boinging. 'See what I did there? "Yarn!" It's not just you clever writer types who can play with words. Bloody funny. Yarn! Wait 'til I tell Pauline.'

Amy said nothing as Barry examined the completed sheets of typing before taking his leave of her once more.

'Eat up now. Work to be done,' he said as he closed the door and Amy heard the key turn on her prison once more. She could hear him laughing to himself as he made his way up the stairs.

Getting under the bed covers once more, Amy drank the soup – cream of chicken, so not ideal, but she simply had to get something into her poor, griping stomach. As much as she wanted to wolf down the cheese roll too, she knew that it would simply be too much for her already protesting insides to cope with.

Once the soup was finished, she took the roll over to the vile chemical toilet and broke it into tiny pieces before throwing them in. No way was she being force-fed by that monster. *You could do with losing a few pounds, anyway*, she told herself as she dropped the bits in, trying not to gag at the smell.

Not wanting to incur the wrath of Pauline for any other reason, Amy used the toilet, reluctantly, and returned to the typing.

We were happy in those early years, me and Barry. Sold my place in York and moved into Barry's house in Clifton. We tried for a baby for ages, but it wasn't meant to be, so I carried on nursing. Probably for the best. I don't think Barry would've liked sharing me with a bairn. We were perfect as we were anyway. Had a nice life. My savings paid for holidays in the

sun. Had a little timeshare on the Costa Brava for
a few years.

Pauline paused, and Amy wondered if she'd finished, her fingers hovering over the keys. No such luck …

I *was* happy, I really was, and I don't want you
thinking otherwise, Amy Archer. I'm not having you
judging me and my Barry and finding us lacking. We
weren't lacking for anything. It was just me. There
was something in me, niggling away at the back of my
mind all the time. Well, not all the time I s'pose,
sometimes it would shut up for a while … but I started
to feel … sort of … I dunno … unfulfilled. Or incom-
plete. I knew there was something missing. A feeling,
a desire, a need. A craving, more like. Like a druggie
must feel when they've had a high.

Amy had a feeling she knew what was coming.

Ever since that night when I was seventeen, the
night of the fire when my family died … I'd never
felt a high like it. I felt so alive, really alive,
my blood fizzing in my veins. Oh, it was the power of
it! I'd never felt anything like it before, or since.
I even thought I might be one of those adrenaline
junkies you read about, but I must confess I've never
felt inclined to jump out of a plane or throw myself
off a platform on a rope. No, it was different. It
was having power over life, I think. Now, don't be

accusing me of playing God, now. I'm not some sort of
maniac with one of those complexes. I just like the
thrill I get from taking a life.

Of course, I know it's wrong to take a life, and I
knew it was wrong, what I did to my family; I'm not
daft. And I tried to ignore that little voice nagging
at me to do it again. And that was when I had the
idea at work, when I was on the wards with the old
folk and the terminally ill, that maybe I could get
my thrills *and* be doing a kindness. Putting those
poor souls out of their misery and suffering was an
act of kindness.

It was the easiest thing in the world to finish
them off. Didn't even take huge doses of the drugs.
We all had keys to the drugs cupboard and it was
simple to just fudge the initials on the paperwork.
Some of those patients were so weak already. Pitiful
creatures. In some ways it was even better than the
fire. I got to watch the life leave their eyes, leave
them. Oh, Amy, what a feeling! I swear on my life
that I could see their spirits leaving their bodies.
And they were smiling! Truly, they were smiling. And
they were grateful. I could feel it. It was what you
would call a win-win situation.

Amy paused briefly as she wondered if she should hyphenate win-win. Compound words were a weakness, and normally she'd check with a quick search on Google. 'For fuck's sake, woman,' she reprimanded herself. 'Does it really matter?' With a sigh she pressed play:

Nobody suspected a thing. All those old, sick people were close to the end anyway. They didn't bother with autopsies for cases like that back then. Waste of money as far as them in charge thought. Got a bit hairy when they did the stocktake of the drugs cupboard, but I just shrugged and played innocent. No proof it was me, was there? I did cool it for a while after that. But I missed the thrill, didn't I?

So, I started up again and chose my … I don't want to call them victims … chosen ones really carefully. I only helped the ones who were the closest to the end. But I have to admit it wasn't quite so rewarding, and I suppose that's why I got a bit careless.

His name was Harry Jones. I recognised him when he came in. We'd had a run-in a few years ago when he'd come in after a heart attack. Horrible man, he was. Abusive to all the nurses, smarmy to the doctors. Wasn't any point complaining back then either. We were expected to put up with all sorts of sexism. If you said anything, you were just laughed at. None of that 'me too' stuff you have nowadays. We just had to put up and shut up. If we didn't like it, there's the door.

Well, old Harry came in after a second heart attack and it hadn't improved his manners any. I heard him say to one of the other nurses, lovely girl she was, from Jamaica, and the old bastard said, 'I'm not being touched by a wog!' Well, that was too much. Poor Yolanda was in tears, and Management did nothing. So I did.

It was the first time I'd done it to someone who would have recovered and been discharged. Silly of me really, but I cannot stand injustice! Someone had to stand up for Yolanda, and that someone was me! It was on a nightshift too, so that was a bit daft of me. I always used to do it during the day when the hospital was fully staffed. I'd slipped Harry and the rest of his ward a sleeping draught in their bedtime cocoas. He wasn't as docile as the others and I was worried he'd wake up when I went to him.

Anyway, he was fast asleep and snoring, and so were all the other patients, when I pulled the curtains around his bed. I watched him for a while, his chest rising and falling, and wondered how to do it. I had a syringe of midazolam all prepared, but it felt too easy, too impersonal. I wanted to put my hands around his throat and squeeze the life out of him, if I'm honest. I couldn't, for obvious reasons, but I really wanted to. Then I thought about suffocating him with a pillow. In the end, though, I stuck with my tried-and-tested method, with only a slight variation. Instead of injecting the drug into his cannula, I stuck the needle though a freckle on his chest, straight into his heart. I was disappointed I couldn't look into his eyes as I did it. I wanted him to see me, to know who was taking his life away, attacking his frail heart, but we can't always get what we want in life, can we? Or in death.

I didn't hang around his bedside as the alarms were going to start going off pretty quickly. I trotted off into one of the private rooms and pretended to be coming from there.

Of course, there was a postmortem this time, wasn't there? I was a bit cross with myself for losing my cool and taking a life that wasn't ready to end. Not because he didn't deserve it, the sexist old racist pig, but because it led to an inquiry. Of course, the spotlight fell on the nightshift staff, and on me. I'm not going to lie, Amy, it got a bit hairy there for a while and I really thought I might go to prison but, ultimately, they couldn't prove it was me and I got off.

Of course, we had to move away, didn't we? Mud sticks, and we had to up sticks and relocate to the other end of the country. Well, I think that's enough for today, Amy. Don't want to wear my voice out when there's so much more still to tell.

Amy leant back in the chair and closed her eyes, repulsed and relieved all at the same time. She didn't want to think about the day when her work would be finished, Pauline's tale told and its scribe no longer needed.

She padded over to the heater and huddled over it for a few minutes before getting back into bed and pulling the covers up around her. Letting her thoughts drift, Amy brought to mind images of Jenny and Willem the last time they'd all been together at the quiz, laughing at something Jenny had said. Tears pricked the corners of her eyes. She knew she needed to be strong, to stay strong, for whatever came next, but she felt small and weak and vulnerable. Helpless and hopeless. *What would Jenny do?* she asked herself, not for the first time. What would Jenny do? And what was Jenny doing? What was she doing right now? Surely she would be out there looking for her best friend, frantic with worry. Had she involved Willem? He must know by now that she was missing. Amy prayed he didn't think she was ghosting him after everything that had happened between them. She couldn't bear that. She would give anything to see them both right now.

Surely even Jenny would be stumped in Amy's situation. There was nothing she could use as weapon, unless she bashed Barry over the head with the word processor. Or gave him a really nasty paper cut. But Jenny would fight! Wouldn't she? With every fibre of her being. She wouldn't take this lying down. Amy felt so weak though. She honestly didn't think she could overpower either Barry or Pauline. Whoever came down had the Taser, and she didn't doubt for a moment that they'd use it. It was hopeless and Amy curled up and closed her eyes.

Amy couldn't hear anything much from the cellar. Occasionally she heard footsteps above, doors banging. She'd heard a car engine a few times, presumably Pauline or Barry coming and going. She'd heard a dog barking, but it didn't sound close by. It was bad enough thinking about overpowering two insane people, without adding a big, aggressive-sounding dog into the mix. She didn't hear the buzzing of a drone overhead as she lay there in that cold, dark room. If she had, it might have given her hope that maybe, just maybe, Willem was hot on the trail of her kidnappers. But she couldn't hear the drone, and soon she'd drifted into an exhausted sleep, only to dream of being dragged back up the cellar stairs and stabbed repeatedly with a knitting needle by a crazed Pauline, while

Barry looked on in admiration, his big red belly juddering joyfully as he morphed into a giant Jelly Baby.

CHAPTER 35

Bedtime reading

Amy woke with a start to the sound of creaking stairs. She could tell from the tread that it was Pauline coming down this time, and she held her breath. She was much more scared of Pauline than the rather more jovial, and infinitely weaker, male half of the partnership. Besides, she knew what Pauline was capable of, what she'd done. She held her breath and waited for the door to open.

'Good evening to you, Amy, dear,' Pauline said, bustling into the room. Amy could see the Taser in her right hand. 'Have you had a productive day? I do hope so. I'm looking forward to reading today's instalment. I think it's got the makings of a bestseller, don't you?' She smiled at Amy as if it was the most normal thing in the world to have an author locked in your cellar typing up the story of your psychotic life.

Amy just blinked at her captor. She had no words.

'Cat got your tongue tonight, dear? Well, not to worry. Barry says you ate all your lunch today. Very good, Amy. Can't have you starving yourself now, can we? That wouldn't do at all. Got to keep your strength up to write our bestseller, haven't you?'

As Pauline clearly didn't require an answer to any of her mainly rhetorical questions, Amy stayed schtum.

'As a reward for all your hard work, I brought you a present,' Pauline continued. She held out a book to Amy. An image of

Stephen King's novel *Misery* flashed into her mind and she couldn't hold back a nervous giggle.

Taking the book from Pauline's outstretched hand, Amy saw that it was one of the *Agatha Raisin* so-called cosy mysteries: *Agatha Raisin and the Busy Body*. She'd read one of the series once, but it hadn't really been her sort of book. She normally preferred her crime reading to be a little more gritty. But right now, she'd take cosy over callous.

'Thank you,' she said, not wanting to antagonise Pauline.

Pauline smiled broadly. 'You're very welcome, dear. I saw the title and thought, I know who'd enjoy this! You being such a busybody and all. Well now, Barry will be down shortly with your dinner and to remove the machine until tomorrow. I'll take the pages you've typed up now. A bit of light reading for bedtime,' she chuckled.

Sick bitch, Amy thought, suppressing a shudder. Then, suddenly remembering the foul toilet, she spoke up: 'Oh! Pauline. Um … I hate to ask, but could you empty the loo? Please. I did ask Barry, but …' her words faded.

Pauline shook her head and chuckled again. 'Of course, dear. No sooner said than done. Barry has many wonderful qualities, but a strong stomach is not one of them. Even picking up after the dog used to make him retch.'

Mention of a dog gave Amy palpitations. As much as she loved dogs, and had handled some difficult ones when she worked at the vet's, she knew only too well how protective they could be of their owners. She took a deep, steadying breath and wondered if she could whack Pauline with the word processor when she bent to pick up the loo.

As if reading her mind, and not for the first time, Pauline

stood in the doorway and yelled up the stairs. 'Barry! Could you pop down?'

Barry soon creaked his way down the steep stairs and appeared in the cellar. 'Yes, my angel, your wish is my command,' he tittered.

Amy felt sick at the sight of the pair of them. If ever there was a match made in hell.

'Just make sure this one doesn't get up to any naughtiness while I empty the toilet,' Pauline instructed him, handing him the Taser.

Barry held the gadget towards Amy and did his usual, hilarious, 'Bzzzz,' and stood beside Amy grinning, while Pauline huffed up the stairs with the portable toilet.

'I'm too old for this shit,' Pauline could be heard saying, as she slowly mounted the stairs.

They both guffawed at that, and Amy felt a flush of embarrassment on her face. If she ever got out of this, she was never, ever going to use a portable toilet for as long as she lived. In fact, she was going to get a gold-plated one installed in her bathroom. Thoughts of her bathroom reminded Amy how bad she smelled. She hadn't been able to wash for ... how many days? Was it five days? Six? She longed to stand in her shower, to wash her hair, scrub every inch of her body, and clean her teeth, which felt furry and gross. Maybe she should ask if she could wash? At this rate she was going to die from the unsanitary conditions long before Pauline had a chance to do the job.

Back at his house, Willem had downloaded the footage he'd taken with the drone above the house and surrounding area in Capel. He'd gone as low as he could risk without being spotted, but wasn't overly optimistic about seeing anything much.

At least on his computer he'd be able to zoom in and get a bit more detail. He rang Jenny when he'd been through the recording.

'Alright, triple D?' Jenny had answered.

It took Willem a moment to realise what she meant. Dodgy Dutch Dude. 'Yes, thanks, Catwoman.'

'Miaow. What news? And please note, I'm only accepting good news for the rest of the day.'

'Bye then,' Willem said.

'Bugger.'

'I s'pose it's not entirely bad news. We can rule out the outbuildings, I reckon. It's clear from the air that they're pretty run down – bits of the roofs missing and so on. I don't think you could keep someone secure in them.'

'Okay, and what about the in-buildings? Can we rule them in?' Jenny asked.

Willem paused again as he tuned himself in to Jenny's wavelength. 'It was hard to make out much from the air, to be honest. I zoomed in as much as I could, but I didn't want to risk the drone being seen and arousing suspicion. If they have taken Amy, the last thing we want is for them to suspect we suspect, if you see what I mean.'

Jenny was quiet.

'I think the main house might have a cellar though. It looks like there's a window below ground level, but I can't be sure,' Willem continued.

'What do we do now?' Jenny asked, finding her voice again. Willem thought he detected a slight wobble.

'I don't know, Jenny. I just don't know.'

'Should we go back up there tonight and have a look round the outside of the house?'

Willem thought for a moment. 'No, not tonight, Jenny. We go tomorrow night when Pauline and Barry should be at the quiz.'

'Good thinking. We'll make our excuses to the others – make sure they let slip to Pauline that we're away or something. Then go and have a proper recce.'

'Sounds like a plan. Shall I pick you up about nine forty-five?'

'Yeah, that's fine,' Jenny agreed.

'I hate the idea of Amy alone and scared somewhere,' Willem said.

'I know, me too. But I'll take alone and scared over the alternative.'

A chill ran down Willem's spine. No, he was not going to entertain the possibility that Amy was dead. 'I'll see you tomorrow night then.'

'Okay. I'll put a message in the quiz chat.'

Back in the cellar, Amy was crying over a bowl of macaroni cheese. She was so hungry, but there wasn't a meal in the world more likely to upset her stomach than pasta and cheese. In desperation, she swallowed down a few mouthfuls of the glutinous mass to try and stop the griping hunger pains, but she knew if she ate the lot, it would end up in the toilet. Cutting out the middleman, she tipped the remainder of the food into the newly cleaned loo, hoping that it would disintegrate before Pauline realised the next time she emptied the bucket.

When Barry had brought her dinner down, and removed the Dictaphone and word processor, she'd timidly asked if she could have a wash, hating herself for being so bloody subservient. Amy just didn't see any point in antagonising her captors.

Barry had laughed in her face. 'I don't like your chances,' he said.

'I promise I wouldn't try and escape,' Amy pleaded.

'Well, I'll ask, but don't get your hopes up. Or your arms. Have you smelled your armpits lately?' Barry laughed again, and Amy felt hot shame and hot tears on her face.

Barry had left her then, and she faced another night alone in the cold, damp cellar, knowing that every passing day was a day nearer her death.

CHAPTER 36

The quiche of death

The following morning saw yet more tea and toast for Amy. She'd asked if she could have her tea black, but that request had obviously been ignored, or denied. Her whole body ached, her head was pounding, and her poor stomach was tied in permanent knots.

She ate one piece of toast and licked the jam off the other. It wasn't really any sort of compromise her insides would be happy with, but she didn't know what else to do. The tea was at least hot and helped to take the chill away. She didn't know how much more she could take, but she felt so completely wrung out, mentally, physically and emotionally, that she really didn't think she could summon up even an ounce of fight.

Hearing Barry's steps on the stairs, she hurriedly tossed the remainder of the toast in the loo before scurrying back to sit on the bed, the bloody thing creaking loudly under her weight. As usual, Barry's belly entered the room before the rest of him, closely followed by the Taser. He took Amy's breakfast dishes and put them outside the door before carrying in the word processor. Amy thought just for a split second about rushing him, but she didn't know if the dreaded Pauline was still in the house, and the moment passed before she could make up her mind and act.

'New tape in the Dictaphone for you,' he instructed, as he made to leave her again. 'Oh, and request denied. For a wash.

Pauline sent these for you though,' he added, tossing a packet of Poundland baby wipes, which had been balancing on the word processor, at Amy. 'I'll bring you a peg for your nose if it helps.' With that, he left the room, chuckling to himself.

Getting to her feet once more, Amy padded over to the window, peering through the dirty glass to the steep bank of earth opposite, and the thin sliver of sky above. The sky was wintry white. Amy wondered if it was going to snow. Her heart sank at the thought of the cellar being even colder than it already was.

Retrieving the pack of baby wipes from the bed, Amy used one on her face and the back of her neck. It came away pretty grimy. She must look an absolute state, and was grateful there wasn't a mirror in the room with her, as she thought of the luxurious skincare products on her dressing table at home. Peeling another couple of wipes from the packet, Amy reached up under her jumper and scrubbed at each of her armpits. The thought of removing her clothes had made her shiver. Besides, she didn't want to risk Barry returning and catching her in her underwear. Running her tongue over her teeth, Amy paused with yet another wet wipe in her hand. 'Sod it,' she exclaimed, as she wrapped the wipe around her finger and began rubbing at her teeth. It was better than nothing, she concluded, although when she tried to clean her back teeth it made her gag. Then, using the loo once more, Amy finished washing herself as best she could, and then tossed the used wipes into the chemical gloop.

Feeling marginally better, she sat herself down at the table with a deep sigh and prepared to work. She figured the only thing keeping her safe for now was doing as she was told. As she put paper in the machine, and pressed play on the Dictaphone, Amy wondered if she would ever feel the sun on her face again. The sound of Pauline's recorded voice brought her back to the present moment once more.

So, that was when we moved to Suffolk. Yes, Amy, I know, I told you a little fib, didn't I? Bristol indeed. Mind you, the two accents do sound quite a lot alike, you know. You thought you were being so clever, didn't you? All that pretending you were looking for ideas for your book character. Pff. As if I'd fall for that. I didn't arrive on the last banana boat you know. I knew you were onto me as soon as you mentioned Suffolk. When did you first suspect, I wonder? We'll have to sit down and have a long chat about that sometime, won't we?

Anyway, Suffolk. I think you know the Suffolk story already, so I won't dwell on it. We were pretty much forced to leave Yorkshire following those allegations, and I got a job in an old people's home in Ipswich. Suffolk was alright. A bit flat, but we had a nice enough life. I couldn't resist helping a few of the old codgers shuffle off though, could I? Couldn't help myself, Amy. Angel of mercy, that's me. Barry sometimes calls me his angel.

Amy thought she might vomit up the scant contents of her stomach at that. The woman was a fucking psychopath.

Long story short, we had to skedaddle again when

things got a bit too hot there. I wasn't too sorry to leave Martlesham. By that time, I was longing to see some bloomin' hills. As much as we'd have loved to go back up North, we decided to continue our journey south and move to the seaside. And that's how we came to be living here in Folkestone. Well, Capel. Couldn't resist being at the top of a hill, could we?! Ha ha! Goodness, Amy, if we have to move again, we'll be in France! Not sure me and Barry would like France. They have some funny ideas over there, don't they? Could never find a proper loo when we went over. Had to squat over a hole in the floor. Heathens! And some of the things they eat. Maybe we'll go west. Somerset, p'raps. Leave some scope for later on … Devon, Cornwall … ha ha. All those lovely cream teas.

Well, Folkestone has been lovely, honestly. We were made so welcome when we arrived. Barry joined the bowls club. I told him he couldn't have picked a hobby he was better suited to if he'd tried. I joined a knitting circle, and we really felt part of a community for the first time since we'd left Yorkshire. Then we started doing the pub quizzes, which were the cherry on the cake. Barry could be Mr Entertainer again, and it was so lovely to see him shine the way he used to all those years ago when he worked at Butlin's. I worked in a care home for a short time, but I realised I wouldn't be able to resist temptation, so I gave that up. I didn't want to burst our happy little bubble.

But then, when all those killings started happening

with that Exhibitionist fella, I found myself feeling a little nip from the green-eyed monster. Seemed like he was having a whole lot of fun. It made me realise there was a part of me missing somehow. I missed the buzz of taking a life. I missed the power. I don't expect you to understand, Amy. Miss Goody Two Shoes, you are, aren't you? You probably wouldn't even swat a fly.

If only you knew, Amy thought.

I toyed with the idea of going back to work. It would have been so easy. But by then I knew it wouldn't be enough. I think I was inspired by the Exhibitionist. You knew him, didn't you, Amy? I heard he belonged to your writing group. Little Miss Detective. Didn't spot a killer in your midst then, did you?

I managed to control the urge pretty well for quite a while. Then, when we had yet another killer on the loose last year, bodies popping up all over the place, the feeling grew again. I could feel it inside me, like some sort of creature trying to escape. I kept it in for a while, but it needed feeding. It demanded it.

It was at one of the Wednesday-night quizzes that I had the idea. Those bloody Scrambled Eggheads had won every week for longer than I could remember, and the morale of the other teams was getting very low. Well, I didn't want half the teams to leave and the quiz to get cancelled. That wouldn't have been good for my Barry, not at all.

So, I thought I could kill two birds with one stone – oh, ha ha, pardon the pun! Barry could keep his quiz, and the other teams could have a chance of winning. So, I'm afraid Stanley's card was marked right away. He was by far the strongest Egghead.

Poor old Stanley. I started making him treats when I was baking. He said my blueberry muffins were the best he'd ever had. I said, ooh, Stanley, you'll make me blush. So, when I took him round a mushroom quiche, he couldn't wait to get stuck in. I didn't hang around, mind you. I was careful not to touch the pie dish or the foil, of course. Left a magazine on the kitchen table, open at an article about woodland foraging, then let the death caps do their work. Not a nice way to go, and I do feel a bit bad about that, but still. Needs must. And I don't have access to all the drugs I used to when I was working.

The police came and spoke to us eventually, us and everyone from the quiz. So very sad, I said, such a lovely man. Was it a heart attack? No? Then one young policeman let slip about the deadly mushrooms, giving me the chance to say, rather vaguely of course, that I'd heard he was into a bit of woodland foraging … couldn't remember for the life of me who'd told me … surprised he'd made such a mistake … I'll stick to buying my mushrooms from the supermarket, thank you very much.

CHAPTER 37

Dead quizzers

Amy was still reeling from the revelations of Pauline's many misdeeds when Barry arrived with yet another lunch of soup and a roll.

'Lunch is served, young lady,' he said, putting the tray down next to Amy.

In her head, she grabbed the tray and smashed it over his head, watching the hot red soup cascade down his fat face. In reality, she just smiled weakly and thanked him.

'You are most welcome,' he said, as if this was all the most normal situation in the world.

Amy rubbed her tired, strained eyes, wishing, for the umpteenth time, that she had her glasses. She could hardly see the words she was typing, and worried constantly about making mistakes she might be punished for.

Barry made to leave her again, pausing in the doorway: 'Nearly forgot,' he said, reaching just outside the door. 'Got you this.' He produced an aerosol can and proceeded to spray the contents liberally into the room, which filled with a horrid artificial floral smell which made Amy cough and her eyes sting even more.

'There,' Barry grinned at her. 'Now you don't need a wash.' With that, he locked Amy in once more and she heard his heavy footsteps fade away on the stairs.

Amy felt like sobbing once more, at the hopelessness of her

situation, and the very real fear of what was going to happen to her. Pauline's memoirs were almost up to the present day, and Amy knew she had to find a way of buying herself more time. As she reluctantly ate the cream-of-tomato soup and a little bit of the bread roll, she started trying to come up with questions for Pauline, answers she could say she needed to really make her story the best it could be.

After she had eaten and used the Portaloo out of necessity, Amy pulled the blanket round her and, with a sigh, pressed play on the Dictaphone once more.

So, that was the end of poor old Stan, wasn't it? Oh, it felt absolutely marvellous, Amy, it really did. That old, familiar rush I'd missed so much. Of course, I couldn't stop then, could I? I knew it was going to be a challenge, but I've never been afraid of a challenge. After all, I married Barry, didn't I?

Pauline cackled with laughter for a few seconds before continuing. If nothing else, it drowned out the uncomfortable gurglings coming from Amy's stomach.

Now, who was next? Let me think … Ah! Yes, Norman. Dear old Norm. These old people are so easy to befriend and I soon found out he was a diabetic, with a weak heart – not much of a challenge there for someone with my nursing background. Poor old boy, must have got in a muddle with his medications. Such a shame, etc etc. I don't think the police looked too hard at Norm's death. Why would anyone want to kill a harmless old man? Well, we know the answer to that one, don't we? I didn't take a great deal of pleasure in that one, Amy. I actually did like Norm, but he had to go; he was just too good a quizzer. So it was his own fault really, wasn't it? Sometimes we have to take the difficult decisions, do the hard things, eh, Amy? You can take the lass out of Yorkshire, but … well … you know the rest.

So … after Norm … it was … deary me, my memory's not what it used to be … Stan, then Norm … Oh yes, Sylvia! Well, the Scrambled Eggheads were still too ruddy strong, weren't they? So Sylvia had to go. I quite enjoyed Sylvia. She was a stuck-up so-and-so, her head so far up her own arse she could wear her tonsils as earrings as my Barry used to say. She was a little more tricky, kept herself pretty fit and well, no underlying health conditions as far as I could make out. Wasn't a helpless old dear I could befriend. I don't think she actually liked me very much to be perfectly honest. Imagine that?! Anyway, had to give that one some thought. Set Barry to following her for a while, see if I could get some inspiration from her movements.

Didn't take too long to establish that she lived on her own and kept herself busy around the property, did all the garden herself and so on. Well, that was her downfall, wasn't it? Literally! (More chortling.) Shouldn't have been cleaning the gutters herself, should she? Didn't check the ladder was steady and reached up just a bit too far. Wobble, wobble, crash!

If only that rock hadn't been right where she fell,
eh? Terrible bad luck. Bye bye, Sylvia.

Amy pressed pause as more cackling came from Pauline. The woman was mad: absolutely, clinically insane. How the hell was she getting away with it? Although, of course, Amy knew a thing or two about getting away with murder, this was on a whole other level. Pauline had been getting away with murder for years, decades. How could the police not be suspicious? Perhaps, with no obvious motives, they'd taken the deaths at face value: tragic accidents. Not for the first time, Amy wished she'd persisted in convincing Jenny that she was on to something. Maybe they could have found the answers the police had missed. After all, they'd done it not once, but twice before. The thought of her fearless friend brought tears to Amy's eyes again and she could feel herself losing hope of ever seeing her again. Or Willem. A sob escaped Amy's lips and she gave in to the tears for a while. All crying did though was make the constant headache worse and create a whole lot of snot. Wiping her nose on some toilet paper, Amy took a deep breath and tried to compose herself once more. The only thing she could do right now was not antagonise Pauline and Barry, and that meant keep on typing up the outpourings of a madwoman.

So, I enjoyed Sylvia, and that did for the Scrambled
Eggheads, didn't it? About bloomin' time too, I say.
Gave the other teams a chance at last. But then that
other team of oldies, Saga Crews, step into their
shoes, don't they? For goodness' sake, I thought,
take a hint you daft old buggers. But no, they had

to go and win, didn't they? Put a target on their backs. And they were clearly much stronger than all the other teams, yours included of course, Amy. I was doing you a good turn.

Jack was an easy choice. He was a superb quizzer. Almost as good a quizzer as he was a drinker. Always thought he had something of the Yorkshireman about him. No nonsense was Jack, said it like it was; called a spade a bloody spade did Jack. I did have a great deal of respect for Jack. But he did stink the place up, didn't he? Needed a damn good wash and to run a comb through his hair, did Jack. Apparently he started drinking after he lost his wife. Cancer took her – might as well have taken Jack too, he never recovered. Numbed the pain with whisky I suppose, poor man. Hmm … you could say I did him a favour too, put him out of his misery. I didn't do it for that reason – it wasn't a mercy killing, Amy. I didn't kill him because of his broken heart or poisoned liver, I did it because of his brilliant brain. Although, to be honest, I'm not sure how much longer his body could have carried on, not the way he was abusing it.

Mixed it up a bit with Jack, didn't I, Amy? Can I be honest with you? Of course I can, silly old me, you know all my secrets, don't you? Well now, I wasn't getting the sort of … satisfaction … the thrill I wanted from dealing with those old codgers. I needed to get up close and personal with the next one. I tell you what though, Amy, getting up close and personal with that old sot wasn't the most pleasant experience. I tried very hard not to breathe in his foul stink when I did Jack. Didn't want to pass out from the fumes, did I? Ha ha! That wouldn't have done at all now, would it? Lying there on the cobbles with a kitchen knife in my hand! But I think I was puffing a bit, you know, from the effort and the exhilaration. And my goodness it was exhilarating! I'm not sure if euphoric is the right word – you're the writer, Amy, I'm sure you can come up with the right one.

'Yeah, how about deranged? Or sociopathic?' Amy muttered.

Jack was a bit of a risk of course. The moment had to be right. I'm not daft and I wasn't going to take unnecessary risks. If there'd been anyone else around I wouldn't have gone through with it that night. But it couldn't have been more perfect. I barely broke my stride as I plunged the knife into his neck. I could feel the warmth of his blood on my face, and I felt more alive than I had in such a long time. Oh the rush! I grabbed his wallet from his coat pocket and was gone before he'd hit the ground. I reckon he knew it was me, but I couldn't hang around to gloat. I'd have loved to have watched the realisation dawn in his eyes before the life left them.

Anyway, I hurried away as fast as these old legs would carry me, to where my Barry was waiting with the car. I must confess, Amy, I still have the knife and wallet. I'm loathe to part with them. Silly really. Have to be sensible though. Keeping souvenirs is never a good idea, is it? Unless it's a fridge magnet from Benidorm! Ha ha!

So, that was the end of Jack. And the end of Saga Crews as it turned out. None of them had the bottle to go on, did they? Oh that's funny, isn't it, Amy? Jack was the one with the bottle! Of whisky!

Amy pressed STOP on the Dictaphone. She couldn't listen to the maniacal laughter for another second. It had grown dark outside, but it got dark so early now, and Amy had no idea what time it was. She knew it couldn't be all that late because dinner hadn't been brought down. Cold, stiff and tired, Amy crawled under the blankets on the camp bed and closed her eyes.

CHAPTER 38

Police inaction

After another sleepless night, Jenny and Willem were on the phone to one another first thing Wednesday morning.

'I told the rest of the team that we wouldn't be at the quiz tonight,' Jenny began. 'Pippa said they might not bother either as three of us would be missing. Ugh, poor turn of phrase, Jenny.'

'Bugger. We need them there to stop Pauline and Barry getting suspicious,' Willem said.

'Well, as it turns out, we don't,' Jenny said despondently. 'It turns out the quiz is cancelled due to illness.'

Willem could almost hear Jenny putting speech marks around the word 'illness' with her fingers.

'Damn it!' Willem exclaimed.

'What are we going to do?' Jenny asked, for the umpteenth time.

And, for the umpteenth time, Willem had no answers. He sighed heavily. 'I suppose I could check with the police – see if they've found anything out.'

'Yeah, good idea,' Jenny agreed. 'They still haven't contacted me, by the way.'

'I hope they're taking it seriously. I'll phone them this morning and let you know what they say,' Willem told her.

'Okay. What are we going to do about going out to the house?'

'I don't know, Jenny. We can't take any chances. If they have got Amy and they know we're on to them, it might not end well. We can't put Amy at risk.'

'We can't do nothing!' Jenny exclaimed.

'I know. One step at a time. Let me speak to the police.'

'Phone me straight after.'

'I will. Bye, Jenny.'

Willem pressed his fingertips into his eyes. He didn't want to let on to Jenny how absolutely terrified he was that they wouldn't find Amy alive. What reason could Pauline and Barry possibly have for keeping her alive? After this long, chances were she was already dead. But while there was hope, however slim, he had to keep trying.

He wondered briefly if it would be better to go to the police station in person, but decided to try phoning first and, after a few minutes on hold, was put through to someone who was familiar with the case.

'Mr de Groot, good morning. I understand you're calling about a missing person case: Amy Archer?'

'Yes, I was hoping you could give me an update? We still haven't heard from Amy and are getting more and more worried.'

'Of course, sir, and I understand that. All I can really tell you at the moment is that we checked Miss Archer's phone records on the day you say she went missing ...'

The day she did *go missing*, Willem thought, but didn't voice.

'So ...' the policeman continued, 'on that Saturday, the phone was in the vicinity of the Old High Street at around 5.30 p.m., and prior to that we had it static in and around the Bayle for about forty-five minutes.'

Willem frowned, wondering where Amy had been. He couldn't think of any reason for Amy to be in the Bayle other than at the Old Town Bar on a Friday night for the quiz. Of course, the Coastal Creatives shop was on the Old High Street, but so were any number of other shops and cafes. He waited for the officer to continue.

'Um ... Mr de Groot, can you think of any reason why Miss Archer might leave town without telling you? Could she have been upset about anything? Was she in a relationship that you know of?'

Willem frowned. He didn't understand why the officer was asking this. He'd told them Amy was single when he'd reported her missing. 'No, no, Amy wasn't seeing anyone. We ... er ... were involved for a short time, but no—'

The officer interrupted. 'So, it's possible she could have been upset at the break-up and just wanted to get away for a while...?'

'She wouldn't leave without telling someone. Even if she didn't tell me, she would have told her best friend, Jenny. They're practically joined at the hip.'

'I understand, sir, but we often don't know people as well as we think we do. Sometimes they behave out of character, especially where matters of the heart are concerned.'

'No, you don't know Amy. She wouldn't. Why are you suggesting this anyway? Do you know something we don't?' Willem pushed, his frustration evident in his voice.

The policeman paused before speaking again. 'On Sunday, Miss Archer used her debit card at Folkestone Central to purchase a one-way ticket to London St Pancras. From there she bought an onward single to Leeds.'

'What? No. She wouldn't ... why would she ...?' Willem began, shaking his head.

'I'm sorry, but we checked the CCTV and a woman matching Miss Archer's description was seen at both Folkestone and London stations. And her mobile was switched on again in the vicinity of London St Pancras.'

'There must be a mistake. It can't have been Amy.'

'She was identified by the coat you informed us she was wearing and which is in the photograph you supplied us with. Same hat, and it looks like her handbag too. I'm sorry, but it really looks as though she left town without telling you. It does happen, I'm afraid. Time after time. Sometimes people just need to get away from it all for a while.'

Willem could feel himself getting more angry and upset by the second. 'You're wrong! Amy wouldn't—' he began, but the policeman cut him off.

'I'm sorry, sir, but at this time we're not treating Miss Archer's case as suspicious—'

It was Willem's turn to interrupt. 'Did you check that she actually got off the train in Leeds? Although God knows why she would be going there. I don't think Amy knows anyone in that part of the country. And what about her mobile? Has that been traced to Leeds?'

'The mobile hasn't been switched back on since its last known location in London, but it's not unusual for someone wanting to disappear for a while to switch their phone off. And we didn't feel it was necessary to involve the West Yorkshire Police at this time. With no evidence of foul play ...'

'No evidence? She's missing! That's your evidence!' Willem exclaimed, his hands expressing his frustration. The thought that he should mention Pauline and Barry flashed into his head, but he dismissed the idea just as quickly. The police officer already thought he was wasting his time.

'As I said, sir, unless anything else comes to light, I'm afraid there's nothing more we can do at this time. Of course, please don't hesitate to get back in touch if new information does arise.'

Willem closed his eyes and took a breath. He could feel it was futile to push the officer further. He muttered his thanks and hung up.

Jenny picked up the phone at the first ring.

'Well?'

'I'm sorry, Jenny, they're not even looking for her.' Willem filled Jenny in on what he'd been told, pausing from time to time to allow for Jenny's exclamations and insistence the police were wrong.

'Useless bastards,' she said, when Willem had finished. 'It can't have been Amy at the train station. How could they mistake someone else for her? Didn't they see her face? Loads of people must have the same coat as Amy.'

'I don't know, Jenny. Maybe she didn't look directly at a camera?'

'It's ridiculous! It wasn't Amy, I know it wasn't! And why the hell would she go to bloody Leeds? She doesn't even know anyone up there,' Jenny said, her frustration matching Willem's earlier feelings.

'Well, whoever it was, they had the same hat and handbag too, don't forget. And Amy's debit card was used. And her mobile …'

Jenny sighed deeply. 'It wasn't Amy,' she said quietly.

'I know it sucks, but I s'pose the police feel they've done their due diligence, Jenny.'

'But you know she wouldn't have gone off like that!' Jenny's belief in her friend was unshakeable.

Willem was silent. Did he know that? For sure? Did he really know Amy as well as he'd thought he did? He knew she was keeping secrets. What if those secrets had caught up with her?

'You do know that, right?! Willem?'

Willem sighed. 'I just don't know anymore, Jenny. I know it seems out of character, but ...' he began.

'No! No buts! She wouldn't! She wouldn't leave without telling me ... she wouldn't,' Jenny kept repeating.

Willem didn't know what to say. He heard Jenny take a deep breath. He knew what was coming.

'Well, if you don't believe me, then sod you, I'll find Amy on my own!'

Before Willem could respond, Jenny had ended the call. He sat with his head in his hands, wracking his brain for answers, for understanding, but came up with nothing. He was truly at a loss.

Back at her house, Jenny was shaking with frustration and fear, her mobile clutched so tight in her hand her knuckles had turned white. She couldn't believe this was happening. How could Willem doubt Amy? Amy always did the right thing by everyone else. Little Miss Reliable, that was Amy. She never wanted to let anybody down, and she would never do something which would cause people to worry unnecessarily. Jenny didn't doubt for a millisecond that Amy was a victim of foul play and, with or without Willem, she wouldn't rest until she found her.

Feeling more resolute, anger and determination took over. Sitting down at her kitchen table, she tried to come up with a plan. It was so much harder without her partner in crime though. Not for the first time in recent days, Jenny wished there was still a gun in her Fruit 'n Fibre. She was also wishing she could drive. Having a car would make this whole situation a darn sight easier. She'd have to get a taxi if she wanted to check out Barry and Pauline's house again. 'Bloody Willem,' she cursed.

Willem, meanwhile, was also at a loss. He knew full well that Jenny wasn't going to give up. Did he really want her on his conscience if she went and did something stupid? He dragged his hands through his hair. He simply didn't know what to do.

CHAPTER 39

Blowing a hooley

In the cellar, Amy had dozed off and was dreaming fitfully when she was woken by the sound of the key in the lock. She could feel her heart pounding as she waited to see who it was. As much as she hated seeing Barry's face appear round the door, his was preferable to Pauline's. Pauline really terrified her. Amy experienced a moment of panic when she realised she hadn't finished typing up the entire dictation that day. She hadn't meant to fall asleep, she'd just needed a little respite from Pauline's crazed memoirs, and a little warmth in her frozen limbs.

She scrambled out from the covers, and swung her legs round to a sitting position just in time to see that it was indeed Barry. Amy breathed out the breath she didn't realise she'd been holding.

'Sitting down on the job, are we?' Barry said, tutting at her. 'I hope you've finished your work then. Can't have you slacking now, can we? Pauline wouldn't like that. I mean, my Pauline's got the patience of a saint – she has to have, being married to me,' he chortled, 'but you shouldn't abuse her good nature now, should you?'

Amy was too scared to admit that she hadn't finished the dictation. 'Um ... sorry, I just needed a minute ... I ... um ... I just need to re-listen to one section I'm not completely happy with. I think I can do better ... and I want it to be perfect ... for Pauline,' she swallowed.

'Well, you're in luck as it happens. Pauline's popped to the supermarket for a few bits she forgot yesterday. Can't have our illustrious guest wasting away now, can we? So you've got about an hour, I reckon, to get your work done. I'll bring your dinner down a bit later than usual.'

'Thank you,' Amy said, with a sigh of relief.

Barry turned to leave once more, pausing in the doorway to give another blast of the horrible air freshener from the can, which was obviously sitting just outside the door. Amy suppressed a cough and watched as the door closed and she was locked in once more.

Not wanting to incur the wrath of Pauline, there was nothing for it but to get back to work. Amy didn't know how much material she still had to listen to on the tape.

As it transpired, Amy had almost finished the tape with Pauline's recounting of Jack's murder. There was only one more paragraph:

```
Well now, Amy, it's been quite a day of confessions,
hasn't it? I think that's probably enough for one day,
don't you? It's thirsty work, this voice-recording
lark too. I think I've more than earned a nice bottle
of Black Sheep tonight. I'll pick some up from the
shops later. Need a few bits and bobs. Roast chicken
on the menu tomorrow and I need some stuffing and
parsnips. Make a nice change to have time for a proper
dinner on a Wednesday with no quiz to go to. Righty-o,
until tomorrow!
```

The tape ended there and Amy leant back in her chair with a sigh. She felt a little hysterical at Pauline talking so matter of factly about her shopping when she'd just confessed to a horrific murder. But now she knew today must be Wednesday. She wondered what excuse had been used for cancelling the quiz. That, of course, led to her thinking of Jenny and Willem and the rest of the quiz team, and Amy was filled with sadness and despair. She had to find a way out of her predicament. She just had to. But how? She felt entirely hopeless. Useless and hopeless.

She was back under the covers once more when Barry returned with her food: spaghetti on toast. Amy didn't know whether to laugh or cry. It was as if Pauline was deliberately picking the worst possible foods for Amy. More wheat for her inflamed insides to deal with. Apparently tonight's roast chicken wasn't intended for her, although her stomach growled at the thought of it, and her salivary glands tingled.

'Could I have some chicken, Barry? Please. Just a little,' she braved the question.

'Well, it's not up to me, lass, but I'll ask the boss. Don't get your hopes up though.'

'Thank you,' Amy smiled shyly, cursing her own pathetic subservience.

'No promises,' Barry added, as he left her once more, clucking and flapping his arms like a chicken as he went.

Amy picked at the food, knowing her body needed fuel to keep warm, but desperately craving some meat and vegetables, and something to drink other than water and tea. She'd give anything to be sat with all her friends at the pub, gin and tonic in hand, laughing over something Jenny had said, safe and warm and happy, not a care in the world other than whose round was it and did anyone know the capital of Azerbaijan?

Barry didn't return with the requested roast chicken. He eventually collected Amy's tray and removed the word processor before locking her in for another long, cold night.

Amy tried to read a bit of the book Pauline had given her, but she simply couldn't concentrate and, after finding herself re-reading the same paragraph over and over again, she gave up, throwing the book down on the floor in frustration.

She was so bloody cold too. The wind had got up and she could hear it howling outside the small cellar window and felt colder than ever. Getting up to investigate, she discovered a small crack in the barred window, which was letting in a bitterly cold stream of air. Retrieving the book from where she'd dropped it, she wedged it against the window to try and stem the flow of frigid air.

'Best thing for it, cosy crime indeed. There's nothing cosy about this situation,' she muttered, returning to the camp bed and pulling the blankets up under her chin. Not for the first time, she wished she had her big puffy coat and woolly hat. When she'd asked Barry if she could have them to help keep herself warm after a couple of uncomfortable days and nights in the cellar, he'd explained that they'd been thrown in a bin in London. Amy had looked at him in confusion.

'What? What do you mean?'

'Ah, Amy, my Pauline thinks of everything. She took a little trip to London dressed up as you. Even took your handbag. Paid for the train ticket using your card, and made sure your mobile phone was traceable up there. As far as anybody knows, you then hopped on a train to Leeds from there,' Barry grinned at her.

Amy shook her head as she tried to get it around what Barry

was telling her. Did this mean nobody was looking for her? That everyone thought she'd left town?

Barry hadn't finished regaling her with Pauline's evil genius. 'She didn't stop at that, though, oh no, not my clever lass. She'd also bought a round-trip ticket for herself previously. After she dumped your coat and hat in one of those commercial wheelie bins in an alley behind a restaurant in China Town, she put your handbag in a carrier bag and off she went again as Pauline – she was mearing her mac under your coat; would've looked a bit odd otherwise, this time of year. Travelled back to Folkestone using her own ticket. Said she had a bit of a job getting the sim card out of your mobile phone, but she managed it in the end. I'd said, couldn't she have put it on the train to Leeds, but she said that it would be too suspicious if it was found. She was right of course, she usually is. Up 'ere for thinking,' Barry pointed to his temple, 'that's my Pauline. I'm much more, down 'ere for dancin',' he pointed to his feet, grinning.

Amy was too stunned to speak. All she could think was that no one would be looking for her.

'Couldn't resist a little trip to her favourite wool shop while she was up there,' Barry chuckled. 'Didn't hurt to get herself seen in the shop, of course. Gave her a reason to be in London too, just in case.'

With nothing else to do, Amy finally fell asleep listening to the sound of the wind, and with thoughts of Willem and Jenny vying for her attention. Surely they must still be looking for her, no matter what Pauline had done? No way would Jenny believe Amy had left without saying anything, even if Willem had his, wholly justified, doubts. The question was, if they were still looking for her, would they find her? And, if they did, would they find her in time?

Back in Folkestone, Jenny had donned her all-black outfit, pulled her black beanie on – making sure to tuck in any stray wisps of pink – fed the cats with promises of 'won't be long', and was now waiting for a taxi which she had booked for 10 p.m.

Soon she was being driven by a rather chatty driver out of the town and up the hill to Capel. She'd asked him to drop her off on the main road, and was planning to walk the rest of the way.

'So, where you off to at this time of night dressed like that, then?' the driver asked, eyeing her in the rear-view mirror. 'Bit of burglary?' he chuckled.

'Yes,' Jenny said seriously. 'I'm a cat burglar.'

The driver roared with laughter.

'Well, I don't live up this way, so I'm not too worried. Just steer clear of the East Cliff area and we won't have a problem.' He winked exaggeratedly in the mirror.

'Noted,' Jenny said, smiling fakely.

A couple of minutes later and the driver was pulling over opposite Capel Court Park. The road was quiet. 'This alright for you?'

'Yep, fine thanks,' Jenny said, handing over the fare.

'Happy burgling!' the driver said, as Jenny closed the car door.

She grimaced and muttered 'dickhead' under her breath. Pulling her coat around her and her hat further down on her head, Jenny cursed the weather. 'It's blowing a hooley, Ames; that's what you'd say if you were here. But you're not here, are you? Where the bloody hell are you? Coz I'm coming to get you. Please God.' Jenny wasn't religious, but she figured she needed all the help she could get. Especially now Willem had bailed on her.

Jenny was about halfway down Winehouse Lane when she heard it. 'Pssst.'

She stopped and looked all around, wondering if she'd imagined the noise, spooked by the wind and the situation. 'Psst.' There it was again. The noise was followed soon afterwards by a dark figure coming out of the field adjacent to the road Jenny was walking up.

'Willem! Christ, you nearly gave me a heart attack!' Jenny thumped his chest with both hands, trying to return the favour.

'Jenny, what a surprise,' Willem said rather sarcastically. 'Thought you might come anyway.'

Jenny looked at him mutinously. 'If you think you're going to stop me …' she began.

'I know better than to think I can stop you doing anything,' Willem said, with a wry laugh.

'What are you doing here then? Lurking in a field in the dark. Trying to live up to your nickname?'

'What? Dodgy Dutch Dude? Always. I regularly lurk in fields in the dark, Jenny. Usually I have a camera though, and a clear sky to photograph.'

'So why …?'

'To keep you safe, jou idioot.'

'You been drinking?' Jenny eyed him suspiciously.

'What? Why would you …? Ah, did I lapse into Afrikaans? It happens when I'm stressed.'

'Idjoot,' Jenny said.

CHAPTER 40

A clue! A clue!

'Are we going then? Haven't got all night.'

Willem sighed. 'Are you sure this is a good idea, Jenny? Chances are high that Pauline and Barry are at home.'

'I do know that, but I can't do nothing. I'm going. What you do is up to you, but I don't need protecting like some bloody damsel in distress.'

'Another thing I do know about you, Jenny. I also know that Amy would never forgive me if I let anything happen to you, and ...' Willem paused.

'And what?'

'Well, I also happen to care about you too, but if you tell anyone I said that ...'

'You'll what? Kidnap me and keep me in your cellar?'

'Well, I don't have a cellar, so no ...' Willem sighed again, before relenting. 'Come on then, let's do this.'

The pair made their way up the lane, battling the strong winds which shrilled around them. Willem thought to himself that at least the noise would mask their approach.

As they neared the house, Willem put a cautious hand on Jenny's arm, urging her to slow down. They had only gone a couple of steps onto the property when a security light came on directly opposite them.

'Shit,' Jenny said, as she and Willem ran back out, talking refuge behind a hedge. Jenny's heart was pounding as she peeped around the end of the bushes. She could just make out a silhouette standing in the window, holding the curtain aside and backlit by the room. She held her breath as she watched, waiting for the person to give up. 'All clear,' she told Willem a short while later.

Willem screwed up his face as if to say he wasn't convinced. 'We can't go in through the front, not with that security light. Come on, let's go around and see if there's another way in.'

Jenny huffed a half-hearted objection, but she knew Willem was right and she followed him away from the drive, hugging the hedge as they went. The hedge was thick and pretty impenetrable, a mix of mainly privet and hawthorn, and the pair were starting to despair about finding a gap when, about halfway along the back boundary, Willem found a possible way in. Turning his back to the hedge to protect his face, he pushed his way through, his thick coat shielding him from the scratchy branches. He grunted as he felt another barrier against his back, discovering a fence-line running inside the hedge. It was his turn to say 'shit'.

'What?' Jenny whispered, her face in his as she followed him in. 'Why've you stopped?'

'Fence,' he hissed. 'Hang on, I'm going to turn round and check it out.'

Thankfully, the fence turned out to be pretty old and rotten and it was easy for Willem to remove a couple of planks and lay them gently onto the grass, creating a gap big enough for them to squeeze through.

Once Willem had set foot in the garden, he held his fist up, telling Jenny to freeze. He wanted to be sure they weren't suddenly going to be caught in the glare of another security light. When nothing happened, he twisted his fist and beckoned Jenny on with a point of his index finger, thumb raised.

'What are you, Special Forces?' she hissed, imitating Willem's army-style hand gestures, before creeping towards the house by his side.

Thankfully there were no more light scares at the back of the house – presumably its occupants thought the double hedge/fence barrier would prevent intruders gaining access there – and they reached the rear wall in a matter of seconds. They were both breathing hard and Willem could feel a rush of adrenaline surging in his veins. He was grateful once more for the wind noise masking their movements and heavy breathing.

Feeling Jenny nudging his arm, he looked round to where she was pointing at a small window below ground level.

'Cellar!' she whispered.

Willem watched as Jenny crouched down and crept closer to the window. When she pulled out a penlight he felt a moment of panic, but nothing happened. Jenny shone the light on the window and crouched down to try and see in. A moment later, Willem heard a gasp and he bent double and made his way over to Jenny.

'What is it?' he asked softly.

'Book! Look,' Jenny whispered, shining the torch on the book in the window. Before Willem could react, Jenny was reaching through the bars and tapping on the glass with the torch. 'Amy!' she called softly as she rapped. 'Amy! It's me! Amy, are you in there?'

The pair outside held their breath, listening intently for any sound from inside. Nothing. Jenny tried again. 'Amy!' No response.

Willem tried next, loud-whispering Amy's name and praying for a response. Nothing. When he looked at Jenny, he could see silent tears streaming down her face in the glow of the torchlight. She sounded desperate as she tried one more time, tapping the torch on the glass and calling Amy's name.

Just then, Willem saw out of the corner of his eye a light going on in the room just to their left. He could see it had frosted glass and assumed it was a bathroom or toilet. He touched Jenny's arm, and put a finger to his lips when she looked up at him, frowning as he pointed to the lit room. The pair froze and waited for the light to go off again, which it did soon after the sound of a toilet flushing.

'We need to go,' Willem said quietly, gesturing back the way they had come in. He could tell by the expression on Jenny's face that she didn't want to leave, not when she was so convinced they had found their friend, but he pulled her away. 'We have to go, Jenny, come on. We won't be able to help Amy if we get caught sneaking around here.'

Jenny allowed herself to be led away, but Willem could feel her resistance every step of the way. He didn't bother trying to replace the fence slats, hoping that Barry and Pauline would blame the wind if they noticed. Jenny and Willem didn't speak as they walked back to the main road and to Willem's car. Jenny got into the passenger seat and turned to Willem; he saw tears and snot mingling under her nose. She wiped them away roughly with her sleeve before she spoke.

'She's there! I know she is! Why didn't she answer? For fuck's sake! Why didn't she answer?!' Jenny said, half angry, half scared.

'We don't know that for sure, Jenny,' Willem said, trying to sound calmer than he felt.

'Yes, we bloody do! That book! The book in the window. It was a clue. From Amy,' Jenny insisted.

Willem frowned at her, not understanding.

'It was one of those Agatha Raisin books she hates so much!'

Willem shook his head, still not on Jenny's wavelength.

'Cosy crime!' Jenny exclaimed, throwing her hands up. 'She hates it. She put that book in the window to let me know she was there! Don't you see?!' Willem didn't really see, but Jenny seemed utterly convinced. 'She knew I'd look for her and she found a way of telling me exactly where she was.'

'Okay, so what do we do now?' Willem asked. 'Do we tell the police?'

'What's the point? They'll say we've got no proof. But I know. *I* know. We can't rely on the police,' Jenny shook her head.

Willem pressed his fingers into his tired eyes. 'Well, we can't do any more tonight. Let's go home and try to come up with a plan.'

Jenny agreed reluctantly and Willem spun the car around and drove back to Folkestone.

CHAPTER 41
Yorkshire tea

With their author-in-residence, Pauline and Barry's morning routine had had to adapt somewhat. However, they still began their morning with a cup of tea in bed. Actually, make that beds.

Barry was the morning tea-brewer and woe betide him if he got it wrong. He'd had plenty of training, and practice, over the years though and rarely messed it up now. He'd learned the hard way when Pauline had scalded him with the contents of a mug which were not exactly the correct shade of caramel. Now there was a handy colour chart on the wall in the kitchen with mugs of tea pictured ranging in colour from *Has tha' just milkt cow?* to *That's coffee*. Pauline's preferred tea colour, *Tha knows*, fell between *Ey Up* and *Builder's brew*.

Anyway, the kettle had to be filled with fresh water (Pauline could somehow tell if Barry skipped this step) and the teapot warmed before the teabags (Yorkshire, naturally) were put in. Pauline had only recently succumbed to using teabags, for which Barry was eternally grateful. He'd hated all the faff with loose leaf tea and strainers. Pauline still kept a tin of loose leaf for those occasions when she fancied a bit of reading the tea leaves. Barry thought that was bunkum, but he most certainly never voiced that opinion to his wife.

Once filled, the pot was given a good stir and the teabags a bit of a mash, before the tea-cosy – a garish affair knitted by

Pauline, of course – was popped on. While the tea brewed, Barry selected the morning's mugs. He had a selection of much-loved snooker and darts ones, which he would replace as fast as Pauline could 'accidentally' break them. On this particular morning, Barry's mug read: *One hundred and eight-tea!* and Pauline's: *When I'm sitting, I'm knitting*.

Barry wasn't allowed to take sugar in his tea. He'd risked it once and Pauline had surprised him with a spot check, demanding she taste his tea. He didn't do that again, but every morning he mourned the absence of a sweetener in his breakfast brew. When Pauline was out, he'd have a sneaky mug sometimes, but he was terrified his face would give him away when she came home. She could always tell when he was lying or keeping something from her, and quite frankly, it wasn't worth the risk most of the time. Besides, he knew Pauline only had his best interests at heart. He came from a family of diabetics, after all.

As he waited out the last few seconds of brewing time, Barry stood at the kitchen sink, looking out into the back garden. There had been a stiff wind the previous night and he was alert for fallen trees and the like. He could make out something on the lawn at the back of the garden and, squinting, he saw that there were fence slats down, revealing the hedge behind. Frowning, Barry turned back to the teapot – it wouldn't do to let it stew too long – and poured two mugs before carefully adding a splash of milk to each, not too little, not too much.

Satisfied with the colour of the brew, he padded back upstairs to the bedroom. Pauline was sitting up in one of two single beds, knitting. She looked up as he came in, immediately detecting a look of 'something' on her husband's face.

'What's up, me duck?' she asked, watching as Barry placed

her mug carefully on the coaster on her bedside table, with the handle turned towards Pauline.

'There's a bit o' fence down int garden, at the back there. Just the wind I 'spect,' he said, going back round to his own single bed, putting his mug down, and making to get in under the knitted patchwork bedspread.

One look from his wife stopped him in his tracks. 'I'll go and have a look then, shall I?'

Pauline just huffed and returned to her knitting, as Barry made his way back downstairs, grumbling very quietly to himself.

Pulling on his garden shoes, which lived by the back door, Barry trudged across the back lawn to where the fallen fence lay. There were just a couple of planks lying on the grass, and nothing much else to see. He looked all around, but the rest of the fence was intact, and there were no fallen trees or anything which could have caused the damage. He peered through the gap in the fence to examine the area behind more closely, before heading back indoors, prising his shoes off after wiping them on the mat, and returning to the bedroom.

Pauline looked up. 'Well?'

'Um ...' he began, earning another look from Pauline, 'there are a couple of planks on the lawn. I think maybe the hedge behind's been disturbed too. I can't see how the wind could have brought any of the fence down, it's too sheltered there.'

Pauline nodded. 'Hm ... I see. That's not good, is it?'

Barry shook his head.

'Especially bearing in mind the front security light came on last night,' Pauline continued.

Barry swallowed. He knew what was coming.

'You ruddy well should have gone out last night to investigate, shouldn't you?'

Barry nodded and looked at the floor.

'Couldn't drag your lazy, fat arse out though, could you? What good's peeking round the curtain, eh? I ask you.'

'No good,' Barry apologised, shaking his head.

'I don't know why I put up with you sometimes, Barry Bulmer.'

Although he secretly wished that sometimes she wouldn't put up with him, Barry didn't dare disagree.

'Drink your tea,' Pauline said. 'I've got enough on my plate without dealing with you right now. You can fix the fence later.'

Barry got gratefully back under the covers and took a big slurp of tea. He knew he'd had a lucky escape. 'Yes, my angel.'

'And put another security light up out the back,' Pauline added, as an afterthought.

'Yes, my love.'

Pauline put down her knitting and lifted her mug, pausing with it halfway to her mouth. 'Maybe we should get another dog?'

'Whatever you want, dearest,' Barry nodded, secretly dreading the prospect as he knew full well that he'd be the one left out in the cold if they got a dog.

'Hm ... I'll have a think. We need to do something. Can't have people poking about out there unchecked now, can we?'

Barry didn't bother replying. He knew his opinion wasn't required at this point.

'I bet it was that friend of her downstairs. That madam with the filthy mouth and the pink hair. Jenny. And possibly Wilhelm. Which is a pity. I like Wilhelm.'

Pauline was quiet for a few moments, lost in thought as she sipped her tea.

'Well, it won't be a problem much longer, will it? My story's almost finished, and then we just have to get rid of Little Miss Nosy Parker downstairs. Then they can snoop all they like, can't they? Because there won't be anything left to see.'

Barry looked over at his wife. She had a self-satisfied smile on her face, and he knew he'd be a fool to say anything to disagree with her, but ... well, he'd grown rather fond of Amy.

'I s'pose there's no other ...' he began.

Pauline looked round and glared at him. 'If you're about to say what I think you are, Barry Bulmer, then you can jolly well stop right there!'

Barry stared into his mug. *What had he been thinking?*

'Of course there's no other way! For goodness' sake! What? Did you think she'd just live in the cellar forever? Got a soft spot for her, have we? We both know it couldn't be a *hard* spot, could it now? Pathetic!' Pauline said spitefully, sneering at her husband.

Barry didn't say another word. He finished his tea to the angry clacking of knitting needles, and then got up to begin his chores for the day, the next one being to take Amy her breakfast.

CHAPTER 42

A bad feeling

When Amy awoke in the cellar the next morning, Thursday, she found she'd pulled the covers up over her head, probably to combat the cold. Pushing them away from her face, she lay looking up at the ceiling, trying to recapture the thread of a dream she'd been having. She rarely remembered her dreams – often thinking it was probably just as well – but this one's tail was just within grasp as she opened her eyes. Someone had been knocking on a door, or a window, but she couldn't grab the dream before it slunk away, a nocturnal creature afraid of the daylight. Not that there was much daylight in Amy's prison cell. She exhaled with frustration before getting stiffly up and using the vile toilet. She didn't know what time it was, but her inner clock was telling her that breakfast would be on its way soon, followed presumably by more typing. Her heart sank at the prospect of both.

When Barry came down with Amy's breakfast, he seemed a little distracted. *Definitely not his usual jovial self,* Amy thought, and she wondered if something was wrong.

'Is everything okay, Barry?' she asked, as he set down the tray, wobbling a bit and spilling a little tea from the plastic mug.

'Nothing for you to worry your pretty head about, Amy lass,' he said.

But she was worried. Something had changed. And Amy was pretty sure it was something she *should* worry about.

At her house, Jenny was slumped at her kitchen table, half-heartedly prodding with a spoon at a rapidly solidifying bowl of porridge which she simply couldn't eat. Just the thought of swallowing food made her feel sick to her stomach. She was saved any further thoughts of breakfast by the sound of the doorbell, and she hurried to answer it.

'Morning, Jenny,' Willem said, when she opened the door.

'Morning,' Jenny sighed, her usual insults notable by their absence.

'Can't eat?' Willem asked, when he saw the uneaten oats. 'Me neither. Did you manage to get some sleep?'

Jenny just shook her head.

'Me neither,' Willem said again.

'I can't stop thinking of Amy locked in that cellar. I can't bear it! I just don't know what to do.'

'We don't know for sure that she *is* there, not really,' Willem said gently.

'You might not,' Jenny said, 'but I do. That book wasn't there by accident. I know Amy. I know her ...' Her eyes dropped to the floor to hide the tears that were threatening again.

'Okay, okay,' Willem said, holding up his hands. He didn't want to further antagonise Jenny. 'Anyway, I've had an idea.'

Jenny's eyes flicked up at him. 'What? Tell me!'

'Well, we need to go back to the house, right? But it needs to be when we know there's nobody home.'

'How the hell are we going to know that?' Jenny interrupted.

Willem calmed her with his hands: 'I'm going to put up a camera. I've got a trail camera that I can set up on a tree opposite the entrance. I can monitor it from anywhere and see when they go out. Then I go in.'

'*We* go in, you mean,' Jenny said firmly. 'You're not doing this without me.'

'Okay, *we* go in,' Willem relented. 'It means we'll have to be together somewhere close by … we'll need to be able to act quickly.'

'I can do that,' Jenny nodded, ignoring the images of her cats which flashed into her head. They'd be fine – she'd just put extra food down and another litter tray.

'Okay. I'll put the camera up tonight …' Willem began. He saw the look of impatience on Jenny's face: 'I can't do it in daylight, Jenny, it's just not possible.'

Jenny sighed and nodded.

'Okay, that's the plan then. I'll find a good place to park up and monitor the camera, and pick you up first thing tomorrow. Eight-ish?'

Jenny nodded once more. She didn't know how she was going to get through another day. It suddenly dawned on her that it was Thursday, Amy's usual day in the shop. 'Do you think Pauline's covering the shop today?' she asked.

'What? Oh, it's Amy's day, isn't it? I don't know. Let me ask Finn. A quick call to Finn revealed that Pauline had messaged him to say she wasn't available to cover Amy's shift in the event she was still poorly.

'Bugger,' Jenny said. 'I reckon we could take Barry, but Pauline scares the shit out of me. If she'd been at the shop …'

Willem shook his head. 'We can't do anything reckless. We have no idea what we'd find in the house. They could be armed … or they could hurt Amy … Anyway, I need to go and do some work. I'll see you tomorrow morning.'

Jenny nodded and Willem left. It was going to be a long day.

In the cellar, Amy had started work again, ignoring the unhappy noises and griping pains coming from her insides. Just the sound of Pauline's voice on the tape made her feel sick, without a stomach full of wheat. Was it her imagination or was Pauline's voice getting more animated with every gruesome tale she recorded? She sounded as though she was working up to a crescendo, and Amy was seriously worried that she knew what that crescendo would be. Shaking the terrifying thought away, Amy tried to focus on Pauline's words so she could type up the next chapter of the madwoman's murderous life story.

Now, where was I? I'd just despatched Jack, hadn't I? Jack was such a thrill. I wasn't sure what to do after Jack … Who else was worthy of my attention? I'd taken out the Scrambled Eggheads - I'm sure there are some jokes you can make about them, Amy; use your clever way with words, won't you? You must be able to say something about them being beaten, ha ha! Well, I mustn't do your work for you, you're the expert. I know you won't let me down. Then of course the Saga Crews team sailed off into the sunset … Oh, there I go again! Ha ha! Forever Jung didn't survive the loss of Norm, did they? Not with him forever dead!

Of course, the next team to draw my attention had to be the Drinking Team. They were the last hurdle to be overcome to leave the way clear for my team to win. Now Amy, the prospect of making any of those lovely young people a target was not a happy one. A delightfully bright and funny bunch, especially young Jon with all his cheeky banter. I really felt quite motherly towards him.

Amy paused briefly, allowing a memory of Jon winding up Kev on a Friday night to surface. How could this evil, evil woman talk about feeling motherly about him, and then kill him just so her team could win a pub quiz? Amy took a deep breath and continued.

```
Well, you could have knocked me down with a feather
when I heard that Jon had died!
```

What? Amy hit rewind. Had she heard that right? She couldn't make sense of what she was hearing. Had Pauline not been responsible for Jon's death after all?

```
That beautiful young man, taken far too soon. Such
a loss, a real tragedy. I was upset, Amy, really I
was. But then I thought, well it saves me a job! I
didn't find out about his epilepsy and that he died
of a fit until a few days ago. I gave myself a slap
on the wrist for thinking it must have had something
to do with drugs. One shouldn't make assumptions about
people, eh, Amy? Just because he had that long hair
and wore those flip-flops all the time.
  I started to think it must have been a reward for
all my hard work clearing the way for our teams, Amy.
What do you think?
```

'I think you're an abomination,' Amy muttered.

I thought I could have a little breather then. Enjoy the fruits of my labours for a while. But then Barry had to go and spoil it, didn't he, saying mightn't people get suspicious with all those brilliant quizzers dying unexpectedly, but nobody dying in our team when we started winning. Well, I thought, he might just be right. But what to do? How to stop people picking up on my scent – which is Tweed by the way, Amy, in case you were wondering (more cackling laughter). Well, of course I knew what had to be done: a member of my team had to die.

It wasn't a difficult choice, to be frank. Esme got on my last nerve. She was another one who could have worn her tonsils as earrings. These arty types, Amy, pretentious so-and-sos if you ask me. She didn't bring much to the team anyway, besides too much perfume and that simpering laugh of hers. Always flirting with my Barry, she was, too. Well, we'll see about that, I thought.

While Amy couldn't imagine anyone flirting with Barry, she still didn't think it warranted a death sentence.

Well now, I didn't have the time, or the energy quite frankly, to plan another execution, as I like to call it. I'm not getting any younger, you know, Amy, and these things take it out of you. So, I asked Barry to find an old banger – ask no questions is my motto where that's concerned – and then got him to ask Esme (another old banger … oh, that's funny!)

to meet him one evening, out in the country. Silly cow thought he was interested in her. 'Oh! Barry! Be still my beating heart! I thought you'd never ask!' He got her to drive out into the countryside to meet him. Well, he wasn't too fussed when I mowed her down, I can promise you that. Checked she was a goner and then we took off, me driving our car and Barry the old banger (oh, there I go again! Ha ha!). All the police would find was a burnt-out shell of a car on an old industrial estate near Ashford. Oh, and a beaten-up old wreck on a country lane! (I mean Esme, of course, Amy, in case you didn't get the joke. I have to say this writing lark isn't rocket science, is it? A half-decent brain and a sense of humour and you're halfway there. To be perfectly honest, Amy, you're just a glorified typist now, aren't you. Minus the glorified – Barry says you're causing quite a stink down there.) Anyway, back to my story … it's easy enough to avoid cameras if you know the back roads. After we'd set fire to the car – which was quite exciting I have to say – we drove home together and had a nice cuppa to celebrate a job well done. It was rather lovely being able to involve Barry a bit more. I know he can feel a bit left out. Well, now he knows how I feel about darts and snooker! But we are a team after all! And a jolly good one too, I think you'll agree.

Amy pressed pause on the Dictaphone. Her heart was beating out of her chest. She was too scared to listen to whatever came next. Esme had been the last person to die – as far as she was aware anyway – and there would be no more reason for Pauline to keep her alive. Following swiftly on from that thought came another, equally terrifying: what if Pauline had murdered someone from Stoned Folke while she'd been locked in the cellar? She made it over to the toilet just in time to vomit her stomach contents into it. When she stood up, wiping her mouth on the back of her hand, Amy was trembling and could feel hot tears on her cheeks. The thought that Jenny or Willem had become Pauline's latest victim was more than she could bear, and she realised she would gladly give her life if it meant they could live. Taking a deep breath, Amy pressed play and listened:

```
Well now, I think that brings us right up to date,
doesn't it? I'll give you a bit more time to make
sure my story's the best it can be, and then it will
be your turn. Isn't that exciting, Amy?! I suppose
I'll have to write that chapter myself, won't I?
Killing you really will be two birds with one stone:
remove the meddling writer and a strong quizzer all
at once. Couldn't be better, eh? I'm not certain who
the strongest member of your team is, if I'm honest,
but you happen to be the one locked in my cellar, so
it's more a matter of convenience than anything. I'm
actually quite fond of Wilhelm and young Finn, but I
wouldn't have minded finishing off that vulgar madam
with the pink hair, Jenny isn't it? Someone should
wash her mouth out with soap.
```

The tape ended then, and Amy sobbed with relief to realise that her friends were okay. Closing her eyes, she tried to slow her breathing and steady her shaking hands. She almost felt a sense of peace, of acceptance, wash over her. As terrifying as the thought of dying was, Amy was willing to sacrifice herself for her friends if necessary.

CHAPTER 43

The end is nigh

At a little after eight the following morning, Jenny and Willem were heading out of town in Willem's car. He'd set up the trail camera opposite Pauline and Barry's house during the night, and was confident it was well camouflaged amongst the ivy on the well-established sycamore tree. After finding a good spot to park within the camera's range, but hidden from the main road, he'd fired up his laptop and made sure the camera was working okay. Willem heaved a sigh of relief when a view of the house loaded onto his screen. It was dark, of course, but he was counting on being there in daylight to capture the couple going out. His main worry was that Barry and Pauline wouldn't go out together anymore. They could well be on high alert and extra vigilant after his and Jenny's night-time incursion. He knew breaking the garden fence had been a bit of a risk and they might suspect intruders. All the same, it felt good to be doing something proactive.

Jenny had been unusually quiet on the drive out to Capel. Willem could sense the tension in her, and feel her anxiety.

'You doing okay, Jenny?' he asked, when they'd parked up and were staring at the screen with its view of the house opposite.

'Yeah,' Jenny sighed. 'Well, I'm hanging in there at least.'

'I know,' Willem said gently. 'It's hard to stay positive, hopeful, but we have to try.'

Jenny nodded. 'I've been trying to think of ways to get them out of the house, but I haven't got very far.'

'I hadn't thought of that. You might be onto something.'

'Hm ... dunno ... I thought about saying there was a gas leak or something. You know, pretend we're calling from British Gas and say they have to vacate the premises.'

Willem was unconvinced. 'They probably wouldn't go far though – if they even fell for it. Pauline's pretty sharp too. I reckon she'd want to see a gas engineer with an ID badge before she'd believe that.'

Jenny didn't respond immediately. She closed her eyes for a moment. When she opened them, she said: 'What about a fire? We could start a fire.'

Willem considered it briefly. 'I don't think that's a good idea. It could put Amy at risk,' he said, before adding, 'If she's even in there.'

'She is,' Jenny said firmly.

They went quiet again after that and settled down to watch.

In the cellar, Amy was grimacing as she drank that morning's cup of milky tea and wondering if she could face the toast. She would have killed for a decent coffee and some bacon and eggs. Barry had seemed quiet again when he'd brought her tray, definitely not his usual larger-than-life self. He'd just shaken his head when Amy had asked again if something was troubling him.

'Out of my hands, young Amy,' he'd said. He sniffed the air. 'Doesn't smell too good in here. Still, you won't be in here much longer, eh? I'll be back for your tray shortly. Eat up. I expect Pauline will be down to see you later. She's just got to pop to Homebase first thing for a couple of bits. Said I'd go, but she likes to do these things herself. Says I'll only get the wrong thing. She's probably right. Usually is,' he smiled, rather sadly. Before locking her in once more, Barry gave a blast of air freshener into the room. 'There you go, lass, that's a bit better, isn't it?'

As Amy squeezed her nostrils shut and tried not to inhale the awful floral cloud, she was thinking about Pauline's trip to a DIY store and had visions of rope, and plastic sheeting, and a spade. Terror gripped her once more, and she gave up any pretence of eating the toast and finishing the tea. The condemned woman most certainly did not eat a hearty meal.

Back in Willem's car, he and Jenny had sat up sharply at the sight of Pauline's silver Skoda pulling out of the drive.

'Oh my God, oh my God! Look!' Jenny screeched in Willem's ear, pointing at the screen as the car nosed out between the hedges.

'Yes, I can see, thanks, Jenny,' Willem said. 'Although I can't hear very well in my left ear now, thank you,' he muttered.

'Damn it!' Jenny exclaimed, when they saw that there was only a driver in the car. 'Why couldn't they both go out?'

Willem was squinting at the screen. 'I think that was Pauline.'

Jenny exhaled, feeling deflated. 'You don't think Barry's lying down on the back seat, do you? Or in the boot?'

'What?! No, Jenny, I don't think either of those things,' Willem declared incredulously.

'We could take Barry. Can't we go and knock on the door?'

'What, and say we were just passing and thought we'd pop in for a cuppa?'

'No, just whack him on the head with something, and rescue Amy.'

Willem shook his head.

Jenny sighed but said no more.

Amy had heard the engine start and the car leave, and assumed it was Pauline heading for Homebase. She was wondering if she had the strength, and the courage, to tackle Barry when he returned for her tray. This might be her only, her last, chance but she felt weak and exhausted, and seriously afraid that she wouldn't be able to overpower him. She didn't have the word processor in the room to bash him with, and there was no way she could inflict any real damage with a plastic plate and mug. Looking around the cellar, she took in the few objects in the room. Glancing up at the window, she saw the *Agatha Raisin* book but, while the idea of beating Barry around the head with the cosy-crime novel was appealing, it was a non-starter. She didn't think she had the strength to wield the chemical toilet. So far, the tray was looking the most hopeful, Amy thought, holding it with both hands and giving it a good swing. The trouble was, of course, that Barry always had the Taser ready to strike. She needed something she could wield from a bit further away.

Turning her attention to the chair, Amy crouched down to examine it more closely, thinking she might be able to break off a leg to use as a weapon. That's when she saw it: the can of air freshener! Barry had left it on her side of the door! Her heart skipped a beat, and the thought that he'd done it deliberately flashed into her mind, but she dismissed it just as quickly. Even if he didn't agree with Pauline's plans to kill Amy, he'd never go against his wife. More than his life was worth, Amy was sure. So, she could only assume that he'd been so distracted he'd done it by accident.

Grabbing the aerosol, Amy returned to her bed and sat on its edge. She waited. And she listened. And she tried to remember to breathe.

In the car, Jenny stifled a yawn and stretched, narrowly missing Willem's face with her outstretched arm.

'Urgh, do you mind,' he said, pushing her arm away.

Jenny wriggled uncomfortably in her seat. 'I can't bear just sitting here waiting,' she moaned.

'Well, what would you suggest?'

'Grab the wheel-nut-removing-thingy, drive up to the house, ring the bell, and whack Barry. Hard. Simples,' Jenny said.

'Wrench,' Willem said.

'What?'

'Wrench. It's called a wrench. The wheel-nut-removing-thingy.'

'I don't care if it's called Patricia. You've got one, haven't you?'

'Yes, of course. But we're not doing that.'

'I'm perfectly happy to do it on my own then. Where is it? The wrench.'

Willem ignored her. She huffed a bit and then fell silent once more.

CHAPTER 44

Run!

While Amy and Jenny were thinking about suitable objects with which to bash Barry on the head, Pauline was pushing a trolley up and down the aisles in Homebase, humming to herself. If anyone of a certain age had got close enough to hear her, they might have recognised the tune as one of Engelbert Humperdinck's finest.

She was smiling to herself as she perused the plastic-sheeting options: 'This could be your song, Amy, eh? Please release me, let me go ...' she sang, before chuckling. Pauline was delighted to spot a plastic drop sheet reduced from fourteen pounds fifty to just eight pounds. 'Ooh! I do love a bargain. You can take the girl out of Yorkshire ...' she said, as she threw the packet into the trolley, before continuing down the aisle.

She hadn't decided how she was going to deal with Amy yet, and wandered around the store looking for inspiration. She had so enjoyed the up-close-and-personal way the old drunk, Jack, had been handled, but Pauline was sensible enough to realise the risks inherent in attempting to end Amy's life at close quarters. Amy was a caged animal and would undoubtedly fight back, all teeth and claws. Of course, they could Taser her, but where was the satisfaction in sinking a knife into the flesh of an inert body? No, that wouldn't do at all.

Pauline continued her circuit of the DIY store, occasionally stopping to pick up a tool, hefting it in her hands before continuing on. She was sticking with Engelbert and now quietly humming 'Spanish Eyes', thinking a trip to Spain was long overdue, and very much deserved, for her and Barry. Be nice to get out of chilly old England for a couple of weeks. Let the hoo-hah of the dead author die down too.

In the cellar, Amy was sitting on the camp bed, gripping onto the air freshener and listening intently for the sounds of Barry's footsteps on the stairs. She'd thought about lying on the floor and pretending to have passed out, thinking Barry would be caught off-guard and, when he bent over to check on her, she could simply blast the spray into his eyes. She decided there were too many variables in that scenario – what if he collapsed on her or grabbed at her? No, she needed to be on her feet and ready to fight, and run.

'Come on, come on,' she muttered, in fear and frustration. She was praying that Barry appeared before Pauline got back. There was no way she could take them both on. Pauline terrified her.

Thankfully it wasn't too long before Amy's ears detected the creak of the stair tread she'd grown accustomed to hearing when one of her captors came down to the cellar. She pulled the neck of her jumper up over her mouth and nose and held her breath as she got to her feet and took up position just to the side of the door, leaning back into the shadowy corner. She was planning to hit Barry in the face with the spray the instant he opened the door, hopefully before he had time to register her presence. He was used to her being docile and compliant, so she was counting on it being a total surprise attack.

Amy's plan worked perfectly. She heard herself yell as she

depressed the top of the aerosol and saw the spray hit Barry squarely in the eyes. She didn't hang around to watch as he dropped the Taser, flinging his hands up to his face, screaming as he clawed at his eyes, coughing.

Amy's heart was in her mouth as she pounded up the stairs where, mercifully, the cellar door was standing open. She hadn't let herself consider what she would do if Barry had had the foresight to lock it behind him. The surge of adrenaline which was powering through her gave Amy the strength to run in spite of her weakened state, and she wasted no time in getting out of the house. Luck was on her side again, thankfully, and the key was in the back door.

Standing in the back garden, Amy looked all around, trying to get her bearings, and in a matter of seconds she was out onto the lane, running as fast as her legs could carry her, panicked sobs escaping her throat. *Run, Amy, run!* her brain was screaming at her.

Amy was soon on Winehouse Lane and heading towards the main road, ignoring the screaming in her leg muscles and her chest. *Just keep going! Just keep going!*

In the car, about half a mile away, Willem and Jenny had just witnessed Amy's escape.

'Oh my God! Amy! It's Amy,' Jenny cried, jabbing at the screen. She yelled at Willem to start the engine. Only with more expletives.

Fumbling with the keys, Willem's hands were shaking as he finally managed to start the car, shoving the laptop at Jenny who was beside herself beside him.

'Come on, come on,' she screeched.

Willem yelled back at Jenny as he crunched the gears, wondering momentarily if he was having a heart attack, as he tried to calm his breathing and trembling sufficiently to function. Finally, the car was in first and Willem pulled out and set off towards Winehouse Lane.

Back in the cellar, Barry was in a sorry state, his eyes red and streaming, his vision blurry. He knew he had to get Amy back before Pauline got home. The consequences of not doing so didn't bear thinking about. He shuddered as he recalled the episode involving a dog kennel, bowl and chain included, when he'd last incurred his wife's wrath. And that time he'd only walked mud through the house: 'Behave like a dog, you get treated like one.' Imagine what she'd do to him if he lost Amy.

Barry made it up to the kitchen and paused only long enough to splash his face with cold water at the sink, before he too was out and running. He wasn't built for running. 'Built for comfort, not for speed,' Pauline used to tell him. But the fear of his wife's displeasure was incentive enough, and Barry puffed out of the drive and in the direction of the lane which led to the main road, hoping he was correct in assuming Amy would head in that direction. He could hear Pauline's voice in his head as he ran: 'To assume makes an ass of u and me.' But he assumed, and he ran. As he rounded the bend, he was relieved to see Amy on the road ahead, some distance in front but at least he was going in the right direction, and he kept on going, red in the face and wondering if he was having a heart attack.

Pauline was almost at the turn into Winehouse Lane, merrily

singing, and happily contemplating ways to kill Amy. Just as she flicked the indicator for the left turn, Amy came charging out onto the main road, straight into the path of Pauline's car. Pauline automatically slammed on the brakes, and managed to stop just before she hit the other woman. She heard Amy scream and their eyes met across the bonnet, where Amy's hands now rested. Amy looked like a crazy person, eyes wide and filled with hatred and fear, her unwashed hair clinging to her face, which was now flushed with exertion, chest heaving and breath ragged.

Before Pauline had the chance to wonder why she hadn't just kept driving and slammed into her, Amy was off and running again, straight over the main road and heading for the cliffs.

Just as Pauline was waiting for the opportunity to make the turn in the car and follow Amy, Barry came staggering out of the lane, his face even redder than Amy's.

'Get in the car!' Pauline screamed, leaning across and opening the passenger door.

Barry collapsed into the seat and slammed the car door, and Pauline indicated right and made the turn.

'I'm sorry, she ...' he began, barely able to get the words out and clutching his chest. He really thought he was having a heart attack now.

Pauline grimaced but said nothing and just kept on driving. Ahead of them, Amy had reached the vegetation which topped the length of the cliffs, a jumble of trees and tangled undergrowth, and was showing no signs of stopping. Pauline looked for a place to abandon the car, tugged at her seatbelt and was out of the car, ready to set off in pursuit. Barry just sat in the car, puffing and gasping.

'What are you waiting for, you great oaf?' Pauline shrieked at him. 'Come on! We've got to stop her! Unless you want to go to prison for kidnap and murder? Come on!'

Barry groaned. 'I can't …' he wheezed. 'I … my chest …' But one look at his wife's face, and Barry tumbled out of the passenger side with a groan, following Pauline into the undergrowth.

Amy was panicking and second-guessing herself. Should she have stayed on the main road and flagged someone down? She'd thought in the split second she had to make a decision that there would be more places to hide along the cliffs. But now Pauline and Barry were right behind her and she didn't know what to do.

Amy wasn't to know that had she stayed on the main road and tried to flag down a car, that car would have been Willem's, as he and Jenny had been approaching from the opposite direction to Pauline and had missed witnessing the near collision by a matter of seconds. They were, however, close enough to the junction to see Barry appear out of the lane and get into the silver Skoda before it turned right towards the cliffs.

'There, there!' Jenny pointed, screaming in his ear again.

Willem resisted the urge to scream back at her, took a deep breath and followed the route taken by the Skoda.

Arriving at the end of the lane, they immediately spotted Pauline's car parked halfway up a bank, and Willem pulled his car in behind it. Jenny was out before he'd even turned off the engine.

'Jenny! Wait,' he called after her.

'What? Come on, come on!' she exclaimed.

'Jenny, just stop a sec. Think!'

Jenny stopped, in spite of her instinct to just run, and glared at him. 'We have to go after her!' she cried.

'I know. We will. But think ... We're right by the cliff edge here. It's chalky and pretty unstable in places – I've walked along here with the camera enough times to know you have to be really careful.'

'Sod careful! It's Amy!'

Willem closed his eyes for a moment. 'If we go rushing in, and they've caught up with Amy first, what do you think they're going to do?'

Jenny said nothing.

'If they're too close to the edge, they could ...' Willem began.

A sob escaped Jenny's mouth and she pressed both hands into her face as the realisation dawned on her.

'What do we do then?' she asked, wiping tears away.

'We go quietly and we ... I don't know ... we pray we find her first ...'

'Christ, this is a nightmare,' Jenny said.

'Try and think positive. She's alive, Jenny,' Willem said softly, smiling with more optimism than he felt.

Jenny smiled bravely and nodded.

'Let's go and get her then,' Willem said, and the pair walked up the low bank and onto the grassland. The area between the road and the cliffs had plenty of places to hide, but it was only about forty feet from the cliff edge.

'Should we split up?' Jenny asked after they'd gone only a few feet.

Willem paused to think about her suggestion. 'Good idea,' he nodded. 'Double envelopment.'

Jenny screwed her face up. 'What?'

'Sorry, pincer movement,' Willem said.

'Bloody hell, don't go all sodding Special Forces on me again,' Jenny groaned. 'You go left, I'll go right, meet you in the middle. How about that?'

'That's what I said,' Willem hissed, thinking for about the hundredth time that day what a pain in the arse she was.

Jenny just pulled a face and set off to the left.

Willem shook his head and turned in the opposite direction.

Neither had gone far and they were still in sight of one another when they heard voices ahead of them. Willem managed to get Jenny's attention and they crept back to the middle again.

'They must be very close to the cliff edge,' Willem whispered. 'We need to be really careful not to spook anyone.' He thought for a moment and sighed. 'I think the best thing to do is make our way round as we were, but keep low and don't give yourself away.'

'Then what?' Jenny asked. She looked terrified, and Willem reminded himself that Jenny loved Amy too, however annoying she was.

'Then I think we just have to play it by ear a bit. See what the lay of the land is, where they're standing ...'

'It's not much of a plan,' Jenny said.

'Well, what would you suggest? We can't just go charging in, Jenny. Not this close to the edge of the cliff.'

'Amy hates heights,' Jenny said, her voice wobbling.

'I know. Look, just keep your eyes on me and I'll give you a signal ...'

'Don't go all—' Jenny began.

Willem held his hand up to silence her. 'If I hold my hand

up like this, that means stay down. If I do this,' Willem made a thumbs-up hand and gestured with his thumb, 'that means I need you to cause a distraction, draw their attention over to you. Okay?'

Jenny nodded. 'How should I do that?'

'Doesn't matter. Anything. Just get them to look your way.'

'What are you going to be doing?'

'Trying to get to Amy before she goes over the cliff,' Willem said grimly.

Jenny swallowed, but nodded her understanding and the pair separated once again.

They'd only gone a few paces when they heard the screams: one low pitched and one high. That was enough for the pair and they ran full pelt to the origin of the screams.

CHAPTER 45

Bye bye, Barry

'One down, one to go,' Pauline grinned evilly at Amy.

The pair were standing at the edge of the cliff, and Amy had just witnessed Pauline push her husband over the edge, where he had surely fallen to his death, his screams fading as he fell. Amy had seen the look of shocked surprise and disbelief as he'd fallen backwards after Pauline shoved him hard in the chest with both hands. He'd seemed to hang in the air, floundering for what seemed like an age, but could only have been a second, before he dropped.

Amy had heard herself scream and was shaking like a beaten dog. If she had been thinking clearly, she would have run – she could easily outrun Pauline – but she was frozen in shock and fear. Her brain simply couldn't compute. Finally, she managed to squeeze out a single word: 'Why?'

Pauline put her hands together in prayer position and began to speak. 'Oh, officer, thank goodness you're here! It was so awful! It was him, Barry, my husband ... I tried to stop him, but I was so scared of him. He kidnapped this poor woman! I set her free and we ran, we ran for our lives, but he followed us ...' Pause for theatrics and fake tears. 'And then he grabbed hold of poor, dear Amy ... and they struggled and ... oh my God ... it was so terrible ... they both went over the cliff! Oh, officer!' Pauline stopped speaking, grinning at a stunned Amy. 'What do you think? Should have been an actress, eh? I'll tell them it was all Barry, that he was controlling and abusive and I feared for my life every day. But that taking you was the last straw. I couldn't have him hurting someone else, could I? Blah blah blah, as they wrap me in an emergency blanket and take me off for a nice cup of tea and a biscuit.'

'You crazy bitch,' Amy said, shaking her head in horror and disbelief.

'Now, now, Amy, there's no need for vulgarity. Don't be like that foul-mouthed friend of yours, her with the pink hair. Filthy mouth she has on her, that one.'

That was when Amy struck. She flew at Pauline, grabbing her shoulders and trying to spin her towards the cliff edge. 'Don't ... diss ... my ... friend,' she said through gritted teeth, as she tried to summon the strength to overwhelm Pauline. But the older woman was shorter and squatter than Amy, and surprisingly strong. Just as her strength was fading, Amy dredged up one last ounce of energy and shoved. Pauline began to lose her footing on the chalky ground and she stumbled backwards. Amy let go momentarily, and then reached out and shoved once more.

As Pauline fell, she scrabbled with her hands and managed to grab hold of Amy's ankle. Amy went down and screamed as she was dragged towards the edge. She tried to grab at something herself, but her hands were met only by grass, which came away in clumps in her fingers. She knew she was going to die. Pauline was simply too heavy. Images of Jenny, and of Willem, flashed into her mind. *Not like this! Please, God, not like this. I'm not ready! Jenny needs me, and I need to tell Willem how I really feel!* It felt to Amy as though everything was moving in a horrible sort of slow motion, but it could only have been milliseconds.

She kicked out and grabbed with her hands, but to no avail.

Then, suddenly, two pairs of hands grabbed hold of hers and she heard Jenny's and Willem's voices saying her name.

'Amy! Amy, you're safe, we've got you, we've got you!' Jenny cried.

'We've got you, Amy,' Willem repeated.

As they pulled her back to safety, Amy felt Pauline's hands let go of her ankle, and she scrabbled herself back and into a seated position, sobbing as she fell into Jenny's arms. Willem wrapped his arms around them both, shushing Amy as her breathing began to return to normal, and the three of them stayed like that for a moment or two

It was only when Willem stood up and peered over the edge of the cliff that he realised Pauline was still hanging on. She'd managed to dig her fingers into the chalky dirt and wrap the fingers of one hand around a root. Her face was purple and she was gasping like a fish out of water as the strain took its toll.

When she saw him looking down at her, she found the strength to squeeze out a few words: 'Should have killed the bitch days ago!' she spat.

Willem didn't hesitate. He reached out with his right foot and stamped on Pauline's hand as hard as he could. Then he stamped on her other hand. It took a couple of good stomps, but it did the trick. Pauline didn't scream as she fell to the rocks below, almost as if she didn't want to give Willem the satisfaction.

Turning away from the cliff edge, Willem looked at the two friends, Jenny's arms still wrapped around a trembling Amy. Both were looking at him wide-eyed.

'Holy shit,' Jenny said, finally.

Willem just raised his eyebrows, stepped over to the two friends and reached a hand down to Amy.

'Come on, let's get you to the hospital,' he said, scooping her into his arms as though she weighed nothing.

Amy started to wriggle and protest. 'No, I'm fine, I don't need to go …'

'For once I agree with Willem,' Jenny said. 'You need to get checked out, Amy.'

'But …' Amy tried again.

'No buts, Amy,' Willem growled, turning towards the road.

The three friends made their way slowly back to the car. Jenny insisted on sitting in the back with Amy, holding Amy's frozen hands in hers as Willem drove them back into Folkestone and to the Royal Victoria Hospital. Dropping them right at the front door, Willem said he'd find a parking space and then come and find them in the urgent treatment centre.

Jenny dealt with the receptionist and found seats in the waiting area. Amy had gone very quiet and was shaking badly. When Willem reappeared a few minutes later, he asked for a blanket to wrap around Amy, who had clearly gone into shock.

Unbeknownst to the two women, he had phoned the police from the car and been told that someone would come to the hospital to speak to them. Neither Amy nor Jenny had mentioned what had happened with Pauline, and he needed to make sure they all said the same thing to the police. Looking at Amy, he wasn't convinced she could take any instructions on board, not with the state she was in.

'Jenny, can I have a quick word,' he asked quietly, nodding to the other side of the waiting area, where they wouldn't be overheard.

Jenny could tell by the serious tone that now was not the time to refuse Willem, so she gave Amy's shoulders a squeeze. 'Won't be a minute. Okay?'

Amy looked scared, but she nodded, and Jenny followed Willem.

'Look, Amy's obviously in no state to speak to the police right now, but we can't put it off. Someone will be here to talk to us soon and I need to know that we're in agreement. Pauline pushed Barry over, and then slipped and fell trying to do the same to Amy. Yes?' Willem looked Jenny straight in the eyes.

Jenny didn't respond immediately as she took in what Willem had said. Realising she didn't have a problem with it, she agreed. 'I don't know what Amy's going to say though. I don't know if she even realises what happened.'

'I know,' Willem said, through gritted teeth. 'Hopefully, we can say she's confused and not in a fit state to answer their questions today. Give them the gist of what's happened for now.'

Jenny nodded. 'Presumably there'll be evidence at the house of what's been going on, you know, to back up Amy's story.'

'I'm happy to take the police to the house, if you can stay with Amy?' Willem said.

'Of course. I'm not leaving her side, not for a minute,' Jenny said, glancing over at her friend. 'She can stay with me for as long as it takes. I can't begin to imagine what she's been through. Those fuckers!'

'I know, Jenny, I know. But we've got her, and she's going to be fine. She's strong, and we'll get her through this.'

Jenny nodded again. Willem squeezed her arm, and they walked back to Amy, sitting themselves either side of her. Willem put his arm around Amy's shoulders, and Jenny held her hand, as they waited to be seen. Jenny glared at anyone who dared to look in their direction. Amy looked dreadful, and smelled worse, but Jenny was ready to do battle with anyone who even looked at her friend in the wrong way.

Amy's trembling had eased a little by the time her name was called by the triage nurse. Jenny insisted on going into the cubicle with her, leaving Willem in the waiting room. He didn't object. He knew it was more appropriate for Jenny to go with her friend.

Willem didn't have long to wait. The door to the triage area opened a few short minutes later, and Jenny beckoned to him. The nurse had put Amy in a private room after hearing what had gone on. She had taken some details and assessed Amy's immediate health condition before leaving them, informing them that a doctor would be in to see them as soon as possible. Willem alerted the nurse to the imminent arrival of the police, and she said she would inform security and the receptionist to expect them.

'Can she have a drink?' Jenny had asked the nurse as she was about to leave them.

The nurse nodded and left them alone.

'Tea then,' Willem had said, glad to be able to do something useful. It was breaking his heart seeing Amy like that. If Pauline and Barry weren't already lying at the bottom of the cliff, he would have killed them.

'No sugar for me,' Jenny said, pulling a face as she recalled the number of times she'd been given sweet tea for shock in the past couple of years.

CHAPTER 46
Clean

The doctor arrived at the same time as two police officers, one of whom was a woman. The doctor shooed them all out while he examined Amy, who was now lying on a gurney. Jenny had refused to leave Amy's side, and glared mutinously at the doctor when he asked her to wait outside. Amy, speaking for the first time, had asked that her friend stay and the doctor had relented. Clearly, Jenny's reputation had preceded her. Or it might have been the look on her face.

When the doctor declared that Amy was dehydrated and malnourished, but basically okay, the police were allowed back in. Willem pushed in behind them; he was not going to be excluded, and was determined to protect Amy if the questions upset her too much. Willem needn't have worried as the doctor immediately told the police that Amy was still in shock and shouldn't be distressed.

Jenny sat next to Amy, and Willem stood to attention at the foot of the bed with his arms folded, a stern expression on his craggy face. Jenny couldn't help thinking he'd gone all Special Forces again, and would probably tackle anyone to the ground if they upset Amy.

As it turned out, they couldn't get much more than gibberish out of Amy, who began to sob as soon as she started to recall what had happened to her. Jenny and Willem filled in what little they knew, and Willem explained what had happened at the cliffs. He looked at Jenny for back-up as he recounted how Pauline had slipped and fallen in the life-and-death tussle with Amy, and she didn't let him down.

'I can take you to the exact spot they fell from, and to the house,' Willem told the officers.

'That won't be necessary, sir. If you just give us directions to the site and the property, we'll do the rest.'

Willem opened Google Maps on his phone and pinpointed Pauline's house and the area of the cliffs at the far end of Winehouse Lane. He also told them that the silver Skoda parked there belonged to the kidnappers. He wondered as one of the officers took notes if Barry's and Pauline's bodies would still be at the base of the cliff, or if they would be gone with the tide before they could be retrieved. He didn't much care, to be honest. The bastards were dead, and deservedly so.

With Amy in no fit state to answer their questions, the police agreed to wait twenty-four hours, saying they would visit her at home the following day.

'She won't be at her house,' Jenny had told them. 'She's coming home with me.'

Amy looked up at her friend to object. 'I'll be okay ...' but one look at Jenny told her the matter wasn't up for discussion, and she closed her mouth and simply nodded.

The police took details from all three friends and said they would be in touch. A brief discussion took place over whether to issue Amy with a Family Liaison Officer, but Amy objected and, as her kidnappers were both dead, it was agreed that it wasn't necessary, although they were given the female officer's contact details and told to phone her at any time.

When the police had gone, the doctor returned to re-check

Amy's blood pressure and other vitals.

'I'd like to keep you in for observation,' he said. 'Just for twenty-four hours.'

Amy objected once more, saying she just wanted to 'go home', and the doctor agreed on the condition that she wasn't left alone and made an appointment to see her GP as soon as possible.

When the three friends were alone in the room, Jenny was the first to speak.

'Right, stinky, let's get you back to mine.'

Willem glared at her, but Amy managed a small smile. She knew she smelled gross and the first thing she wanted was a long, hot shower, with gallons of shampoo and shower gel. Possibly followed immediately by a long, hot, bubbly bath. And coffee. And food. And then maybe, hopefully, sleep, in a clean, comfortable, warm bed.

'Come on, let's get out of here,' Jenny said, helping Amy up.

Willem led the way to the car and it wasn't long before he was pulling up outside Jenny's house.

'Are you coming in?' Jenny asked him, as she helped Amy out of the car.

'I'm going to leave you both, just for now, but I'd like to come back later if that's alright?'

'Yes, of course,' Jenny said, smiling at him.

'Maybe I could pick up some food? Just let me know what you fancy.'

Jenny nodded. 'That would be great, thanks.' She paused. 'And Willem, thank you, from the bottom of my heart, thank you for helping me get her back.'

'There's no need to thank me. And I'm sorry for doubting

you. You were right.' Willem smiled at Jenny.

Jenny smiled right back.

'Bloody hell you two, get a room,' Amy chuckled, sounding more like herself than she had since they'd found her. The sight of her two best friends, usually so antagonistic, smiling at one another had brought her back to herself, a little at least.

Jenny and Willem laughed, both relieved to see a glimpse of the Amy they knew and loved. The three friends knew that they had a lot to talk about but, for now at least, all was relatively well in their world.

Willem waited until Jenny closed the front door and then set off for Capel once more. He wanted to make sure the police found the house and the fall site, and that they had made the scenes safe. He wasn't taking any chances on what happened next. He knew that he'd die for Amy, and that he would go to prison for her if necessary, but he would rather neither of those things had to happen. He had no regrets over his actions but, at the end of the day, he could have saved Pauline if he'd wanted to. He hadn't wanted to. And he was glad. He would deal with whatever fallout came his way; even if Amy didn't want to be friends with a murderer, he could live with that. Because she was alive, and that was enough.

With Willem off policing the police, Amy took herself off upstairs to Jenny's bathroom. Jenny was running round her like a mother hen, fetching clean towels and dry things for Amy to put on.

'Shout if you need anything,' Jenny said, as Amy shut herself in the bathroom. She sniffed her armpit and screwed up her face, embarrassed as she thought of everyone seeing, and smelling, her in such a state. Standing at the sink, Amy looked at herself in the mirror. She almost didn't recognise herself, and tears leaked down her face as she pushed her lank and greasy hair back, and examined the state of her face. She looked as though she'd aged ten years, not ten days, with dark shadows under her eyes, and an unhealthy pallor to her skin.

With a sigh, Amy turned on the shower and, when it was hot enough, stepped under the steaming spray. She stood there for ages, letting the hot water ease her aching bones and muscles. She ran her hands over her body, noticing the changes which had been wrought on her by the virtual starvation diet and lack of exercise. It was a pretty extreme way to lose weight, Amy thought, as she soaped her flat belly for the second time. After scrubbing herself from head to toe, Amy was starting to feel a little more human. Turning off the shower, she wrapped herself in the bath sheet Jenny had given her, and made a turban for her hair with a smaller towel. She decided against having a bath as well, thinking she simply didn't have the strength to climb in or out of the tub. Next, she cleaned her teeth with the spare toothbrush Jenny had provided, and relished the smooth, clean feel of her teeth when she ran her tongue over them. Amy made use of Jenny's deodorant, the spray can triggering a flashback to the cellar as she blasted Barry in the face. She shook the image away as she lavished moisturiser on her face and body. Finally, dressed in a pair of Jenny's jogging bottoms, warm socks and a fluffy jumper (with cats on), Amy made her way back downstairs where Jenny was waiting, an anxious look on her face.

'You okay?' Jenny asked her friend.

'Better,' Amy nodded. 'Thank you.'

Jenny's bottom lip wobbled, and tears welled in her eyes. 'Oh, God, I was so scared! I knew they'd taken you, I just knew it! I didn't know what to do, Amy! I'm sorry, I'm so sorry!' she babbled. 'I should have got you out sooner!'

'Hey! Hey! Stop it,' Amy shushed her. 'You saved my life. You and Willem. If it wasn't for you, I'd be at the bottom of the cliff with Pauline and Barry. And, quite frankly, I'd had more than enough of their hospitality.'

'But ...' Jenny began.

'No, no buts,' Amy smiled, squeezing her friend's hand. 'You saved me. Thank you.'

They hugged for a while then, and Amy could feel Jenny's heart beating rapidly against her own chest.

'There's less of you to hug,' Jenny said after a while.

'Yep, extreme weight loss the Barry and Pauline way. Not to be recommended. I never want to see another cheese roll as long as I live. Apparently kidnappers don't cater for food intolerances,' Amy said wryly. She was definitely sounding a bit more like Amy, Jenny decided.

'Speaking of food, what can I get you?' Jenny asked, breaking out of the hug.

'Coffee and a fry-up would be heaven, please.'

'Coming right up. Then we need to let Willem know what we want to eat later.'

Amy nodded, and leant back into the sofa cushions as Jenny headed off to the kitchen.

When Jenny returned with a mug of coffee a few minutes later, Amy was fast asleep, curled up on the sofa. Jenny carefully draped a blanket over Amy and sat in an armchair to watch over her. She texted Willem:

She's fallen asleep. I'll sit with her in case she wakes up. Maybe just pick up a curry or something when you come?

Glad she's sleeping. Sounds good. See you later.

Jenny sent a thumbs up and then put her phone on silent. She didn't take her eyes off Amy, watching as she began to twitch, shushing gently when she began to murmur, stroking her when her arms and legs began to scrabble about, and then holding her when she finally woke up, startled and disorientated.

'Oh! I was dreaming, I think,' Amy said, shaking her head as if to try and dislodge the unwelcome images. 'I was in the cellar ... and then I was running ... and by the cliffs ... Barry ...'

'Shh, it's okay, it's over.'

Amy closed her eyes briefly. 'She pushed him. Pauline. She pushed Barry off the cliff.'

Jenny nodded. 'I know, Ames, I know. But she's gone now, the crazy bitch.'

'I should have run. I don't know why I didn't run,' Amy said, shaking her head.

'Don't beat yourself up. You were in shock. Bloody hell, Amy, you'd just seen someone fall off a cliff! I don't think rational decision-making comes into it.'

'You'd have run,' Amy said to her friend. 'You wouldn't have just stood there like a muppet.'

Jenny shrugged her shoulders. 'I don't know what I would have done. Nobody does until they're actually in a life-and-death situation.'

'Maybe,' Amy sighed. 'I still think you'd have done something, anything, to try and get away. I just said please and thank you and typed that bloody psycho-bitch's memoirs. And then froze when I could have got away. If you two hadn't turned up when you did …' Amy swallowed. It didn't bear thinking about.

'Typing her memoirs?' Jenny asked, wondering if she'd heard right.

'Yep,' Amy nodded. 'I was right about her, Jenny. All those deaths were down to her, all the quizzers. And they weren't her first victims either. She killed her own family!'

'Fuck.'

'And I was going to be next.' Amy buried her face in her hands as the emotions threatened to overwhelm her.

'But you weren't! You got out!'

'I'd almost made peace with it,' Amy admitted softly. 'I knew you and Willem and the others were safe, so I was kind of prepared to die. But I could hear you in my head telling me to fight. Then, when Barry left the air freshener in the cellar, and I knew Pauline was out of the house, I knew it was my only chance to try and escape.'

Amy told Jenny everything then, detailing all Pauline's crimes, and how she'd finally made her escape.

'She nearly hit me with her car,' Amy said. 'I think she must have braked automatically. There's no way she wouldn't have mowed me down if she'd had a moment to think about it.'

'That must have happened just before me and Willem arrived. We saw Barry run out of the lane and get in the car with Pauline.'

'Thank God you did.'

'We'd been watching the house. That's how we knew. Willem set up a camera. He's been brilliant – he cares about you so much, he really does.'

Amy nodded sadly, remembering how badly she'd treated

him, and how things had ended.

The friends were quiet for a while. It was Jenny who broke the silence.

'We came to the house one night, me and Willem. I knew you were there, I just knew it. And when I saw that Agatha Raisin book in the cellar window, I knew you'd put it there for me to see! You did, didn't you?! You knew I'd see it if we came looking for you.'

Amy was looking at Jenny in disbelief. 'You were at the house? Oh my God, I can't believe it! Why didn't you knock on the window or something?'

'We did! We knocked and called out, but you must have been asleep. I didn't want to leave, but … we didn't know what to do, Amy! They could have hurt you if we'd tried to get in. It was bloody awful, knowing you were so close but not being able to get to you.' Jenny's face was screwed up as she recalled the pain of that night.

'It doesn't matter now,' Amy told her. 'All that matters is that I'm here now.' She smiled at Jenny. 'That book – the one in the window – I put it there to stop a draught!'

It was Jenny's turn to look surprised. 'No? Really? And there was me thinking it was a clue!'

Both women were laughing now.

'I'll have to change my opinion of cosy crime now, I suppose. Maybe it's not such a waste of paper after all!' Amy chuckled.

'Speaking of waste,' Jenny began, 'do you still want that fry-up? It's probably a congealed mess now, to be fair, but …'

'After what I've had to eat recently, a bit of congealed fat sounds like heaven.'

CHAPTER 47

I could murder a whisky

As soon as Willem was alone in his car, he began to shake. 'Get a grip, man,' he snarled at himself, releasing his fingers, which were, rather ironically, white from gripping so tightly to the steering wheel.

Starting the car, he set off to Capel. He didn't know what he expected to learn, he simply felt the need to see what was going on, and make sure the police were taking the whole matter seriously. Calming his spinning mind as much as he was able, and focusing on the road ahead, Willem drove up Winehouse Lane and turned in towards Pauline's house. He didn't need to go all the way up to the property to see that the police were indeed in attendance. He sighed with relief. They would surely find everything they needed to back up Amy's story, as far-fetched as it must have sounded.

Turning the car round in a lay-by, Willem headed for the coast and parked at the edge of the road, from where he could see the area of the cliff where the earlier drama had taken place. There was a single police officer standing next to a cordon of blue-and-white tape. Nodding with satisfaction that at least the scene was protected, Willem assumed that the police's resources were spread thin and that they were focusing on the house where Amy had been held captive.

Realising there was nothing else he could do, Willem drove home.

Cat was lurking in the hallway when Willem opened his front door, and the animal wrapped himself around Willem's legs, mewling his usual reprimand about the lack of attention from his human servant.

'Ach! I should send you to live with Jenny,' Willem told the cat, who looked at him disdainfully. Willem bent down and, risking life and limb, gave Cat a tickle behind the ears. 'Come on then, I suppose you want food.'

Willem headed to the kitchen, closely followed by Cat, and shook some dried food into a bowl, which Cat took one sniff at before turning tail and stalking out of the room.

Willem barely noticed. He'd pulled out a chair and was seated at the kitchen table, his head in his hands. He was shaking uncontrollably, and sobbing.

Cat turned back briefly at the sound, but decided it wasn't his problem, and carried on going.

Willem stayed like that for some minutes, the delayed shock finally showing itself now that he was home, and alone.

When the crying and shaking finally burnt itself out, Willem reached for the kitchen towel, dried his face, and blew his nose.

His head and heart gradually began to pound less as the adrenaline left his body, but Willem felt absolutely drained, physically and emotionally. He was old enough and ugly enough to know this would happen, that the high stress of the situation would catch up with him, and he'd wanted to be far away from Amy when it did. He had to be strong to help Amy, and her crazy friend, through the next days and weeks. His own fears were unimportant. All that mattered was Amy.

Exhaling loudly, Willem got up and filled a glass with water, which he downed in a few gulps. Then he poured himself a whisky, and downed that too – just a small one as he knew he would still have to drive. Before he went back to Jenny's, he needed some time and space to think. As much as he didn't want to relive what had taken place on the clifftop, Willem needed everything clear in his own mind.

Whichever way he looked at it, though, he had killed Pauline. He could have grabbed her hands and pulled her to safety, but he had chosen to send her to her death. Would he have saved her if she hadn't said what she'd said about killing Amy? He honestly didn't know the answer to that. And now he never would. He asked himself if he regretted what he'd done, and the answer was no. What he regretted was that Amy and Jenny had witnessed it. How the hell were they going to feel about being friends with a murderer? Would they both be able to keep secret what had happened? To lie to the police? He might be able to plead it down to manslaughter, but Willem didn't want to spend his last good years in prison.

With an enormous sigh, Willem got up and poured himself another whisky. He'd walk to Jenny's.

At Jenny's house, Amy was feeling better by the hour. Warm, clean, and fed, she was thankful to be alive, and to be back with Jenny. Now she was calmer, the events which had taken place on the cliffs were coming into focus. She knew how close she had come to death, and shuddered as she remembered wrestling with Pauline, before the older woman went over the edge. It could so easily have been her.

She didn't even want to think about what would have happened had Willem and Jenny not shown up when they did. When Pauline had grabbed her ankle, Amy had known she was a goner – there was nothing to grab onto as she was pulled towards the edge of the chalk cliff.

But they had arrived. And they had saved her. Amy closed her eyes as she recalled the moment. When she opened them, she turned to Jenny:

'He killed her, didn't he? Willem, I mean. He killed Pauline.'

Jenny looked directly at her friend and nodded.

Amy was quiet for a few moments, her face pensive.

'I'm glad,' she said, finally.

Jenny exhaled the breath she hadn't realised she was holding. 'Phew! I wasn't sure how much you'd taken in of what happened. You were in such a state.'

'I did see. And I don't blame him. I should probably be shocked, shouldn't I? He could have saved her. He stamped on her hands instead of grabbing them.'

'Only because he got there before me. I'd have stomped on her bloody hands too, given half a chance,' Jenny told her.

Amy smiled weakly at her friend. 'I reckon I'd have done the same thing too if the roles were reversed.'

'The world's better off without that psycho-bitch in it.'

Amy nodded. 'And Barry. I actually felt a little bit sorry for Barry.'

Jenny looked at her in surprise. 'Felt sorry for him? The man who kept you prisoner in a cellar and helped his wife murder umpteen innocent people?'

'Yeah, I know, it sounds crazy. But he was always basically nice to me. He was absolutely terrified of Pauline.'

'Well, you're more of a man than me, Gunga Din,' Jenny harrumphed. 'I'd have kicked him in the balls before I ran off.'

Amy laughed. 'He simply wasn't strong enough to stand up to her.'

'Maybe she got to his balls before me?' Jenny said. 'Along with his spine.'

'Pauline definitely wore the trousers in that marriage,' Amy agreed.

'Beige knitted ones,' Jenny added.

'Well, her knitting days are over, thank God.'

'Yep. The head of the knitting-nana mafia is sleeping with the fishes,' Jenny said in her best Marlon Brando voice, nodding with satisfaction.

When Willem arrived with Indian takeaway later that evening, Jenny let him in, and took the bags of food from him before ushering him into the lounge, where Amy was still curled up in a blanket on the sofa. On seeing him, Amy pushed the blanket aside and went to him, wrapping her arms around him.

'Thank you,' she whispered in his ear, squeezing him tightly. She could feel his body start to tremble.

'But ...' Willem began.

But Amy shushed him, and pulled him onto the sofa to sit beside her. She called Jenny, who reappeared with plates and cutlery in her hands.

'Sit down, Jenny. Please,' Amy said.

Jenny did as she was told, for once, and she and Willem looked at Amy expectantly.

'So,' Amy began, 'this is what happened: Pauline was trying to throw me off the cliff, and we fought, and she lost her footing and went over the edge. That's when you two showed up. Pauline grabbed my ankle when she fell – that will explain any bruising on my ankle – but I managed to kick her off, just as you both grabbed my arms and pulled me to safety. And that's what we're going to tell the police. Okay?'

'Fine by me,' Jenny nodded.

'Willem?' Amy asked. He was looking at the floor.

'But I ... I ki ...' he began, unable to look at Amy.

'Ssh,' she said, putting a finger to her lips, and reaching over with the other hand to tip his face up to meet hers. Their eyes locked on, his watery and blue, hers green and resolute.

'I know,' she whispered.

THE END

Acknowledgements

Thank you for reading *The Wipeout Round*. I hope you enjoyed reading it as much as I enjoyed writing it. I've loved developing the characters of Amy, Jenny and Willem in this third book of *The Write Way to Die* series, and seeing where they take me. As I don't plan my books, I never know what's going to happen until it happens, and characters do take on a life and will of their own at times. There's certainly never a dull moment with Jenny around!

As always I want to thank the amazing and talented Charlotte Mouncey at Bookstyle for her brilliant typesetting and cover design. Charlotte never fails to impress. A big thank you to my wonderful proof-reader, Emma Brown, who gives me such confidence before the book goes off to be published. Thanks also to my partner, Dirk, who reads and listens, bounces ideas around with me, and supports my writing career every step of the way. I thank my son, Sam, for new shared experiences, one of which was getting a tattoo! To Kathy, thank you for being such a good friend, for making me laugh, listening, caring and never judging. And last, but absolutely not least, thank you to my readers for reminding me why I stick at this crazy writing lark.